# The Manchester Hub

## Created by
## J A Manarola

# The Manchester Hub

A catalogue record of this book is available from the British Library
ISBN 978-1-670-03470-0


Acknowledgements and thanks:
Cover created by Jo Parry
Editors: N Grimshaw and A Shafiq


Thank you to Paul,
Steve W and my friends who know
they have helped me along the way

# THE MANCHESTER HUB

It's true to say that a café can provide a hub for its community. Where people from all walks of life, and at different life-stages, come together to share their experiences with each other. Where friendships are formed and help is at hand or you can choose to be as anonymous as you like. As teenagers we didn't realise that one café we walked past every day on our way to school would become significant to us. The four of us met at a grammar school in the days when the 11+ managed to sift children to set them on different life paths: supposedly one path for the children who passed the 11+ and another for the ones who didn't – some of whom ridiculously classed themselves as having 'failed'.

Bea, the daughter of a seamstress and a handyman who became friends with Vivie despite knowing that she was the only child of a Catholic mother (which in the 1970s was not an acceptable occurrence; frowned upon even). Their other two friends, Caroline, the daughter of two doctors and Elle, whose family life led her to be a quiet and introspective girl at school, forged their friendship at the 'difficult to get into' Catholic grammar school located smack bang in the middle of Manchester. Here is their story.

# Chapter 1 - Welcome to the Hub

Have you ever strolled past a café, then self-arrested only to return to wonder about the misty lives of the people inside?

Nosiness can be seen as a failing in others but Bea, as everyone called her, not her beautiful Spanish name Bernicia, liked to think of herself as fascinated by folk. Her interest in people was so intense that when she saw a *for sale* sign outside an empty shop on the outskirts of central Manchester she managed to persuade her husband Frank that it would be an ideal setting for a café. Their café. A place at the hub of people's lives. They bought it and unimaginatively named it the *Manchester Hub*. It wasn't Bea's wildest idea as she had always worked with the public and Frank was a trained chef. They viewed it as their chance to work alongside each other, for better or for worse.

Despite working and living together for twenty-four hours a day, almost every day of the week, Frank Walker occasionally gazed at Bea in silent admiration. Had she known that, she would have been astonished because he rarely spoke about *feelings*. His wife was dynamic and no matter what, always saw the best in people. Her manner was forthright, which some may find intimidating, but she was kind-hearted to such an extent that she drove him crazy. She made sure that surplus food from the café was given to Manchester's homeless people through local charities. Bea was tireless in her endeavours for this cause and had even roped Ben and Bella, her friends' children, into helping. Bea always made time to listen to people no matter what her commitments. This often made her late to events but how she loved to *chitter chatter* as Frank put it. Her husband on the other hand, was a customarily quiet man.

Although often thought about, Frank had never told Bea how glad he was that they had bought the café. It had given him a sense of freedom, he was curator of his own destiny, able to demonstrate his superb culinary skills daily; a talent nurtured during his sea-faring days.

Affectionately known as the Hub, the café is at the west side of a main street. Here the red brick terraced buildings were built on long, narrow plots. Outwardly the café is inauspicious with its one large, shiny front window downstairs and a door. Unfortunately for its customers, Frank recently fitted the glazed front door, edged in glossy black wood, which now only ever opens ¾ of the way. A design fault, Frank says. If you ever manage to push open the door and step inside the entrance your eyes might be immediately drawn to the well-trodden oak floor because there's a small area which houses mosaic tiles ingrained with worker bees, which Frank had organised in honour of Bea. He copied that idea from Manchester's Town Hall. Despite the outward plainness, once inside the place swathes you with its comforting character.

On this grey day, by 10 a.m. Frank had been particularly busy. Not only was he preparing food, he had also ejected two lads for being drunk in charge of a tea pot. The miscreants were probably on their way home from a great night out in Manchester but Bea had become agitated when the scene turned ugly and they threatened to return and "torch the place". As the Hub was also their home she felt vulnerable. There had been a couple of other disturbing incidents recently. A menacing looking, gangly youth had come into the café and asked Bea for protection money.

This was such a ludicrous request, especially as they hardly made any money that she had laughed hysterically thinking he was joking.

As he walked away, the youth peered back at her ominously. Bea had a horrible sense that she had not heard the last from him. There had also been the unnerving incident when two mopeds had driven around the main street whilst the pillion passengers had snatched handbags or mobile phones from unsuspecting pedestrians, some of whom were her customers.

In fact, if the truth were known, Bea had felt anxious for a while. This morning her sense of unease was heightened. On top of these unfortunate incidents, her old friend Vivie was having an MRI scan today.

## Vivienne Baker

For as far back as she chose to remember fifty-two year old Vivienne Baker had been known as Vivie to her friends. As she had brushed her short, but wild brown hair that morning, Vivie had that horrible knot in her stomach which told her something she didn't like was about to happen. She often had that feeling of *ominiscity* as she called it, a sense of impending doom. Thankfully she was surrounded by people whose personalities were more positive. Her husband Tom had prepared breakfast and as she gazed at her uneaten porridge, Tom asked if she needed anything. "No thanks. I'm fine" she replied quietly, but he could tell from the fear in her hazel eyes as she looked up at him, and by the frown on her forehead, that she was anxious.

Tom knew when to speak or listen. Now was the time for a Churchillian speech. "In spite of your terror Vivie, you still need to go to the hospital to find out what's wrong. Are you sure you want to go alone?" he asked kindly. "Yes I'm sure. Elle has spoken to me about what to expect. I'm a big girl. I can manage.

You go to the Hub and I'll see you there later. I'll probably feel like eating then." She was disinclined to discuss anything further, so quietly left the kitchen, put on her navy coat, collected her car keys from the key holder and walked to the front of the house. Tom joined her at the door and gave her a kiss. As Vivie got into her Range Rover, Tom watched the car slowly reverse out of the driveway and onto the road. He was still looking as the car zoomed away and the electric garden gate closed softly. Tom decided to call at the newsagents to see his son Ben and then stop at the café for a chat with his old friend Frank. He did not want to be alone today.

When she arrived at the hospital Vivie informed the receptionist of her name and waited for five minutes before a man arrived to escort her to the MRI area. Vivie looked at the stranger who was walking alongside her. He was nondescript with light brown hair and a pallid face. He tried to make small talk with her but she was having none of it. "Have you travelled far?" was the latest interrogation she had endured. "No" she replied. Thankfully, he realised not to probe any more. Silently they walked together along a sage coloured corridor. He pushed open an opaque glass door. "It's this way" he pointed as they continued their journey along another windowless corridor.

When they reached a dark green door he yanked it open. "You can get undressed in here" he said unceremoniously and pointed to a small room. Vivie waited until the stranger had left and closed the door behind him. She took off her knee high navy boots, slipped out of her pale blue dress and removed her bra. Placing her belongings into a tiny locker she quietly closed the door. Quickly she wrapped herself in a paper gown and tied it at the waist. The stranger re-entered the room. "All done then? Good" he smirked.

"Right love, lie down on this bed and put these on" he said. Vivie did as instructed, accepted the headphones offered, placing them over her ears. She felt a weird sensation as the cold, metal bed she lay on moved backwards then upwards. Her eyes were tightly shut but a bright light shone through her eyelids. It wasn't sunshine. Vivie could feel her heart racing, hear her breath quicken and taste the moisture of perspiration on her upper lip. She inhaled sharply. All reason rushed out of her body as she gripped a plastic buzzer which lay on her stomach. She squeezed it with all of her might. "Get me out of here" she screamed in an undignified manner. Almost immediately Vivie felt the bed as it was lowered and moved forward. The earphones were removed brusquely, and she felt a hand grab hers as she was helped from the bed. "I think the next time we try this Mrs Baker you'll need to be prescribed tranquillisers by your doctor first" Mr Insipid said. "There won't be a next time" thought Vivie, "not likely."

The stranger left Vivie to get dressed. When fully clothed, she abandoned the room. In silence the man, who had waited for her, walked alongside, opened the green door and showed her out into a different corridor. He departed and left her alone. 'Off to collect some other poor person to torture', thought Vivie. Retracing her steps back to the car park she didn't return immediately to her car. Instead she sat on a bench in the hospital garden and for five minutes looked up at the grey sky, gratefully gulping fresh air. 'I don't want to face Tom yet. He'll be disappointed in me. I've only got a tiny mole anyway. It'll be nothing. I'll go to the Hub' she thought 'and see some friendly faces. Bea's bound to have a smile and, if I'm lucky, Elle will be there too.'

## Elle Lowe

The industrial grey clouds which lingered above Manchester never usually irritated Dr. Elle Lowe. Today she wished the sun would fight from its encasement of cast iron clouds which shrouded its brilliance and had the nerve to hurl despondency over her beloved city. 'I'm tired of this weather' she grumbled to herself, as she looked out of her Deansgate apartment. 'I can't bear the sombre appearance of these wet, grey streets.' After a few moments she thought 'this weather must be driving me insane. Who in their right mind talks to themselves?'

Elle gave her brown, curly hair a shake and her cobalt eyes looked down at the pink lottery ticket she was holding in her left hand. She stared at the numbers. 'They look like winners to me' she thought. Her personality was usually optimistic and generally cheerful. As she turned from her bedroom window, she spotted her mobile phone where it lay unused on the bedside table.

In silent expectation she snatched at it and quickly keyed in her lottery numbers. 'It'd be great if I won. Please let me win just enough' she pleaded for this foolish idea to come true 'so that I can take all of the others on a fantastic, well-earned holiday'. Her eyes peered as if imploring the tiny screen to relay the positivity that somehow had left her today. Elle paused for a moment as she watched the app communicate its message. You have winning matches in 1 draw, she read. With a thumping heart, "Yes" she squealed "thank you" and punched the air. With her middle finger she scrolled up the screen and saw that she had matched two numbers. 'Prize free lotto lucky dip', Elle smiled wryly. 'Typical. A lucky dip? I suppose it's better than nothing at all' she thought to herself. 'No text from Vivie yet. I'll go to the Hub, she's bound to call in there after her scan.'

For some unknown reason Elle felt restless today. She needed to be outside and feel the wind in her face; to breathe the cold air. Quickly, she put on her outdoor clothes. Her wildly curly hair fizzed underneath her maroon, woollen hat and wrinkled over the collar of her lilac coat which was edged in red. By embracing colour Elle was able to wrap herself in shades that would make rainbows appear pale.

She foraged around her mind to try and remember the stupid word that her friend Vivie often used. *Ominiscity*. That was it. Today she thought, I am suffering from *ominiscity*. She stuffed her hands into wide coat pockets, clasped her mobile 'phone in case it vibrated and strode off through the Manchester streets. As she walked the path along the industrial canal, she could see three expansive iron jetties which led from the grey cobbled walkways down to the water's edge. Elle counted nine boats of different sizes, three lined up along each jetty.

She thought it had been an inspired idea by the council to exploit Manchester's ship canal, which used to transport goods around the world, to one where workers from the suburbs could travel by boat to and from the city. Waxi was an ingenious name, Elle thought. She wondered if it would become a useful form of public transport and help cut down on the congested roads.

As Elle reached the imposing Victorian Town Hall, set peacefully amidst new, high rise glass buildings, she stopped, brushed tiny rain drops from a metal bench, sat and listened to the voices of foreign visitors as they chatted to each other in languages she did not recognise. The Christmas market stalls were being erected which meant that the city would be awash with hundreds of lights and thousands of visitors. As she looked around, Elle spotted at least twenty cranes which peppered the skyline with signs of adjustment.

Candid developers like the Gaph brothers had shared their ideas to cultivate and invigorate this vibrant city. She was concerned about what its gentrification would mean for the current Manchester residents, especially Bea and Frank. Elle continued her journey through the streets of Manchester, towards the outer limits of the city centre. As she marched along wide, tree-lined streets she heard a male voice shouting to her. With a glance she surveyed a new colleague, Dr. Sie Patel who approached her. "Great to see you Elle." He smiled and his large, coffee coloured eyes sparkled.

"You're looking striking in your beautiful coat. Where are you off to?" She blushed slightly. "I'm about to pop into the café" she replied "d'you want to join me?" "Sorry Elle I can't today as I'm on my way to work" he said briskly. I'll text you later if that's ok? Aren't you on call today?" he asked. "No. My shift at the hospital changed this week so I've got the weekend off. I'd like to catch up with you later if you have time." She smiled as Sie bent down and gently kissed her cheek.

Excited at the prospect of meeting him afterwards, she watched as he strode away towards the tram stop. After a few minutes she sauntered towards a red brick building, pushed a black door ¾ of the way open and entered the Manchester Hub.

## Bea Walker

Bea wondered if she was suffering from *ominiscity* as she had a feeling of impending doom. Unusually she had become increasingly annoyed by the industrial grey globules of water which were frozen together and hung over her beloved city.

'It's like seeing gnarled grey hands spitefully snatching away the sun's joyful rays. Oh how my old English teacher, Sister Rose would've been proud of me for creating that sentence' she thought cheekily. 'This weather's just not good for business.' Bea sighed loudly, turned her blonde head slowly, and questioned her friend Elle who had just arrived in the café, cheeks ablaze. "You're glowing" said Bea with a warm smile "and I've been frittering away my time thinking about our terrible school days.

Remember when the nuns at school said we'd never amount to much Elle? Ha, they tried to put fear in us didn't they and for a while we believed them. We were terrified that we'd live a life of purgatory. What the hell did they know?" Ha. Bea chuckled at her own pun. "Here we are in the sparkling city of Manchester on a grey Saturday living it large" she laughed irreverently. "What could we do that's a bit more adventurous for you?" replied Elle kindly. Her cobalt eyes sparkled with laughter as she looked in anticipation at Bea whom she sensed was uneasy.

With her gentle green eyes, light brown skin, long blonde hair and no-nonsense ways, for the 41 years that Elle had known Bea she had been impulsive, kind, wilful and bold. She was a bundle of determination and confidence. At the convent they had attended together from the age of 11, Elle quickly recalled times when she, and their two friends Caroline and Vivie had been in trouble because of Bea's audaciousness. Bea refused to be controlled or manipulated by anyone, which is why many teachers disliked having her in their class. Bea had a mind of her own, and everyone knew it.

Elle had a flashback to when the four friends were at school. So that they could miss a *boring* maths lesson, Bea had suggested that the four of them balance precariously on a toilet seat in a tiny, smelly cubicle for forty minutes. This idiocy was only discovered when the toilet came away from the wall under the weight of the four of them. Water spurted everywhere and the four girls were soaked to the skin. Not only that, they were made to line up for the cane outside Mother Superior's office at lunchtime, in full view of the whole school.

As well as being given six lashes, in the days when six lashes were deemed devout retribution, the Mother Superior had taken great delight in telling their parents about the misdemeanour. This meant they had to make the shameful walk into their respective homes.

Elle recalled that Vivie's devout Catholic mother was beside herself with rage as she wondered aloud how she could ever face their Parish Priest again. She almost forbade Vivie to be friends with Elle, Bea and Caroline but Elle's father had persuaded her to be tolerant of her daughter's passion for life. Elle remembered that Vivie's single mother, already ashamed because her husband had left for another woman, was exasperated by her wilful daughter. She informed Vivie that her bad nerves could not withstand another shameful incident. Vivie said that her mother's bad nerves were like her pimples, always there! Her mother didn't see the irony and gave her a clout. Those were the days when clouts were allowed. Caroline's parents wondered whether they should try to control her wild spirit, whilst Bea's mother and father were more forgiving; they understood their daughter's spirit would soften.

Another time, the four girls had crouched down in their seats as the service bus sailed past their school because the four, at Bea's suggestion, had agreed to play truant that day. Bea and Vivie had said that instead of learning rubbish the girls could spend their time watching the Manchester United team during their training session. This, Bea proclaimed, would be learning about real life, away from being stuck in a *dreary* classroom.

When someone at the Littleton Road training ground asked if they should be at school that day, the four girls had replied that it was a Holy Day of Obligation. This sin was dutifully confessed by each of them at church the following Saturday. None of them felt exonerated, and their feelings of guilt didn't last long.

Today Bea was in an unusual state of agitation. "I'm 52. I want to take a leap of faith, leave behind my usual routine and do something different." She couldn't say that to Frank. He would have seen it as an insult to the life they had forged together. It wasn't their life that she wanted to change, it was work that she wanted to break free from. "We could take a gap year" suggested Bea to Elle. "Give up work, rent the apartments and travel for a year. It'd be fabulous to have different experiences every day."

Bea's musings were punctured by a voice which chirped "You two'll still be doin' the same things next year. Talking about it, but not havin' an adventure. If you do take action, I'll show my backside on the Town Hall steps' stated Frank. He had been listening to the women's conversation. Bea looked at him in defiance. 'Oh no' thought Elle 'after all their years of marriage, Frank must realise that he had thrown down a gauntlet to Bea.

Surely he knew that she would take all steps possible to jump to action.' "Depend upon it you two, you'll still be slaving this time next year" said Frank as he burst into boyish laughter which belied his fifty four years. 'All I need now is for Vivie to turn up then the three of us can connive to concoct a plan which means Frank'll be proved wrong' thought Bea as her piercing green eyes viewed Frank. How well he knew her. She wouldn't do anything so daring any more, or would she?

As a distraction, Bea chose this moment to ask Tom, who had been in the café most of the morning, if Vivie had been in touch. He told Bea he had called in to have a chat with Frank about football but Bea knew Tom was really worried about Vivie. Tom replied that he had not heard a word from her. 'Vivie was always the quietest one', thought Bea, 'and she ended up living a glamorous life in New York. I wonder what it's like to live in that vibrant American city. I'll never know' she mused as she looked around. 'I wonder how Vivie has gone on' she thought.

The Hub always exuded a comforting atmosphere. Despite the tiny blobs of rain which had begun to cascade gently, Elle's opinion strengthened that this café had its own distinctive warmth which enveloped her every time she entered it. This enterprising business represented to her the opportunity to share the daily trials and tribulations of ordinary lives. 'But what is ordinary?' she thought. 'Normal? Usual? Conventional? Familiar? All of those things are comforting to me.

Extra-ordinary means something peculiar or bizarre has happened.' Elle was certain that strange events in her personal life were unwelcome to her. Unusual often meant not good as far as she was concerned. She had enough variety in her work at the hospital. That was as much as she wanted to handle.

Elle looked around the café and took in the familiar and calming scene but inside she was worried sick about Vivie. As a doctor she was aware that news following the scan may not be positive.

On the glass in the front door, was displayed a command in blue writing to 'follow us on Twitter'. This was the kind of place where talk resonated around a tiny room, and customers were encouraged to speak to each other rather than use the Internet on their tablets or mobile phones.

Even so, recently Elle had been curious to know what was trending on the café's Twitter account. She found that the Mayor of Manchester had visited, that incredibly an eclectic mix of items from canal barges to Christmas trees were sold outside the shop, (how could that be?) and that there were fundraising activities for local causes. Elle knew that social media played a huge role in the promotion of any business these days. Hard to think that when she was at school she had to rely on the local telephone box for her electronic communication. These days most of the world appeared to be interconnected through tiny mobile devices. It was good to be with Bea, Frank and Tom. Even so, Elle wondered where Vivie had got to; she was looking forward to seeing her old school friend.

It wasn't difficult to hear conversation abound in the café. As she waited patiently, Elle sat at one of the tables parallel to another at which sat four business people. They were already tucking in to a beautifully presented English breakfast. Elle eavesdropped as they reminisced about their younger days. She half turned to watch a bald man say "At school I could never understand maths. It was only when I left, I realised that decimals had a point." Elle smiled.

As the talk of education abounded, and proud of his daughter, whom he said was the first in the family to go to university, the man continued "Our Jasmine has just finished at Manchester Uni. She's thankful to the Student Loans people for getting her through and doesn't know how she can ever repay them."

With a twinkle in her eyes which Vivie spotted, the woman opposite to him replied "Yeah, I remember at school being made to study Greek. It was my Achille's elbow." This was just the kind of gentle banter which reverberated around the café every day. It helped Elle to stop worrying about Vivie or thinking about Sie Patel.

Whilst her husband Frank chatted about football to his long-time friend Tom at the counter, Bea sat beside Elle and looked through the huge glass panel at the front of her café. Her window to the world. The sparkling pane was dotted with tiny raindrops. Bea peered past a dangling mesh wooden heart she had carefully placed a few days ago, towards the exclusive bridal shop immediately opposite the café. In the downstairs window were three white wedding dresses. In the room above, one black suit stood to attention as if guarding the upper window. She thought it appropriate that it was a single suit in a wedding shop, perhaps looking for a partner. There was no name on the shop frontage as the owner did business through word of mouth recommendation rather than the social media of WhatsApp, Instagram, Twitter or Facebook.

'It's a shame' thought Bea 'that fewer people are getting married these days.' This fact had led the owner, Francine, to reconsider her options and had chosen to retire sooner rather than later. Her beloved shop would re-open as a hairdressers.

"Not that we need another hairdressing shop in Manchester" moaned Frank "the place is awash with them and nail bars. Women don't half waste their money" he'd jibed.

Bea liked to watch people going into and out of Francine's bridal shop. She imagined what the wedding would be like and which guests would cause the most problems. Her guilty pleasure was watching a television programme which enabled her to observe prospective brides try on their potential gowns. She had to switch channels quickly when Frank entered the living room. If he saw her watching a programme like that, he would tut and look at her in bewilderment. It was such fun, she thought, seeing a wide array of wedding dresses and being appalled by the behaviour of some bridal party members.

She wondered how her friend Caroline and daughter Bella were faring at the bridal gown try-on across the road. Bea had seen the two of them enter the shop at least two hours ago. As this thought occurred to Bea, she turned to Elle and said "I thought Caroline would've been here by now. Bella will need to get her dress today, 'cos the wedding's only three months away." Elle nodded in agreement. As the two women looked out of the rain-globule beset window they saw a sleek red Range Rover draw up and spotted the driver park deftly in the road opposite. Immediately they both recognised Vivie who was looking pale and a little sad.

Slowly Vivie crossed the road, pushed open the café door to ¾ of the way, walked towards her husband Tom and kissed him on the cheek. He could tell that it was not the time to ask about her hospital visit.

Vivie moved clumsily past the café tables, hugged Bea then Elle and sat down heavily on a wooden chair. "How did the scan go?" asked Bea. "I couldn't go through with it. I panicked. I'm such an idiot" replied Vivie. "It's a difficult thing to face isn't it?  Next time we'll go with you" suggested Elle. "You're both kind.  Thanks.  I appreciate the offer" said Vivie "but there's no way I'm doing that again."

For a few minutes there was silence "and I'm certainly not telling Tom that I chickened out.  He'll be mad at me for being so soft" confessed Vivie, "I'll just tell him I'm fine".  Her hazel eyes filled with tears as she bent her head to mask disappointment in herself.

## Ben Baker

As the three women sat in silence, Bea and Elle, who were facing the café window, observed a young man negotiate the busy traffic and wend his way through cars parked on either side of the road.  He was sporting a beard which some might think was a gritty, unpolished, dishevelled look, but they knew that this man was considered by most people to be stylish and handsome.

The owner of Baker's newsagents was in his early twenties and worked as a part-time model.  His sartorial style was elegant and he wore a blue, black and green plaid suit with a sky blue silk square placed in his top pocket.  He was wearing a navy roll-neck cashmere sweater and his multi-coloured socks were encased by navy suede Chelsea boots.

Ben Baker, Vivie and Tom's son had recently set up his own Internet clothing business which, as a new-comer to the retail industry, was causing him anxiety.

Sipping café latte both women sensed a change in the atmosphere to one of curious expectation when Ben entered the Hub. This happened often when his handsome face appeared.

Silence descended as people turned to look at Ben. His eyes lit up as he flashed a casual smile around the busy room, seeking out his parents. Deftly negotiating his way through the tightly packed furniture he joined Tom at the counter.

"Hello son. Did you manage to collate that big order?" enquired Tom. Plonking his bottom on a stool at the counter, Ben replied "I'm still working on different clothes orders dad, trying to get them out in time for delivery tomorrow. Just thought I'd have a quick bite to eat before carrying on. The shop's been mad busy too. I'm exhausted and I promised Bea that I'd help tonight with the food donations."

Within two minutes of Ben's arrival, Bea approached him and said "You amaze me Ben you're driven and ambitious like your parents. Do you ever stop working?" Bea thought if imagination and determination were acknowledged as important, Ben would be considered a shining star. She looked at him, this young man who viewed life as having endless possibilities. "According to the weather forecast, we're going to have a monsoon in Manchester later on! Ha. What a ridiculous statement. When have weather forecasters ever been right?" "Let's wait and see" was his pragmatic reply.

Ben smiled and placed his food order which was simple, salad with quiche and a drink of tea. After a few minutes, Ben joined his mother and Elle.

Once she had delivered the order, Bea sat at the table. Vivie waited for her son to speak as it was difficult to gauge his mood, though he often made perceptive comments. Ben was frugal with his remarks and able to elude his mother's questions about girlfriends to the extent that she had given up asking him. She refused to spy on him using Instagram, instead she relied upon the second-hand surveillance of her friend Bea whose gregarious son Alfie was Ben's friend and innocently passed on information.

Alfie had reported that Ben was suffering from a broken-heart. His first love had decided that Ben did not earn enough money so would not be able to keep her in a lifestyle which she wished to become accustomed. Vivie was indignant as her son was a good person, kind, considerate and hard-working. Oh the trials of being a mother. She had been annoyed by the greed of some women but confused too as she thought that Ben had appeared to be more light-hearted recently. She was sure that Ben had a girl on his mind, but who? Vivie looked at Bea who seemed to be preoccupied. Bea was worried as her parents were usually at the café by now.

## Robert and Matilde Riva

Bea's parents, Robert and Matilde Riva lived in a four-storey Victorian terraced house next door to the Hub. Robert was proud of the house which he claimed "had all its original features" including a clothes rail on the ceiling. In her younger days, Bea had been embarrassed by these original features in what she called, old fashioned living.

She had been keen to live in the newer houses which had been built nearby and had all modern conveniences with integrated appliances in the kitchen and en-suite bathrooms.

Robert said they were built of paper and not worth the money. He and Matilde were a constant source of support to both Bea and Frank and their efforts were appreciated. When the place was busy Frank or Bea would knock on the adjoining wall to her parents' house, an indication that help was needed.

Bea was becoming anxious because her parents, who were usually always on hand, had not responded to Frank's call. With a heart full of unease she peered at the ¾ opening glass door, just as Robert and Matilde bustled in bringing the rain and cold air with them. "Oh Bea we nipped to the shops and there's been a bomb scare near to Piccadilly Station. We had to be evacuated from the shops and some of the streets have been cordoned off by the police. There was such a kerfuffle but you can't be too sure about suspect parcels these days can you? Sorry we're late love" exclaimed Matilde.

Bea looked at her parents in alarm. "I'm glad you're both ok. We've not heard anything so I assume it was a false alarm?" she questioned. "No it wasn't" retorted Robert. "There was a suspect package in one of the shops so the police had to blow it up." "What? Blow up the shop?" asked Bea in horror. "No you daft thing, the parcel, not the shop" replied Matilde.

Bea's parents always appeared to know everything that was going on in the town even when they didn't venture out. "Did you hear that for the first time ever there will be armed police at the Manchester Christmas Markets this year?" asked Robert. "No" replied Bea "but I suppose it's only to be expected. The world seems to have gone mad." Her heart felt heavy.

In silence Bea surveyed her tiny café and pondered whether now was the right time to sell up and do something different. Was it ludicrous to think that she and Frank could begin a new life abroad? Is that what was unsettling her? Did she really want to leave behind her wonderful parents and dear friends?' She shuddered. For the past ten years Bea and Frank had both strived hard to create an invitingly warm atmosphere in the café which they knew offered a safe haven for people. Maybe living so close to a big city was too perilous these days. It felt safer to push these thoughts to the back of her mind. Maybe this morning's contretemps with those two lads had unnerved her. She had left it to Frank and Tom to ask the lads to leave when they had become aggressive. With their diabolical expressions and threats, she had become unusually frightened.

Full of ominiscity Bea sat with Elle, Vivie and Ben but overheard her father's conversation with other people in the café. 'Oh no' thought Bea, 'my dad's not discussing Brexit again.' She could hear him as he said "I told you if you voted to leave the EU that the price of stuff would rise, that you wouldn't be able to afford to go on holiday 'cos the value of the pound would plummet against the euro and the dollar.

This is on your own head. Look at this news item on my mobile. The Footsie has fallen, Alpine resorts are reporting a drop in British bookings for the winter season so no skiing for you this year mate and no more holidays in Italy as the Italians are now marketing their country to the Japanese. No-one needs the British." Frank looked crestfallen. He had hoped, as a small business owner, that moving away from European rules and laws would offer him more freedom.

"The world doesn't need the UK mate, companies will market their efforts at other countries in the EU, or look wider to the continents of Asia, Africa or America. You mark my words." Frank considered this but had a more optimistic outlook "Brexit will have a big impact on domestic visitors won't it if people stay in the UK? That means that more people will eat locally and I've already seen an increase in trade during the school holidays as people aren't travelling abroad for their holidays. Staycations they're called Robert. Staycations, that's the way forward. People will decide to take their holidays in the UK and keep money in this country. That's so they can enjoy our glorious weather – like today. Every cloud has a silver lining" replied Frank cheerily. Robert sighed. "Idiot" he said quietly to himself. Bea scowled at her father, and at the same time wondered how Caroline was getting on.

## Caroline Butler

As it happened, across the road at the bridal salon, cocooned in an orange velvet chair, Caroline Butler was sipping champagne. She sat back, crossed her legs delicately at the ankles, checked the time on her Breguet watch and surveyed her daughter on the catwalk.

Bella's flashing coal-coloured eyes beamed down at her mother. She swaggered in a glittering, fish-tail wedding dress. She felt beautiful and looked exquisite. This was the eighth wedding dress that Bella had tried on. Caroline was exhausted by all the drama. She knew that she should be excited to be helping her daughter choose a wedding dress, but she wasn't.

Caroline wasn't quite sure that Bella was ready to get married. She had a sneaking suspicion that Bella felt that too which was why she was dithering about choosing a dress. Caroline had a heavy feeling in the pit of her stomach. She knew that her long-time friend Vivie would say that she was experiencing *ominiscity*. A much used word in Caroline's life. She sipped more champagne to try to obliterate this gnawing feeling, but it just would not shift. "What do you think mum?" Bella asked cheerily. "It's beautiful darling. You look stunning in all of them. Do you really need to choose one today?" replied Caroline. Bella looked relieved. "You're right mum, I'll leave it for another day." Caroline's heart sank. Something was wrong. That feeling of ominiscity would not leave her.

Bella walked back towards the changing room. She sat down in the current wedding dress, opened her bag, dug out her mobile 'phone and considered sending a text to her fiancé Charlie. Fifteen minutes later, she changed back into her skinny jeans, red cashmere jumper and red shoes. Caroline was still sipping champagne when Bella left the changing room, in a state of abject misery. Caroline gave her head a shake and looked at the third glass she'd drunk that morning. 'Thank goodness this experience had ended' she thought, but felt ashamed that she was also a little relieved. 'The gleam from those diamantes is giving me a headache. Not to mention all that champagne I've quaffed.' She looked at the exiting figure of her daughter. It took a while to absorb that Bella had been in tears. 'Damn' thought Caroline 'what the hell is wrong now?' She watched as Bella crossed the main street, furiously pushed open the front door ¾ of the way and steamed into the café.

## Bella Butler

As the door opened, Elle watched as Bella Butler, whom she had spotted rush out of Francine's shop, flounced into the café. Bella's flustered face scanned the room and spied that there was only one seat available in the café at the table where Elle, Vivie, Ben and Bea sat. She approached them. "Please may I join you?" she asked glumly. "Not at all" replied Ben chirpily, as he stood up to leave. He wasn't good with tears, or four women come to think of it. For a few minutes Elle, Bea and Vivie were undecided whether it was time to leave too, or time to stay and offer solace as Bella cried. Obviously, curiosity got the better of them and they chose to stay.

Bella's waist-length brown hair was scraped back off her petite, olive skinned face. In her early twenties, her coal coloured eyes were red and her large lips which these days could have been inspired by Kim Kardashian and created by Botox, were blotchy. A soft blue scarf was draped around her neck. She tore off what looked eye-catchingly like two carats worth of diamond engagement ring and continued to sob. Vivie sensed the atmosphere change as people shifted uncomfortably in their seats.

"Do you need any help?" Vivie asked kindly. With spirit, Bella looked up at Vivie, "No thanks. I've just been planning my wedding since I was seven years old. I've read every wedding magazine, been to loads of bridal fayres, attended weddings of ALL my friends, and now I'm NOT getting married" she stated emphatically.

Bea, Elle and Vivie were shocked by this news especially when Bella placed her head on the table and sobbed loudly. The women looked at each other awkwardly.

Everyone turned around and looked at the door as it was pushed open ¾ of the way. The room fell silent. Caroline always had that effect. Elegant, middle-aged, 5' 7" tall with a slender frame this woman was eye-catching. Her dark brown hair was scraped into a chignon balanced by a light fringe swept to the left of her olive-skinned face.

Caroline's glittering diamond earrings shimmered in the dim light. Her loose fitting, flame red collarless coat was buttoned to the neck and her hands held red leather gloves. Her enormous doe eyes were framed by long black eye lashes and her lips were Chanel red. As she entered the café her low heeled, black leather boots reflected the lights which were placed around the edge of the floor. She sat at Vivie's table and spoke to the top of the sobbing young woman's head. "Bella, what the hell is going on?" she implored. The atmosphere changed to one of impending doom. Ominiscity Vivie would say.

# Chapter 2 - Can chocolate clarify thinking?

Every Saturday Bea made sure that the café shut at 12.30 p.m. so that she and Frank had some time at the weekend to spend with their family. Today was an exception. Bea placed a '*closed*' sign in the shop door and, fifteen minutes earlier than they would have liked, and much to their indignation, two customers, along with Frank, Tom and Ben were bundled out of the Hub. The only people who remained were four friends and one daughter.

Caroline, Vivie, Elle and Bea sat in stunned silence with Bella who was still weeping. They eyed each other cautiously in an attempt to signal that each did not know what had happened. Finally, in an anxious state Bella spoke. "I've sent a text to Charlie. I did it after I'd tried on eight wedding dresses. I wasn't satisfied with any of them. I kept finding fault with all of them. After trying on the last dress I realised that I wasn't unhappy with the dresses, it was me I was unhappy with. I sent Charlie a text" Bella sobbed. "What about?" demanded Caroline. "To tell him that you looked beautiful in all of the dresses and couldn't decide which one to choose?" stated Bea as she tried to lighten the mood. "No" said a terse Bella "to tell him that I didn't want to get married, EVER."

In unison Bea and Vivie exclaimed "have you lost your senses?" A fused sigh was audible from the four older women. "His family are loaded. They own that national flour milling company. She's mad" whispered Bea to Vivie. "Shh" replied Vivie. "I just sent him a text to say that we're not getting married" repeated Bella.

This was serious business as Bella and Charlie had been inseparable since they had met on their first day at university six years ago. Caroline sighed and shook her head. Her wilful, headstrong, intractable daughter. What on earth had possessed her to do such a thing? By text? Unbelievable. At the very least it was bad manners, she thought.

Caroline wondered if Bella had concealed something from her. She had never been an easy child to cope with, well, not since she turned seven anyway; she'd been adorable up until then. Bella looked up and her miserable expression made her mother's stomach churn. They had never broached the subject of Bella's wedding to Charlie. It had just been accepted that one day the two of them would get married. That was that. No questions asked. Until now. Caroline's usual confidence eluded her. She looked beseechingly at her three friends. Surely one of them must know the right thing to say. It was like having a huge elephant at the table with the five of them in squashed attendance. 'Funny' thought Caroline 'if an elephant had been in the room, it would be the first thing that they would talk about. I wonder where such a stupid expression came from.'

Caroline looked at Vivie, who could always be relied upon to say something, anything, the first thing that came into her head. Usually something popped out of her mouth, even when it was not wanted or needed. She was generous with comments, a bit like Frank in that respect. But, just when Caroline needed her, Vivie was silent. Caroline then turned her gaze to Elle. She was inordinately sensible, surely she could say something.

Caroline gave Elle a nod of the head as if to say 'go on, you talk some sense into Bella'. Elle took her cue and cleared her throat. "Well Bella.

Obviously we're all surprised, no, stunned to hear your news. Has Charlie done anything wrong?" "No. It's just that I don't want to marry him" Bella said in a truculent tone. It's not him, it's me. I don't want to get married."

Caroline thought that Bella was just experiencing pre-wedding nerves. It was natural to have doubts about getting married. She looked at Bea. Caroline's eyes locked on Bea's face. Bea took the hint. "Well, that's that then isn't it? No wedding. I'll have to take back the dress I bought at House of Fraser. As if they're not having a bad enough time anyway, and Frank'll have to give back his new suit to Ben. That won't do his Internet business much good will it? Hmm? There'll be lots of people asking questions now won't there?" she said. Caroline raised her eyes to the sky. Good grief. Just when you needed friends, they made things worse, not better. She sat back in exasperation. Concentrate on breathing' she thought 'otherwise I'll pass out. Whenever I've needed my husband, he's never been around.' Right at this moment, fainting seemed like a wonderful escape. She really did contemplate trying it, but holding her breath only made her face as red as her lipstick.

Taking charge, Bea attempted to elicit an explanation from Bella as she could tell by Caroline's reaction how upset she was at the news. "Why did you do that Bella? You're due to be married in three months. How do you think the poor lad'll feel, being dumped by text? That seems callous and not like you at all."

Caroline snatched the mobile phone out of Bella's hands. She opened a text that Bella had sent to Charlie and read it aloud "Hi Charlie, I'm so sorry but I'm not ready to get married.

---

Not ready to get married?" Caroline questioned. "His family will come to the Hub, they'll know that we'll all be in here. They're bound to feel a bit crusty" cried Bea. "They'll smash the Hub to pieces and ask for their dough back." "They won't know Bella's here you idiot" said Vivie "but you're right, they'll think you're taking a rise out of them."

Elle raised her eyes to the sky and stifled a very tiny giggle. Typical of her friends to poke fun even when they shouldn't. "They can't force Bella to marry Charlie can they?" stated Elle. "Well they can make life pretty awful though" retorted Bea. "What do you mean?" replied Caroline. "They're well connected aren't they? I bet his family can be odious gits if they have a mind to be and those uncles are great boxers, or so I've heard" said Vivie fearfully. She decided to carry on by stating "that family is used to getting what they want". Caroline aimed her a warning look. 'So is Bella' she thought ominously.

"I think you should delete all your social media accounts Bella, and the tracking app on your 'phone otherwise Charlie will know where you are. Do it now" urged Elle. "Remember when that weird man stalked me? He kept turning up everywhere I went until I realised he was tracking me through my social media accounts. Be warned. I'm not saying Charlie is strange, at all, but he will want to speak to you at some point. Take yourself off social media" urged Elle. "It's too late isn't it?" queried Bea "He'll already know she's here." A ripple of anxiety waved through the Hub.

"We need a plan" said Bea. Vivie appeared surprised at this statement "A plan? What kind of plan?" "I don't know yet do I? I've not had time to think.

We're four resourceful women, we must be able to come up with a plan." "A plan for what?" asked a startled Bella as she knew that her mother's friends were enterprising and feisty ladies. "We need to keep calm" interrupted Caroline.

"We do nothing at the moment." "Ok, let's do what we used to do at school then and discuss this over hot chocolate and some Prestat gin truffles which y'know I keep for special occasions" suggested Bea. "Remember Caroline we used to pinch the gin truffles from your mother's kitchen when we were younger? We used to pinch the gin too and top up her gin bottle with water thinking she would never know. She used to go berserk.

I'll make the drinks, Vivie you get the truffles. It'll give us time to think and indulge in chocolate." Bella sat in mortified silence. It was bad enough that she had dumped Charlie, now four women were scheming about it. "Oh goodness" she thought "what an awful day and what a mess I've made." She was filled with unaccustomed gloom.

The five women sat in silence, bemused and incredulous. As they congregated around one of the wooden tables in the dimly lit café an angry voice said "we could always shoot him." Turning to Vivie, and speaking in a high pitched voice Bea asked her "Are you insane? Where will we get a gun?" "There must be someone in Manchester who would be willing to shoot him. We could have him shot. Just a little bit."

Disbelieving faces turned at the same time to look at Vivie's earnest face. "You can't shoot someone a little bit you idiot.

May I point out that we are not acquainted with someone who might do that kind of thing?" retorted Bea, 'although the lads she encountered this morning might do just that' she thought, 'just not by her request'.

"We could make discreet enquiries. Your Frank is bound to know someone" replied Vivie. Shaking her head, Bea replied "what are you trying to imply about my Frank, Vivie Baker?" "I'm saying that he might have heard about shady people. People who, for an amount of money, would shoot someone just a little bit" she said patiently. A sensible career woman, and well versed in life, Elle interjected "stop this talk of shooting Charlie. If we do that, we'll all end up in prison and none of us wants that. Our freedom is too good to waste. Anyway, who's to say that there will be recriminations from him or his family, or that he will come here?" Vivie rolled her eyes.

Anxious to invoke a workable and legal solution, Caroline entreated them to stay calm as she saw that Bella was becoming more, not less agitated by their conversation. "Let's drink the hot chocolate and stuff our faces with truffles." She certainly thought that chocolate was good for thinking, if nothing else and she needed to buy some time. "We need to think. Sensibly not irrationally." As she said this she stared at Vivie, Bea and Elle then shook her head. "This is a grave situation. Somehow I think we are going to be in for a long day." Outside the wind offered its cacophonous agreement only adding to their current feeling of alarm.

There was definitely no satisfactory conclusion to be had. The four women had talked over Bella's head as she sat in a dazed silence, emitting the occasional sob and shiver.

Her mind was in a whirl as she remembered the good and bad times she and Charlie had spent together. Why did she not want to marry him? It made no sense. Well, if were to be truthful with herself, it did make sense. It made a lot of sense.

Bella recalled that she had definitely been quieter and more pensive this week as something, or someone, was on her mind. She had been working tirelessly with Bea and Ben at the homeless shelter, could this be what was bothering her?

A long time ago one of Bella's teachers had taught her to breathe deeply when she became anxious, but now, even doing that could not stop the images of her time with Charlie flittering through her mind in rapid succession. The day they met and their holiday in New York appeared involuntarily in her mind's eye, like watching a video, dragging her back in time.

## Charlie Jones

"Come on mum, we'll be late arriving at St. Andrew's if you don't hurry up" Bella shouted impatiently to her mother. "I'm almost ready Bella. Have you got everything you need?" Caroline replied as she stared at her reflection, shocked to see how much she had aged. It seemed only two minutes since she was eighteen and leaving home to study at university far away from home. She gave her head a shake. She needed to let go, to enable Bella to make her own way in life. At the bottom of the stairs Bella's coal-coloured eyes stared up as her mother appeared. Bella was keen to leave home but realised with a jolt that this would be the first time her mother had lived alone. Ever. She was sure Caroline would not like it.

Arriving briskly at the bottom of the stairs, Caroline feigned chirpiness "I'm looking forward to seeing my alma mater.

Let's head off." Once the house was locked, and the door was checked twice to make sure it was secure, they both stepped elegantly into the Aston Martin. The car was stuffed with enough belongings to furnish two apartments, never mind one student's room.

The journey was long. Once they crossed the Forth Bridge, acres of open land stretched out ahead of them. As they approached St. Andrew's, the drive through the medieval town led Bella to experience an overwhelming wave of sadness. She watched mothers and fathers unload scant belongings to help children move into the student accommodation which was dotted throughout the town. She found it difficult to cope with this glimpse into family life as images of her beloved father, with his bright green eyes sparkling at her, flooded her mind. When she turned and saw her mother's pale face, Bella jolted into reality. She wished to be able to sob uncontrollably; she had not done that since she was seven, but Bella was not prepared to make this parting difficult for her mother. Caroline had been through enough, she did not need Bella to lose her poise and dignity now.

As they drew closer to the university halls, Bella sensed the tension rise in her mother. "It's such a beautiful and peaceful place Bella, you'll love being here and at least you'll be in the same time-zone as me!" The car stopped outside Saint Salvator's Hall. Unaware of admiring glances from students and parents, the two Latino beauties got out and unpacked the sleek, black car, before entering Bella's future home.

Bella's large bedroom had a mullioned, leaded window overlooking the quad. The bright yellow curtains hung either side of it, reflecting optimism and cheerfulness which Bella decided augured well.

A wooden work table had been anchored to the bottom of the window and Bella was thrilled to realise that she would be able to gaze out at the changing seasons. As she viewed her room, home for at least a year, she spotted a large double bed which seemed lost in such an immense space. "Why don't you leave open the door to your room Bella?" asked Caroline as she put out plenty of wine and nibbles "It's a way of breaking the ice with anyone who fancies popping in. That way you can get to know the other students on your corridor." 'Trust my mother' thought Bella 'practical as ever' but she remained to be convinced.

The wooden work table almost sagged under the amount of food and drink that Caroline had brought. Once finished, she turned to Bella and said "ok darling, I'm leaving now. I need to visit the Edinburgh office. Take care of yourself and keep in touch". With that, she hugged her only child and left swiftly; Bella could see Caroline was crying.

Surprisingly to Bella, her room began to fill with students shortly after her mother left so she did not have time to wave at the window as Caroline drove away. It was on this occasion, the first day of her new life, in her bedroom that she met Charlie. It was a cursory introduction. "I'm Charlie Jones" he said casually. "Here, let me help you serve drinks" he offered. 'Attractive rather than gorgeous, and what stunning green eyes' Bella remembered thinking.

His athletic frame was covered by a black and white spotted, silk short-sleeved shirt combined with cream coloured shorts and cream Vans.

'His outfit would have looked ridiculous on anyone else', thought Bella, 'particularly in Scotland where the temperature does not usually call for short-wearing', but on Charlie it sort of appealed.

"Did you get dressed in the dark?" she asked cheekily. He laughed. She could sense he was watching her as she refilled glasses, hosted the make-shift welcome party and chatted to other undergraduates in an animated fashion. Charlie made sure he was the last in her room.

In the early hours of the morning they decided to go out for a walk. They wended their way down the narrow Granny Clark's Wynd which led to the Old Golf Course towards one of the most famous of golf bridges, the Swilcan Bridge. "What are your plans after you leave university?" Bella remembered asking Charlie as they walked, with no end in mind. "Whilst I'm here I'm going to work on the computing side of my family's business. We are flour millers and, thanks to the incredible invention of the Internet, which I am sure began in your home town of Manchester, I'll be able to do my degree and work for the family at the same time."

Bella had been impressed by his fortitude. She looked up at him, he bent down to kiss her. Some may say this was presumptuous; others may think it was love at first sight. Cautious by nature, Bella would not put it so boldly but that was how she remembered their first meeting. Vividly. In technicolour. Together at Lewis Hamilton speed.

The video playing in her mind, shut out what was happening in the Hub. The babble of voices and the noise of clinking coffee cups disappeared as if frozen in time. An unwanted thought crept into Bella's mind.

She had wanted to be the centre of Charlie's attention, but that had proved impossible. He had too many other commitments for her liking. To dissipate that thought, Bella chose to fast-forward the video in her mind to their holiday in New York.

"Come to New York Bella. I've got to negotiate a deal for our business and if I'm successful, 2,000 employees will keep working for the family firm. You'll be able to see the sights and I'll meet up with you in the evenings." Bella had agreed readily as the last time she had been in New York was with her parents.

Their flight was uneventful, unlike the yellow cab journey from John F Kennedy airport into Manhattan. The speed at which they were thrown around the huge vehicle made Bella feel dizzy. She could hardly see any sights as the car buzzed, like an annoyed wasp, in front of enormous cars and wagons while drivers honked horns for no particular reason. The driver was oblivious to her loud complaints. When the cab stopped on Park Avenue outside the Waldorf Hotel, realising they had arrived unscathed, Charlie and Bella breathed a sigh of relief. As they exited the cab, both found the energy on the streets palpable. Around the grand hotel in Midtown, skyscrapers were even larger than they had seemed on television.

Their senses were assaulted the minute they stepped on to the sidewalk by smells, noise and heat. Around them, people marched individually, seemingly with a purpose. The majority held disposable coffee cups and appeared to belong to an army nourished by Starbucks.

The hotel doormen, of which there were four, smiled at the couple and vied with each other to carry their bags whilst expecting a tip.

With a great deal of noise and shouting, their luggage was quickly drawn out of the cab and taken to their room. Bella's red suede shoes, bought especially for the trip, stepped across the mosaic marble tiles. She stopped abruptly to absorb the story of the Wheel of Life which depicted the drama of human existence from birth, to old age then death. The memory made her shiver. Bella was worried about Charlie; she knew he would feel humiliated. She was searching for reasons why it didn't seem right to marry Charlie, but she didn't have to dig too deeply. She knew there was one overriding reason, no matter how much she tried to avoid it, why she couldn't go through with the wedding. She pushed that thought out of her mind and forced herself to think about the trip to New York. Bella continued running her internal video.

The Waldorf Hotel had no ordinary reception area. "Look at that amazing design Bella" Charlie had said as they were both drawn to the nine foot tall, gold coloured clock created to commemorate the discovery of America by Christopher Columbus.

Despite a busy reception area, their check-in was prompt and they were shown to a magnificent room on the fifth floor overlooking Park Avenue and the Helmsley Building.

Double doors led to their suite. "Look at this onyx fireplace, and a flat screen television on the wall above it. Oh goodness, touch these sofas, can you believe there are two made of gold silk and such a stunning glass coffee table." Bella walked over to a wall cabinet. She could not believe that Lalique glass and a Fabergé egg were there within touching distance, displayed in a cabinet.

Bella walked through a second set of double doors which led to the bedroom. "Gosh, look at those stunning white orchids. They look like they're standing to attention on the dressing table."

She touched an oak writing table. "I wonder which guests have taken the opportunity to write postcards at this table?" she quizzed. Turning around she looked at a simple king size bed, with a gold coloured Egyptian cotton bed cover to the right of the room. This suite was ostentatious but Charlie would not have noticed, as this was how he lived.

Bella recollected that the holiday had passed in a whirl of activity. At this moment, if the four women were watching her face, they would have witnessed a smile flicker across Bella's lips at the memory of her first meal in New York with Charlie. "Let's eat in an American diner Charlie" she suggested. "I didn't think we would be eating in a mini-supermarket Bella" grumbled Charlie as he sat glumly and ate among the toilet rolls and washing conditioner whilst locals made their grocery selection and gawped at the two tourists. "Eating from paper plates, using plastic cutlery is not my idea of fun Bella" moaned Charlie. Bella laughed so hard at his disquiet that tears rolled down her cheeks.

On her own during the day Bella had a tendency to walk slowly to absorb the many attractions New York had to offer. She made her way along Sixth Avenue, one of the wide boulevards which criss-crossed Midtown Manhattan and headed towards the Rockefeller Centre. As they turned into West 50th Street Bella could feel her spirit soar as she looked up at the looming historic landmark. She booked tickets for the last day of their holiday so that she and Charlie could go up 'The Top of the Rock' to the Observation Deck at dusk.

At the front of the Rockefeller Centre the magnificent statue of Prometheus shimmered in bronze to represent defiance of established authority. Right now, Bella longed for the same courage.

Uninterested in shopping, she visited Saint Patrick's Cathedral every day. Charlie had told Bella that the Cathedral had opened in 1879 and each year more than five million people of different nationalities and faith visited this neo-Gothic building. Standing inside the voluminous space Bella was in awe of the splendid stained glass panels and enchanted by the replica of Michelangelo's Pieta. She felt a sense of peace and calmness overtake her.

One evening, Charlie had booked a meal at the famous Oyster Bar in Grand Central station. They could both hardly contain their excitement to see the famous clock and marble staircases. Inside the Terminal Bella was overwhelmed with her first vision of the grand hall "wow look at the light streaming through those enormous arched windows and the chandeliers.

Oh, oh and look up, look up" she implored Charlie "look at the blue vaulted ceiling and the myriad of twinkling lights.

Do you know that it's a back to front mural to represent various constellations?" she had asked Charlie. He kindly pretended not to have seen any of this magnificence before.

Keen to spend a day in Downtown New York, early one morning Bella caught the number 5 bus to Greenwich Village. She was not disappointed to find it reminiscent of a film which depicted Victorian England rather than brash and bustling 21st Century New York. She had not expected to see small, independent, neighbourhood shops nestled at the bottom of handsomely built, curved edge buildings, along tree lined boulevards.

Walking along Bleeker Street, just beyond the bright red canopy of Murray's delicatessen, was sure she could see her father in the distance.

She bellowed "dad" at the top of her voice only to be disappointed when about a dozen people turned around and not one of them she knew.

Discombobulated, Bella walked in the direction of the Freedom Tower. As she neared the 9/11 site, she was shocked to be pestered by vendors plying memorability of the disaster. Quickly she turned away from them and headed towards the two black memorial pools. Bella found herself alongside throngs of people, even though no word was spoken, she felt strangely peaceful. Intent on reading the names at the north and south pools, she placed a tiny wooden acorn that Bea had made into one of the stencils on a bronze parapet. It was a symbol of life, growth, and immortality. At length, Bella decided to leave and walked towards Battery Park so that she could gaze out over the glistening water towards the Statue of Liberty resplendent in green, her gold crown shimmering. Bella stayed there until dusk.

On their last day in New York Charlie had finished his negotiations and wanted to spend some time just relaxing in Central Park. As soon as they arrived Bella felt as if she were in a film. In this swathe of green everything looked so familiar and she pointed out to Charlie all the interesting places she had spent hours researching on the Internet.

In the late afternoon they held hands and strolled down a tree-lined mall arriving at Bethesda Terrace. They leant on the balustrade and absorbed the vision of an eight foot bronze angel holding a lily atop a fountain. Below the angel, four small cherubim stood back to back around a bronze pole to symbolise health, purity, temperance and peace.

Even at the closing of the day, the air was still warm so the couple headed towards the conservatory and rented a model radio-controlled boat which they had great fun navigating. When Bella brought the boat to the water's edge a small box was perched precariously on the bow. The top of the box had the initials HW engraved in silver. Curious, she bent down to pick it up.

Perplexed she turned to show Charlie. "Open it Bella, let's see what it is" he advocated. As she opened the navy, leather box, courtesy of Harry Winston, a stunning diamond ring glistened in the fading light. At that moment, in Central Park, Charlie knelt down on one knee. "Bella, will you marry me?" he asked. Overwhelmed by this extravagant gesture, she cried and said "yes". Bella remembered thinking 'wow, now I'm going to be at least two carats heavier'.

In the Hub, Bella's chain of thought was interrupted. She shivered. "Are you cold Bella love?" asked Bea gently. "I'll put the heating on."

The four friends had sat in silence whilst Bella's internal video had run through her first meeting with Charlie and their engagement. "I am Bea" replied Bella quietly. "I am cold. Inside and out. How could I have been so reckless with Charlie's emotions?" With a jolt she looked around the café, and began to sob uncontrollably. Bea, Caroline, Vivie and Elle looked at each other remembering turbulent and happy times in their own lives. Exchanging knowing looks, as in many cultures which impart wisdom from old to young, they decided it was time to share with Bella their own wheel of life surprises.

# Chapter 3 - We can travel far, but still stay close

In Manchester the afternoon was growing dark which cast a portentous mood on the group. The wind howled down the street, gnarled fingers of branches tapped against the window like an embittered old man, leaves swirled and the rain battered the pavement. Bea switched on the café lights and closed the blinds in an attempt to shut out the world. "I'm sure that the weather forecasters predicted a monsoon in Manchester. Surely that's not going to happen is it? A monsoon in Manchester. Unthinkable. What I do know is that more coffee is needed so we can consider how we've dealt with things in the past. That might influence what we do now" said Bea as her willowy blonde figure sashayed into the kitchen. This time she was accompanied by Elle.

"What are we to do? Do you think it would be useful to Bella if I told her my story?" Bea glanced at Elle's expressive blue eyes which relayed a quiet confidence. "Yeah" said Bea, "I think that's a good idea." They returned to the table with two large coffee pots, poured drinks for the five women as dim lights reflected a subdued atmosphere. "I know everything appears bleak at the moment, both inside and outside the café", said Elle addressing Bella as the rain hammered on the window and door. "Everything passes. Good and bad. You'll not always feel sad. When I was a little younger than you I came through a difficult experience. I came through it Bella, do you hear me?" Bella gave a faint smile. "Yes I do and I'm sure that I'm going to hear about it aren't I?" she questioned. Thus Elle began her tale.

## Elle again

"Unlike Vivie and Bea who couldn't wait to leave school and left the convent when they were 16 years old, your mum and I stayed on at the convent until we were 18 years old. We thought we were lucky when we were each offered a place at St. Andrew's University and I think that's one of the reasons you chose to go there Bella isn't it, to follow in your mum's footsteps?" Bella nodded in assent. "At the convent most of the nuns kept telling us we'd never amount to anything but one nun believed in us. Sister Angela said we had the chance to live a life of endless possibilities. We applied to St. Andrew's, were amazed when we were both accepted and managed, with some jiggery-pokery to share the same hall of residence. We had great fun didn't we Caroline?" Both women laughed.

"During the second weekend of November we joined in the age-old tradition of Raisin Weekend which takes place in St. Andrew's. I know that the locals don't join in but they do allow roads to be closed and tolerate the stupidity of students. We had great fun. The theme was Disney characters so I dressed up as Piglet and Caroline dressed up as Winnie the Pooh. It gave us an excuse to make loads of things to eat using honey and food was our great way of getting to chat to people.

Regardless of what you might think, it isn't just Bea who can cook but she's always been better at being creative. If you'd've come with us to university Vivie you could've been Roo as you were always into mischief and Bea you would've been Kanga as she is nurturing and motherly."

Both women laughed at the image. "Anyway our aim was to meet as many people as we could." "Mainly boys" interjected Caroline and Elle smiled. "I fell for a young man dressed as Eeyore" said Elle. "Did he turn out to be a right donkey Elle?" asked Bella with a wry smile. "Ah ha, you haven't lost your sense of humour yet I see" replied Elle with a twinkle in her eyes. "Listen and you might find out" said Elle mischievously. The women were enjoying the banter.

"Shall I continue?" asked Elle. "Yes please" retorted Bella. "Ok. So we met up with second year students who took us under their wing and went to a place called the Drouthy Neebors pub, y'know the one on South Street? As we arrived I heard a boy dressed as Eeyore say that *'people who do not use punctuation deserve a long sentence;* which my eighteen year old self thought was hilarious." "You didn't really did you?" asked Bella. "Yes, I was very easily amused!

He told us a joke which I can still remember, *I accidentally gave my wife a glue stick instead of a chap stick. She hasn't said a word to me since.* I howled with laughter! Is that better Bella?" "No" Bella replied emphatically. "I'll tell you one more joke that Eeyore told and then I'll stop *I've always believed that ironing boards were surf boards that just stopped pursuing their dreams and got a job."* Bella shook her head and judged the joke to be "terrible. 'I can't see why you fell for him." We thought it was hilarious didn't we Caroline? Caroline said "you did" and rolled her eyes.

We partied all weekend and on the Monday all the students congregated in the quad at St. Salvator's College to participate in, what I think must be the world's largest outdoor shaving foam fight.

As happens when you've got freedom from home and go mad a bit, or a lot, Eeyore and I became an item for a while. He was a nice lad, a bit geeky." "He was a lot geeky Elle, he was a mathematician who told terrible jokes, had a ruddy complexion, wild hair and poor taste in clothes" exclaimed Caroline. "You shouldn't judge people by how they look, he was kind, thoughtful and plain looking. We saw each other for about four months and then our relationship fizzled out but we remained, and still are, good friends.

Anyway. To continue my story. Much to my horror, a little time after our relationship ended I found out that I was pregnant. At the time I decided not to tell Eeyore." Bella looked at Elle with incredulity. "I never knew that." Elle, Bea, Caroline and Vivie looked at each other. "You don't know everything about us Bella. We did live a life before you joined us y'know" retorted Vivie. "So I gather" said Bella with a smile. "I'm glad you find this amusing Bella.

"In those day things were not as easily accessible as they are today. Your mum and I saved up the money to buy a pregnancy kit. Now St. Andrew's is a small place and everyone knows everyone else's business so we caught the train to Edinburgh one Saturday morning. We dared each other to go into Boots and, on the toss of a coin, Caroline had to go into the chemist's shop and buy a pregnancy kit whilst I waited outside, on guard. I don't know what I was on guard for because no-one knew us in Edinburgh.

There was a small café close by to the chemist shop so we went in there and had a coffcc. It took me ages to pluck up the courage to take the test.

It was in the café toilet that the news was relayed to me. Oh I was in such a tizzy. In my mind I was destined for great things – I had huge plans. I wanted to be someone and go somewhere now this kit confirmed that I was pregnant which would ruin all of my hopes.

I was terrified about what my parents would say, especially my father. Caroline and I talked things over. We agreed on a plan of how we could both take it in turns to look after the baby when it came and we managed to hide my pregnancy from everyone. I wore baggy jumpers, 'cos you could as a student, look like a real tramp and no-one would question why. I didn't put on much weight because I couldn't eat with the worry of it all. In those days, it was still frowned upon to be pregnant and not married and at that time I didn't even have a boyfriend. Oh I can still feel the shame of it" she said with a bright red face. I feared that the nuns were right, I wouldn't amount to much." "But you did Elle, didn't you? You have amounted to a lot" Caroline beamed at Elle "and not just in your job."

"I decided no matter what, I was going to go ahead with this pregnancy. Bella, your mum was amazing. She was kind and tolerant when I was moody. Then after a few weeks I began to have pain on the left side of my tummy. I thought this was a symptom of being pregnant because, for the first few days it was a mild pain. Something I could tolerate. Then when I lay down to rest I got pain in my shoulder so I thought I must've pulled a muscle.

Your mum made me rest while she got notes from my lectures then read them to me every day so that I could keep up with what was happening in my classes. She cleaned our rooms, cooked light meals for me. I couldn't have survived without Caroline, she was amazing.

Whenever I stood up I began to feel faint, so I lay with my feet on pillows. I had absolutely no idea what was wrong." Elle dabbed her eyes and Bea gave her a reassuring hug. At this point Caroline interjected "I rang Bea and Vivie to tell them the news. In those days I had to ring from a local telephone box and had to wait until no-one was around, so that I wasn't overheard when I made the call.

Bea and Vivie drove for five hours to St. Andrew's and the plan was that they would stay for a few days as I was getting behind with my university work. They helped me to look after Elle while she was ill" said Caroline. "Yes", agreed Bea "we drove up in a battered old Vauxhall Viva. It was teeming with rain, the windscreen wiper fell off. I stopped the car while Vivie ran down a dark country lane to find it.

In a howling gale we tied the windscreen wiper back on with a piece of string and for the rest of the journey Vivie pulled the string to make the wipers work. How we survived that journey I'll never know." Both Bea and Vivie laughed as they reminisced. "On the way back the water tank seized up and we had to put an egg in the tank to make it work. We certainly got home on a wing and a prayer, didn't we?" "Go on" urged Bella in eager anticipation "what happened next?"

Elle took over. "I was feeling pretty grim. The others didn't know how to help me or what to do. By this time the pain in my tummy was unbearable and I couldn't take any painkillers as I was afraid this would affect the baby.

So Bea insisted that the four of us go to the hospital whilst we had access to a car. We didn't go to the hospital in St. Andrew's but decided to travel to Ninewells in Dundee.

It was less likely we would see someone we knew there. Your mum practically carried me into the car and lay me down on the back seat with a blanket. She sat in the back with me. Bea started the battered Vauxhall Viva which chugged along slowly down the country roads until it ran out of petrol about half way to Dundee because the petrol gauge wasn't working properly. In the pouring rain, with weather very much like today's weather, we had to abandon the car." "I'm still sorry about not filling up the car when I should've done Elle" said Bea in muted tones. Elle smiled. "Life's never dull when the four of us are together is it?" she questioned.

"Where was I?" "You were running out of petrol" urged Bella. "Ah yes. So, we walked to the nearest bus stop which was about half a mile away. When I say we walked, Caroline and Vivie practically dragged me along and Bea tried to hold an umbrella over us for protection from the driving rain but she ended up like Mary Poppins, almost lifted into the sky by the fierce wind.

It was a freezing day and the rain was hammering us. We just about had enough money for the bus fare. A bus appeared fairly quickly so we arrived shortly afterwards at Ninewells Hospital's Accident and Emergency unit which isn't the best place to be. We passed a man outside who had a can of beer and an empty bottle of lemonade. We watched him pour the beer into the empty pop bottle and throw away the can. He walked into the reception area before us and told the receptionist that he thought he had a cotton bud stuck in his ear. He was drunk out of his mind.

We checked in. I said that I had a bad tummy ache. I think the receptionist thought that I had appendicitis. Anyway the drunken man went to triage first.

He came out within two minutes, said to the receptionist, 'there's nowt wrong wi' mi' ears' and staggered off.

I was next in triage. The nurse asked me if I could be pregnant. I told her that I was fairly sure that I was. She did a pregnancy test which confirmed what I had told her and then we waited for forty endless minutes to see a doctor." "Were you scared?" asked Bella. "Yes, I think we all were scared." The other three women nodded their assent.

"So what happened?" Bella insisted. "You won't believe it but one of my professors walked into reception with his wife. His wife looked white as a ghost. The professor spotted the four of us in the waiting room and sat next to us when his wife was in triage. It turned out that they had been shopping in Dundee and his wife had fallen over and broken her arm. Of all the people to see, I had to bump into someone I knew. Anyway, Professor Fane's wife was taken away to have her arm put into plaster. He waited in the reception area with us. Then I fainted."

Caroline took up the story. "It was obvious to the Professor and everyone else around that something was seriously wrong with Elle. Her face was pale and her breathing shallow. Two nurses picked her up, put her on a trolley-bed and took away and I went with her leaving Bea and Vivie with Professor Fane." "Yes" said Bea "Professor Fane was a really kind man, very gentle and easy to talk to so we told him everything." "Oh my goodness, did Elle want you to do that?" asked Bella. "She didn't have any choice in the matter did she?" stated Bea. 'Yes, they'd be no good as spies those two.

They'd give up their friend for a cup of coffee" said Elle with irony. Bella laughed and, eager to hear the rest asked "then what?"

Elle blushed and continued. "When I came round I was having an ultrasound scan. Your mum was with me. There appeared to be some difficulties highlighted on the scan, but at the time I didn't know what was wrong. Anyway I started to panic and your mum tried really hard to calm me down. The doctor who was on call that night said she would need to arrange for me to have a laparoscopy for which I needed to be asleep. I had a general anaesthetic and can remember no more about it" said Elle in a perfunctory manner.

"At that point" said Caroline "I went back to the waiting room to be with Vivie and Bea as there was nothing I could do whilst Elle was in theatre. I remember telling Professor Fane that things looked bad for Elle. We waited and waited. Professor Fane's wife joined us with her arm in plaster. She too was kind and very concerned about Elle. They both waited with us for news of Elle. Time passed by very slowly. We had no money as we'd spent it all on our bus journey. The Fanes brought us food and drink and generally acted like our parents would've behaved in the same situation; when they'd overcome their Catholic shock obviously.

Professor and Mrs Fane were just adorable and non-judgemental which made them so easy to talk to. I think that's what you need at times of stress, someone who won't shout at you for messing up. After about four hours the doctor came to see us.

She said that Elle had gone through an ectopic pregnancy which had ruptured her fallopian tube.

As this was a medical emergency, Elle had been taken to the operating theatre and there was nothing we could do but wait." "How awful" said Bella with tears in her eyes.

"After what seemed like an interminable amount of time, Professor and Mrs Fane went home as she looked really tired and worn out by her own misadventure. Before they left, they gave us more than enough money for a taxi which we didn't have any choice but to accept. Remember that this was before a hole in the wall cash dispenser was commonplace.

When the Fanes left, the three of us agreed not to ring Elle's parents until we had spoken to her the next day, knew what the situation was and what help she needed from us." Bella turned to Elle who had begun to tremble and gave her a much needed hug. Caroline continued the tale. "The taxi driver was really kind too as we told him we'd had to abandon the car on the road to Dundee. He agreed to take us to a nearby petrol station so that we could fill up the old Viva with petrol on our way back to St. Andrew's." "I was able to drive back to the university" interrupted Bea "so that we had our own transport." "Yes, and we didn't sleep a wink that night did we?" said Vivie miserably "as we wondered what was happening to Elle."

Caroline carried on the story. "A lot happened the following day. Bea, Vivie and I had spent a restless night in my room. Hospital visiting time was one o'clock so we agreed to leave St. Andrew's at 11 the following morning so that we could arrive at the hospital early just in case there were any traffic problems and to take account of Bea's awful driving.

We decided to have a brief visit to St Salvator's Chapel early in the morning.

I know you've been to it many times Bella as that is, er was er where your wedding was going to be."

Caroline looked apologetically at Bella as she said this. Bella knew the chapel well, with its 600 years old history; an exquisite example of late Gothic architecture.

Bea and Vivie raised their eyebrows to indicate that Caroline needed to get on with the story.

"Anyway" said Caroline "we crept in through the enormous oak door, which I bet even now is not easy to open, walked past the pews which faced each other and headed to the ante Chapel which was hidden behind a decorative stone screen. We didn't know beforehand, but the chamber choir were rehearsing in the ante-Chapel when we turned up. The three of us sat, side by side in an oak pew and listened for an hour as thirty students performed a repertoire of choral music which was meditative and entrancing."

Bea and Vivie nodded their agreement. "It seemed to be just what was needed before we faced Elle. After that we set off on our journey, which amazingly was trouble free." "Cheek" retorted Bea "but I did take a wrong turning out of St. Andrew's didn't I?" she confessed. The four women smiled at each other. "And we thought there was only one road in and one road out" replied Vivie.

"When we arrived at the hospital" continued Caroline, "we went to the reception area to find out which ward Elle was in. It was so unnerving when we were told she was in the intensive care unit. We did panic didn't we?" she turned to Vivie and Bea who nodded their agreement. "We were concerned that the nurses wouldn't let us into the ward because we weren't next of kin, but they did.

Elle was linked to lots of machines through wires, her heart was being monitored, and we could hear the machine bleeping. There seemed to be a disharmony between the noises in the ward as they were at odds with the calmness we'd left in St. Salvator's Chapel. We all tried hard not to cry as Elle lay motionless on the bed. The three of us sat around her bed with the curtains closed for some privacy and eventually one of the doctors joined us.

Se told us the news that Elle would recover but that she would have to be supported in her grief." There was a stunned silence as Bella began to comprehend what had happened. "Oh Elle, you lost your baby?" she asked. "Yes" said Elle looking miserable. "Oh no. Then what happened Elle?" asked Bella. "It's difficult to remember exactly but Caroline, Vivie and Bea came back to the hospital every day and after four days I was moved off the intensive care ward.

Whilst we were all together in the hospital Professor Fane visited me with his wife. We told him what had happened and he arranged for us to have a private memorial service in St. Salvator's Chapel. Strangely on the day of the service the weather was freezing cold but beautifully sunny as we paid our respects to the baby. We didn't have any money, so the Fanes paid for everything.

We decided not to tell my parents to avoid unnecessary added misery. At the time, I couldn't have coped with their disappointment in me at the same time as coping with my own unhappiness. It took me a long time, and a lot of kindness from my friends, to get through such a sad event. Anyway, getting back to the story. The service was attended by the four of us, Professor Fane and his wife. I told Eeyore so he turned up with two of his friends. The choir sang." At this recollection, Elle became distressed so Vivie took over the story.

"It was a beautiful service. The baby was a boy and we named him Salvator after our halls of residence and the chapel. It means saviour. We had a very simple service after which the Fanes took us to their home. They lived in a grey stone Victorian villa near the Old Course at St. Andrew's. They're both fanatical golfers.

Their house was impressive. As we stood in the living room, I remember I had to squint as I looked out to sea as sunrays danced on the water. The sky was a brilliant blue and, for once, the sea looked shimmery and sparkly rather than a murky grey. The bright weather seemed at odds with our sombre mood.

Professor and Mrs Fane had spent ages making a spread of home-made food and the smell as we entered the house was of freshly baked bread. Professor Fane probably made most of the food though because Mrs Fane's arm was still in plaster. It was such a welcoming and warm environment that we stayed all day, just chatting which seemed to alleviate the anguish we all felt. We are all still very close friends with them, as you know." "Ah", replied Bella "I wondered how you came to be friends with them, now I understand." There was a pause of several minutes.

"After that" began Elle, "I put all my efforts into studying." "Hence the First Class Batchelor's Degree, a Distinction at Masters Level and a Doctorate?" said Bella. Elle smiled. "Yes. I was determined to make something of my life. To make a difference. To help people. To be kind and I thought that having qualifications behind me would help to open doors, which it has. That's why I still work with the Ectopic Pregnancy Trust to try and make a positive difference to people.

It's very difficult breaking bad news to a lady who is expecting a happy event. There needs to be lots of support for women, some of whom do end up grieving. We've found that once a woman has an ectopic pregnancy, it might indicate a problem with her fallopian tubes and her fertility might be compromised in the future. Some women may never be able to have a baby and our Trust helps people to deal with that sadness."

"Is that why you studied that particular field of medicine?" said Bella. "I'm sure it is Bella. I had a difficult time coming to terms with losing my baby but I got through it because of the support I received from Bea, Vivie and Caroline. Everyone goes through difficult times Bella. Perhaps it's how you deal with life's challenges that measures you as a person" said Elle quietly.

"Is that why you never married?" asked Bella. "No of course not. I chose to be married to my job Bella. A career woman as my parents call me. If I hadn't lost the baby I would never have ended up working in that field of medicine would I? My job has given me loads of fabulous times, especially when I've been able to help other women.

I've had lots of boyfriends too. I think that there are many people out there that perhaps I could be married to. I don't think that there's just *the one* but I chose to put all my energies into my work rather than into a relationship. Do you hear me Bella? There isn't just one person who will make you happy. In fact, it's dangerous to expect someone else to make you happy. You're in charge of your own emotions.

I don't think it's too late for me to meet someone, but up until now I just haven't felt the need to settle. In fact, I could write a book and call it *boyfriends and why I never married.*

I travel all over the world with my work. I've seen places I never would've visited if it hadn't been for my job so far my life has been great.

Travelling extensively would mean that my partner would have to give up their job to be with me and I'm not sure, even in these supposed enlightened times that a man would like that. They wouldn't like playing second fiddle to my work. Anyway, my friends' lives have kept me entertained over the years with their own highs and lows, joys and tragedies. Haven't you?"

Elle raised an eyebrow as she looked at her three friends. "Which one of you wants to go next?" she said. "What, there's more to tell from you all?" exclaimed Bella "like what?" "I think we need more coffee" said Vivie as she excused herself and walked into the kitchen. Across the table, Caroline shot Bea a warning look and jumped as a gnarly branch tapped against the window and rain hammered on the glass. On the shiny, slippery street, a lone man, wrapped in a black raincoat staggered in the wind towards the Hub where a feeling of ominiscity grew within the group.

# Chapter 4 - You could cause an argument in an empty house

The day grew darker, the wind screeched around the corner of the building, outside the noise of trees swaying to and fro joined the cacophony of noise. Through a small gap between the blinds and the window a steady stream of cars could be seen to light up the dark street as drivers hurried about their business. Suddenly there was a bang on the door. All five women screamed as the pounding on the door continued. Bea leapt to her feet anxious about being held up at gun point as had happened recently at the local petrol station. A terrified silence shrouded the Hub. Full of trepidation Bea walked slowly to the door. She bent down to peep through a gap by slowly and breathlessly lifting a single layer of the door-blind and placed her eye as close as she could to the opening. Peering out, she saw a hunched, dark figure at the café door. Without hesitating, the shadowy figure continued to batter the door.

On and on the walloping continued as Bea looked around the gloomy room at the frightened faces of her friends. She decided to be brave. "What do you want?" she shouted. "Bea, Bea, open the door. Hurry up I'm soaked through" shouted the silhouette. Quickly, Bea unlocked the Hub door, dragged it to ¾ opening and stepped aside as her soaking-wet husband Frank burst in and rain-water from his black coat dripped on the oak floor.

"It's vile out there" said Frank unaware of the terror he had created in the Hub "I've just left Tom and Ben at your house" he said to Vivie.
"I told them I'd only be a few minutes because I wanted to find out what you lot were up to."

The women began to laugh "Frank, I thought we were about to be robbed at gun point" shouted Bea. "Robbed, what are you talking about? I've just come to find out what's going on in here. Not to rob you. I rang your mobile 'phone but it's been turned off and I've been worried about the Hub and what yer all up to."

Frank's actions often spoke louder than his words. Bea was touched that Frank had come out on such a dreadful day just to check that she and her friends were all right. "I'm fine. We're all fine. Well, we're not all fine. Bella has called off the wedding to Charlie. We've been telling her tales about life's dramas in the hope that she realises that everyone's life has its ups and downs" said Bea without taking a breath. "Women. I can never understand them" retorted Frank. "Did you jump when I knocked on the door because you though Charlie had turned up to exact revenge on Bella?" He laughed at the lunacy of his comment. The women didn't join in with his mirth as this thought had flickered through the minds of all of them, including Bella.

Frank sat down at the table oblivious that his presence might be unwelcome. "You're a strange lot aren't you?" he asked as he looked around the table at the five women as if, in his wildest dreams, they might agree with him. None of the women were sure why Frank had chosen to pick on them when they were trying to cheer-up Bella.

"I can remember when we got together Bea, talk about unpredictable and unreasonable. Do you remember how obstinate you were? Still are?"

Frank laughed. "You're an idiot Frank. What I remember is that I went shopping with my mother to the furniture store on the High Street and as we were leaving you walked in.

You said you were sorry to hear that my husband had died and asked if I wanted to go out with you that night. You've never been subtle have you? No wonder I said *no* to you. Then Elle and I went in to Manchester that night and you turned up. We couldn't shake you off. Do you remember that?" exclaimed Bea.

"That's absolute rubbish Bea and y'know it. You followed me into the furniture shop, asked if I ever went out in Manchester and when I told you where I usually spent Saturday night, you and Elle turned up and I couldn't shake you off" said an indignant Frank. "What utter rubbish Frank" replied Bea. "What I remember is that we were in the Town Hall Tavern and the three of us chatted all night. Afterwards we went back to my house. You didn't say no Frank when we invited you in" exclaimed Bea.

"I remember that night" said Elle. "You kept giving me the eye Frank as if you wanted me to leave you and Bea alone but I wasn't going anywhere on my own on a Saturday night. That's why I stuck to the two of you like a limpet" retorted an indignant Elle. Never one to tolerate people Frank responded "eventually you left. Yes, eventually. It was like waiting to get through passport control at Manchester Airport the length of time you were with us! I thought you'd never leave us alone."

Elle looked hurt when Frank, indifferent to her feelings said "Yes, I was very pleased when you left." At that point Bea interjected.
"What he means Elle is that when you left we had our first kiss since we were teenagers and within four months we were living together."

"Yes. So it's a good thing you left Elle because we've been together ever since" said Frank in an objective manner, which Bea thought was objectionable.

Instead of feeling awkward, Elle was placated by this statement and smiled. Bea breathed a sigh of relief. Another potential commotion caused by Frank had been averted she thought. She whispered to herself 'please don't speak again Frank' but he took it upon himself to do just that.

"Charlie. Charlie's been dumped? Hmm well it's probably because of the cost of the wedding I think. He might be rich, but he certainly doesn't like splashing the cash all the time does he? It can't be anything else. I haven't heard that you've got another boyfriend Bella. Or is it a girlfriend?" He paused, then started again. "Or, is he in some kind of bother?" asked Frank. Bea gave him a withering look endeavouring to quell his mighty mouth, but to no avail.

"You're odd Bella, can't think why you wouldn't want to marry him. Is it that you're high maintenance and he's realised it so you're not getting your own way? I never put you down as a moaner who would wimp out of getting married. That's the trouble with you young ones, no commitment. You want everything but you're not willing to work hard for it. You're not gettin' any younger y'know. Your biological clock is ticking away. Tick, tock. Better to hold on to Charlie. That's my advice for what it's worth." Frank looked pretty pleased with himself.

Bea stared at Frank in horror. He was oblivious to the effect his words might have on Bella.

For at least three minutes Bea sat in stupefied hush. The silence was broken by Bella who smiled and said "well Frank, thanks for the support of my character. In your unusual way, you've made me feel a little better. It's me, I just didn't want to spend the rest of my life with Charlie" stated Bella. "Simple as that." "Hope Charlie sees it that way" retorted Frank. "Hope he thinks it's simple." Bea gave him a withering look. 'Idiot' she whispered to herself. "Hope he doesn't come here looking for you. Who knows what might happen" declared Frank.

Immediately changing the subject by opening his mouth once more, Frank questioned "did I tell you about the time I asked Bea to marry me?" He was impervious to the atmosphere in the room. "She was the first girl I ever kissed. We went to junior school together then she passed that 11+ and went on to the Convent so obviously we didn't go to school together after that. I would've had to dress up as a girl to get into the convent, and I wasn't going to do that." Frank paused for comedic effect. Nobody laughed as was usual with Frank's witticisms.

"I used to see her standing at the bus-stop every morning. In the evenings after school, I used to hang around waiting for her to get off the bus but I always pretended that I just happened to be passing the bus-stop at the same time each night. We always walked home together and talked about what had happened during the day. She was so easy to talk to and I loved her from the minute I saw her in the school playground. I told her that one day we'd be married to each other.

On my sixteenth birthday I signed up to work on the cruise ships. I'd always wanted to travel the world and this was such a brilliant, unique chance for me. The way I saw it, I'd be able to train as a chef and travel.

That evening when I told Bea what I'd done she didn't seem excited, she just said *goodbye* and walked away.

Bloody cheek. I don't mind telling you I was really offended by her indifference. We didn't speak to each other again until years later when she stalked me in the Town Hall Tavern. Hope you're not makin' a mistake Bella, like Bea did!"

"That's not telling them how you asked me to marry you Frank" said a shocked and astonished Bea. Rarely had she seen Frank so animated unless he was chatting about football or cooking. She speculated if he'd been drinking with Tom and Ben. "Actually Bea, I never asked you why you just turned and walked away from me when you were sixteen and I told you I was going to work on a cruise liner" Frank questioned.

"I didn't want you to see me cry" whispered Bea. "You were bothered?" exclaimed Frank. Bea put her head down and simply nodded. "I never knew that. I always thought you didn't care about me and then you went and married Jasper." "You've always been an idiot Frank" she answered "never able to see what's right in front of you" she added. Discomposure hung in the air. Frank was forced to look at his beloved wife. He took a deep breath, and said "Why did you marry someone else first then and why did you say no to me when I asked you years later?"

All eyes in the room turned to Bea in eager anticipation of this unfolding drama. At that precise moment the wind let out a lamentable scream and a few seconds later, in harmony, so did the small group. "Good grief" cried Bea trying to change the atmosphere in the room "We're all jittery aren't we?" she said to no-one in particular. "Let's make fresh drinks, some soup and sandwiches. If we all help out, it won't take too long."

Frank was aghast that five women were going to be working in his kitchen but, against his normal character, he resisted the temptation to tell them so.

He watched in agitation as knives were removed from wooden drawers and vegetables were chopped on his precious quartz worktop, without a chopping board, he noted gravely.

Frank folded his arms, silent doubt etched on his face until Bea caught his eye. She indicated inaudibly for him to stay at the table in the café. Instead, he busied himself by lighting candles in the Hub to create a brighter aura as the grey daylight began to abandon the sky by turning it inky. As he pushed three tables together, covered them with fresh chequered tablecloths, Frank wondered why Bea turned him down all those years ago. Until today, he had never asked her. Maybe she'd never tell him.

Slowly the tables were covered with plates of food. Hot tomato and basil soup was subject to the vagaries of Frank's judgement. Surprisingly, his verdict was positive. Unusual for Frank that. Sandwiches made with Serrano ham, fresh tomatoes and paprika were equally well received. Bea had some freshly baked lemon drizzle cake, enough for each to share a piece which they washed down with Navazza coffee. When all had eaten a sufficiency, the tables were cleared, the dishwasher stacked and the kitchen was cleaned to Frank's satisfaction. Due to his excellent training, he couldn't help but be precise where food was concerned. Although uneasy to ask the question, Bella queried why Frank had left home at sixteen.

"I was eager to see the world and it was a fantastic opportunity for me to learn a trade" explained Frank. "I wanted to work with different people and visit places I'd never even heard about in school.

It was hard work. The shifts involved long hours and the corridors for crew members were really narrow. At first I had to shuffle along pushing food trolleys, moving and lifting pallets of food and drink, sorting out the recycling of rubbish. I was happy to take direction and did loads of jobs so that I could learn all about how to be a chef. You wouldn't believe that we had more than forty different kinds of fruit and vegetables to prepare each day.

On the ship there wasn't just one food outlet, but twenty so all in all we had to plate up about 60,000 meals every day. Most of the food, including bread and pastries was made on board so it was all really fresh. Can you believe how hard we worked? The kitchen work area was tiny but I saw there was a chance that I could work towards being promoted. There were 150 chefs on board the ship, so I knew that there was the possibility that one day I could run my own kitchen. At times it could be fraught because we had a brief time to prepare the food so I had to be really organised.

The most hectic time was when we returned to port and had about ten hours to get the ship ready for its next cruise. It was like re-stocking a small city. That was also the most exciting bit, arriving in port as sometimes I had the chance to go on land and explore different cities. My favourite place was Barcelona. I left home because I just couldn't see myself limited by living in one place. I suppose I was restless and there was lots of unemployment at that time.

When I'd been at sea for about seven years, so I'd be 23 then, I'd got some money behind me and visited home for a long weekend. I called in at Robert and Matilde's house, Bea's parents, because I wanted to find out how they were and also to hear about Bea" explained Frank.

In a state of agitation Bea exclaimed "I never knew that". Frank's countenance was resolute. "I know" and he explained his actions. "I wanted to know if you had a boyfriend and your mum told me that you were getting married. I asked her not to let you know that she'd seen me. Pardon the pun, but I didn't want to rock any boats." He glanced at Bea whose face had coloured. "Your mum wanted the best for you. She could see that you were happy and had the promise of a great life with your future husband. I could understand that" explained Frank.

"That's the stupidest thing I've ever heard Frank. You knew I was going to get married and you didn't want me to know you'd visited my family's home" Bea scowled. Agitated, Bea stood up, her emotions in a tangle. She breathed deeply then her face softened "I never realised that you were interested in me except as good friends. You can blame Caroline. She introduced me to Jasper." All eyes turned to Caroline who had the grace to appear abashed as she shuffled uncomfortably in her seat. "I never thought you'd end up marrying Jasper" she forced an apologetic smile "or that Frank would be hurt by that."

"All of this was a long time ago. We were young, impetuous and foolish. It turned out fine in the end didn't it? Mostly?" implored Bea. Bella's curiosity had been stirred "I never asked you Bea how you met Jasper" she probed. As she looked around the table, Bea peered at Caroline. "It was through your mum and her job at the brokerage company" replied Bea. She pointed a finger at Caroline "I'm passing this one on to you my friend. You can explain how it happened and I'm going to sit here and listen. Over to you' she said in a theatrical manner.

Caroline's beautiful countenance lit up in the dancing candlelight as she turned to face her audience.

She began her tale about finding a summer job at a brokerage company based in Edinburgh. "I'd always found working with numbers really interesting and the company formed part of the *milk round* at the university."

"What's a milk round?" questioned Bella. "Oh, I don't think it exists anymore. These days young people are expected to work for nothing aren't they? Doing internships if their parents can afford to keep them. Tantamount to slave labour really. It means that the only people who can afford to take internships are those whose parents can fund rent, travel, clothes and food whilst their children work for nothing in the name of *experience*. It should be illegal to work for longer than two weeks as an unpaid intern. There should be a public outcry but obviously there won't be.

Anyway, the milk round was the name used when companies visited universities to tell students about job vacancies. It was possible to apply for jobs and companies took the cream of the students, hence the name milk round.

I was lucky. I applied for a couple of paid summer jobs and after a brief interview, face to face mind, not over the Internet like today where you peer into a screen and have an conversation looking at some grainy person. I must have persuaded the Human Resources Manager that I'd be suitable for the job because he offered me a role that I took and found really interesting.

I worked for a firm of stockbrokers who advised people and companies how to invest their money and I'd never been involved in anything like that before. My role was to monitor how certain companies fared on the stock market, whether their share price went up or down.

In those days we didn't have the Internet where the information is updated minute by minute. It wasn't so easy to find out whether companies were losing share value or gaining it.

Collecting that information regularly without access to the Internet was a massive job. I worked for a fabulous boss during that summer, Jasper. I spent a lot of time trying to find out about the stock market and people I worked with explained how things worked. It was an interesting business where lots of money could be made or lost, and that still happens now. At work we experienced huge highs and also gigantic lows.

When I returned to university I kept in touch with people in the company and just after I graduated, I was offered a job there" explained Caroline. "Enjoyable story mum but that doesn't tell any of us how Bea met Jasper" countered Bella.

"Well I said that I kept in touch with people from the brokerage firm, so after my summer internship I was invited to their Christmas party in Edinburgh. The only one of my friends available to go with me on that weekend was Bea" Caroline said dryly.

"That doesn't sound good for me Caroline" retorted Bea, "as if I was the last reserve". "Give over. You wanted to go to a posh party where you could dress up and I wanted your company so don't act as if I've hurt your feelings Bea, as if you were second best. Don't be soft" retorted Caroline. "The party was at the Balmoral Hotel." "Yes", said Bea "it has that beautiful clock tower that can be seen from all over Edinburgh city centre." "We'd been allocated bed and breakfast for the Saturday evening so Bea caught the train from Manchester to Edinburgh.

We were only twenty, and a bit nervous about staying somewhere so sophisticated weren't we Bea?" observed Caroline.

Bea nodded her assent "of course, it's not every day that I got to stay in a place like that but Caroline, you were used to five star luxury weren't you, so you weren't as stunned by everything as I was.  I'd never stayed anywhere so grand therefore I was a bit over-awed by it all.  The room was enormous and the view over the city amazing.  We didn't just have a twin bedroom, our room had a sitting area too with prints on the wall of Sean Connery as James Bond, so handsome, and the bathroom was white Carrera marble.  I wanted to stay there forever.

I can still remember the gorgeous oak smell of the bedroom and the feel of the crisp white linen sheets.  We pinched the slippers, obviously and the miniature toiletries of course" said Bea genially.  "I don't think anyone else would want the slippers Bea, but we were very cheeky because we ordered room service and put it on the company's bill" proclaimed Caroline.

"We felt very grown up and sophisticated" she added. "Yes, so urbane that we nicked the toiletries!" she exclaimed. "What're you talking about, as if we don't still do that now?" retorted Bea indignantly.  There was a momentary pause before Caroline took up the story but not everyone was enchanted.  Frank breathed a sigh of impatience and Caroline cast him a warning glance.

"Once we'd seen the room, and found where everything was, we walked into Edinburgh town centre" began Caroline.  "It was a bright, chilly day so we took the time to explore Edinburgh Castle then walked down the hill into the city and looked into the windows of the designer shops along Multrees Walk.

We'd arranged to have a manicure in the town. I chose bright green nail varnish, and Bea chose to have silver sparkly nail varnish. We must've looked ridiculous but we thought we were the bees-knees. We'd already booked two evening dresses from a dress hire shop and were really giddy as we tried on each one just to make sure that they looked amazing. We thought we were movie stars."

As Caroline began to describe the two dresses Frank let out a loud yawn "time for me to leave I think" he stated. "Don't be a misery Frank, this is interesting" said Caroline and carried out regardless of Frank's comment. "My dress had a velvet black halter-neck top attached to an emerald green long satin skirt with a huge bow at the front and Bea's was a sleeveless azure, long silk crepe fitted dress with a sweetheart neckline. We carried the dresses back to the hotel as if they were made of gold and hung them up in our wardrobe as quickly as we could. I bet your mum's still got the photos we took Bea.

Bea curled her hair with heated rollers and then put mine up in a chignon. We sprayed loads of glittery hairspray over our newly coiffed hair, enough to choke the entire hotel floor I think. As we got ready we had a couple of glasses of white wine, Lambrusco I think which we'd bought in the Co-op and sneaked into the hotel in Bea's handbag. Obviously the hotel bar would've been too expensive for us" clarified Caroline.

"Goodness sake Caroline, how long does it take to tell a story?" complained Frank and he feigned a yawn. As long as I like Frank. The door of this café is locked and you're going nowhere because, secretly, you're dying to know what happened next aren't you?" she replied cheekily.

"I remember looking in the long mirror and us laughing at our transformation. Do you remember Caroline?" asked Bea. "If we had access to modern technology then, I'm sure we would've used Instagram to show off pictures of ourselves Bea and we would be mortified now to look back on them" replied Caroline "but we didn't have modern technology, so we used my dad's camera and waited for two weeks before the photographs were developed. That's when Kodak was around, it isn't now because of all the changes in technology."

"Yes there was no deleting photographs or re-taking them was there, or altering them either. We had about twelve photographs in black and white because that's all we could afford. I'm sure I'm right aren't I?" asked Caroline. "Yes, you're right. My mum has definitely still got one of those photos of us somewhere. Remember we had to set the timer and run in front of the camera? Not a selfie like you would know Bella, with your posh, arms-length stick for your mobile." The older women giggled at the thought and Bella raised her eyes to the ceiling.

"Get on with it Caroline" muttered an impatient Frank. Tilting her head at him, with a wide grin Caroline continued, obviously enjoying reminiscing. "There we were, trying to look like a blonde Jacqueline Kennedy, that's you Bea and me pretending to be Audrey Hepburn." Caroline and Bea giggled at the recollection.

"My nerves were fraught Caroline" confessed Bea, "until I drank three glasses of Lambrusco. The only person I knew at the party was you, so I was really nervous about doing or saying the wrong thing and giving a bad impression." "Well you didn't" appeased Caroline "you looked amazing and behaved impeccably." Bea beamed at this praise.

"We walked along the red carpet to a private dining suite which had fabulous panoramic views of Edinburgh. The green of the table displays matched my dress so I didn't want to get too close to the table in case someone thought I was a moving plant" remarked Caroline. "Yes, you did look a bit like a Christmas tree" stated Bea. "Oh great. I didn't realise that" sighed Caroline. Frank looked as though he wasn't troubling himself to listen to the recollections of Christmases past. "Get on with it" he demanded. Nobody listened.

"At the beginning of the evening we circulated the room which banished our earlier misgivings. When we scoured the table plan we saw that we were sat at a table with two brothers, Phillip and Jasper Butler.

Phillip, who was about ten years older than us had started the brokerage business when he graduated from university and Jasper joined him in the company after he graduated. We assumed they were really sophisticated when they helped us with the wine choice, and they didn't choose Lambrusco." All the women laughed. At this, Frank let out a low snort which Caroline ignored and prompted Bea to fire him a dangerous look. "They were really enthusiastic about their business but they didn't talk to us about work all evening.

They seemed to be interested in us and we discussed a range of things such as golf, football, music, art and travel. We had more in common with them than we thought we would. It was a social evening so there was a disco with a few dances thrown in like the Gay Gordon, which encouraged everyone to dance with a partner. We danced most of the evening didn't we Bea?" asked Caroline.

"Yes, we hardly sat down all night so we got our money's worth out of our clothes and hair I think" said Bea. "Is that it?" Bella quizzed.

"Is that the end of the story? You got your money's worth?" she said scathingly. "No" replied her mother indignantly, "there's more". At this, Frank raised his eyebrows and Bea was full of ominiscity.

"At the end of the party we had coffee, brandy and Prestat mint chocolates. I'm sure we were a bit tipsy. A small group of us decided to take a stroll around the grounds of the hotel as they were lit by tiny, twinkling fairy lights. It looked really gorgeous" recounted Caroline.

"It's like listening to a bloody Disney fairy tale" groaned Frank. "It kind of was for us Frank" said Bea with feeling, "remember we were only twenty and it was a special evening. I hope your eyes don't turn any greener with envy Frank" she said pointedly. "Just have the good manners to listen" said Bea impatiently.

"Carry on Caroline and ignore Frank." Caroline continued to narrate her tale. "As we walked around the grounds I noticed that Jasper had moved next to Bea and they were deep in conversation. After a while, when they reached a wooden bench, he placed his jacket onto the seat so that Bea could sit down without ruining her dress or having a cold bottom. I thought that was really sweet. They chatted for a while and I talked with Phillip.

When we left the garden and returned to the hotel foyer, the four of us wished each other goodnight then Bea and I returned to our room. We stayed up most of the night speculating about Jasper and Phillip, as girls do, and finally went to bed about five o'clock.

When we scrambled down to breakfast the following morning, we had the bitter disappointment of searching fruitlessly for Jasper and Phillip in the dining room. We heard later that they'd checked out of the hotel so we spent Sunday in bitter frustration and mild speculation."

"Shame" said Frank spitefully. "I'm still wondering how Bea ended up with Jasper" exclaimed an exasperated Bella. "Ha, wait patiently young woman and you might find out" replied a sagacious Caroline.

"I think we would all prefer to know what happened between you and Phillip" Bea said gently as she smiled at Frank. Bea's smart deflection tactic appeared to work as Bella implored her mother "yeah mum, tell us about the two of you."

Bea breathed a sigh of relief that she had dodged any talk about Jasper. Frank scowled in frustration.

# Chapter 5 - Can the mystery be solved?

"It's strange how things work out isn't it?" asked Caroline to no-one in particular.

"I was keen to become financially independent, so I took the paid summer job at the brokerage company in Edinburgh. It meant that I could stay in my student accommodation during the summer holidays. As the bus ran frequently between St. Andrew's and Leuchars train station I was able to catch the train to and from Edinburgh during the week. It was a beautiful journey along the coastline, so it was no hardship to me to travel for an hour and soak in the Scottish scenery.

There were always loads of holidaymakers on the train and because I was on my own they would usually chat to me, especially the Americans. There were lots of them that summer because the Open golf competition was held in St. Andrew's that year. Most of them were supporting Tom Watson and had travelled from all over the United States to follow his progress in such an historic golf competition in, what everyone told me, was the home of golf.

It was a warm summer in 1984. The tiny town of St. Andrew's was heaving with people, many of whom were hoping that they would see Tom Watson equal Harry Vardon's record of six Open titles.

Professor Fane helped me to get a job during the Open weekend selling golf programmes to visitors and I managed to get Nick Faldo's autograph.

There I was, working at the course which meant I had a ringside position to watch the final day's play. It was incredibly exciting and that's where my love of golf was sparked. A tight contest emerged between Tom Watson and Seve Ballesteros as they were tied at the Road Hole.

Tom Watson made a bogey on the 17th so it was almost impossible for him to win the tournament. Seve struck a beautiful putt on the last hole to win. It felt as though the whole town of St. Andrew's actually shook with shared delight because Seve was such a creative golfer. It was spine tingling. I was lucky enough to be one of the people who partied in the town all night long.

I worked hard at the brokerage but it was great every day to come back to the peace and calm of St. Andrew's after the hustle and bustle of my job. I shadowed different people in the company, watched closely how they dealt with clients and how difficult situations were managed.

For about four weeks I worked on a small project with Jasper Butler, who was a partner in the company with his older brother Phillip. Jasper was gregarious and able to explain the inner workings of the activities very clearly. We got on well together which is why I think I was invited to the company's Christmas party that year, where he met you Bea" she said pointing at Bea, "and I spent some time speaking with Phillip Butler." After a pause of some minutes, Caroline continued.

"I was over the moon when I finished university and got a full-time job at the brokerage company. My parents weren't too pleased that I was going to be living in Edinburgh instead of going back to live in Manchester.

When I got the letter which confirmed I'd got the job I ran around the university quad squealing with delight. Elle looked out of the window of our apartment to shout encouragement to me.

We must've looked ridiculous, but I'm sure the students were used to people doing daft things." "Yes, you did look silly Caroline as you're usually quiet and sophisticated" remarked Elle.

"Shut up" replied Caroline good naturedly. "It wasn't difficult to study hard because Elle was so focused on her academic path, and we supported each other with different study techniques didn't we?' she observed to Elle who nodded her agreement.

"I think Elle it's safe to say that working co-operatively, even though we were studying completely different subjects, helped us both didn't it?" asked Caroline. Elle replied in the affirmative and was unable to resist saying "being able to drink coffee in the library, eat chocolate and ogle boys helped too."

"When we graduated in the summer of 1985 there was a recession in the UK. Elle completed the first part of her medical degree at St. Andrew's so returned to Manchester to finish her studies by working in one of the large hospitals there. The brokerage firm was setting up an office in London, so instead of living in Edinburgh, as planned, I had to relocate to London.

My parents were delighted because they'd inherited my grandparents' terraced house on Gordon Square and it meant I could live in it and look after it at the same time.

The house was close to Euston Station so within easy commuting distance back home to Manchester, or should I say, within easy commuting distance for my parents to keep popping down to London to see me. Living there meant that I'd be able to walk to work as I didn't fancy travelling on the tube each day, boiling hot and smelling strangers' armpits.

I was glad Bea and Vivie when you said that you'd both live with me otherwise I would've been daunted by moving to such a big city after living in the gentle town of St. Andrew's." "We were really lucky. It was a fabulous chance for the three of us to experience city living on the cheap" said a pleased Vivie. "Thankfully our rent wasn't so high because your parents were very generous.

Our lives changed completely when we moved to London. It was the start of everything" she said. "I agree" said Bea. "There wasn't much prospect of work in the north of England because of the recession. There were certainly more opportunities for us all in London.

I remember seeing images on telly of people, usually men who worked in the city of London, waving cash around to boast about how much money they'd earned' said Vivie sadly. "My mother was furious because millions of people around the country, outside of London were being put out of work and finding life tough whilst some ignorant gits were flaunting their wealth without a thought for others and no care about anyone else's predicament." The other women nodded their agreement.

Caroline said "we were grateful to find work weren't we? My grandparents had always lived in Gordon Square and my grandfather had always managed to maintain the house.

Do you remember when we all went to see it and couldn't believe that we'd be living in such a grand house? Three storeys high above a basement and the roof had a dormer window to spray light into the attic room.

I remember standing on the Square to survey the house and wondered how we'd ever get our furniture up the three stone steps leading to that wide entrance hall. The front door was beautiful, jet black, made of oak framed by a brick arch. At night a metal, curved hanging lamp lit up the entrance so we never needed to be anxious about anyone lurking in the shadows whenever we returned home late. Black wrought-iron railings sectioned off our house from the pavement.

We were on a regular bus route but the traffic was so heavy into the city that it was often quicker to walk to work than it was to catch the bus.

Remember the large sash windows on the first and second floors which let the light flood into the rooms and kept out the street noise? We even had our pick of bedrooms. None of us wanted to sleep in the attic room because it had a spooky feeling up there at the top of so many steps. We used that as a guest room and Elle you stayed there whenever you came to London."

"I remember that room. I never felt uneasy in the house and thanks very much that none of you ever said anything about finding it eerie." "Sorry Elle, but we knew that your scientific, logical brain would've put paid to our nonsense anyway" replied Caroline.

"Each room had a beautiful black, cast iron fireplace and gorgeous parquet flooring." Vivie replied "the three of us knew at the time that we were really lucky to be able to live in such a central location in a gorgeous property but we worried about how we'd keep those fires burning. It's fortunate that we didn't set fire to the house the way you used to add newspaper to any fire Bea." "It was my dad who told me to do that. We're all here to tell the tale aren't we?" Bea replied sardonically.

"Caroline, your father made a wise decision not to sell the house. It must be worth a small fortune now" said Bea. "Hmm" agreed Caroline.

"Do you remember that our parents donated loads of furniture to us?" asked Caroline. "I had to laugh when my mother made a big deal about offering us her Stag bedroom and dining room furniture. She'd been dying to update the furniture at home for ages and it gave her the chance to persuade my father to part with their money.

Even though we were in a recession he said that it was wise to spend to help the money cycle." "Your father and mine drove to London in a hired van to transport all their unwanted things" stated Bea "and they got lost on the way."

They all laughed. "We ended up with a real mismatch of furniture didn't we? These days it would be called eclectic and considered cool. We just thought we were poor! We were grateful for anything though weren't we as we couldn't have afforded to buy much seeing as we were just starting out as independent young women" giggled Vivie. "I would describe our furniture as shabby chic" Bea said. "I'd describe it as just shabby" replied Vivie.

Caroline took up the mantle of reminiscence "I started work at the brokerage firm in September and was swept away by a sea of numbers. The financial decisions we had to make hour by hour were phenomenal. I worked long hours, often not returning home 'til ten at night by which time I would crawl into bed and be up again at six the following day. My brain was frazzled.

On the rare occasions when I didn't work late, I would meet Vivie and Bea after work, you nine to fivers, and we went to different bars. Sometimes we would be with other work friends too.

One evening Jasper and Phillip Butler joined us at a local bar and a large group of us decided to go for a meal. Jasper was really pleased to renew his acquaintance with Bea, Vivie was speaking to Tom Baker who was one of Jasper's school friends, and I sat and chatted with Phillip.

We mostly talked about the political situation in the United Kingdom, under Margaret Thatcher's government and the demise of the power of the Unions. We were both shocked by what had happened during the miners' strike particularly the violence shown on television and we discussed the possible impact of privatising the country's national industries. Phillip appeared to be a very thoughtful, intelligent and cheerful man" Caroline recalled.

"It's no wonder Tom, Bea, Jasper and I left the restaurant to go to a nightclub after listening to you two and your serious conversation" said Vivie. "We were relieved when Phillip said he'd walk home with you" said Bea "you were being a bit intense and boring." Caroline laughed and visibly relaxed. "Boring's fine by me" said Caroline and she continued with her tale regardless of whether anyone wanted to hear it or not.

"I remember that night really clearly" she said. "Phillip and I walked slowly through Bloomsbury Square Gardens, past the British Museum onto Gordon Square and I noticed that the closer we got to my home, the quieter he became. When we arrived at the house, he asked me out on our first date and kissed me under the street light." Even Frank remained silent as Caroline recounted her tale and he leant across the table to squeeze her hand.

The rest of the group were deathly quiet, allowing Caroline to reminisce. "By Christmas, Phillip and I were seeing each other regularly at work and socially outside of work. He was my first proper boyfriend and I thought he was the most amazing person. He was driven to succeed but also had a social conscience. Once a month on a Saturday we both volunteered at Centrepoint by mentoring a homeless person. Princess Diana was the Patron then. It's incredible to think that it was all so long ago and now her son, the Duke of Cambridge is the Patron isn't he? Phillip and I always found helping others was rewarding, even though it could be frustrating when people didn't want to be helped!" she quipped.

Caroline's thoughts tumbled out. "On my 22nd birthday Phillip and I walked to Covent Garden and had a meal in one of the restaurants nearby. When the waiter brought our drinks on a tray he theatrically handed me a red envelope with my name printed in gold embossed letters. I was surprised by this, had no idea what it could mean and was momentarily taken aback.

For some strange reason I was nervous when I opened the envelope. My hands were shaking. I looked at Phillip and he was staring at me. Just staring. I couldn't read his face at all.

Inside the envelope was a cream and gold coloured invitation card. I had to read it twice to absorb what it said. I remember Phillip's green eyes peering at me as I looked up. When I read it my mind was in a whirl. I've still got that card and remember the first line vividly: *'You are cordially invited to attend the wedding of Phillip and Caroline'*.

Oh my face was bright red when I said yes. I needed a drink to steady my nerves and goodness knows what the waiter assumed when I burst into tears. My heart was thumping so loudly that I thought everyone in the restaurant would hear it. Phillip seemed to be delighted. He had already arranged everything in the hope that I would be happy with his choice of venue. He wanted us to be married three months later when the banns had been read at Saint Patrick's Church in Soho Square." Caroline paused momentarily then continued her narrative.

"The following weekend I travelled from Euston on the train to Manchester Piccadilly where I met my parents and immediately told them the news.

They already knew as Phillip had been in touch with them, but they were shocked at the suddenness of it all and pleased that I was happy.

Phillip was eleven years older than me and keen to settle down. In those days" said Caroline as she turned to Bella "getting married aged 22 was not unusual.

These days you young people usually live together and rarely think about getting married. Or, should I say, the boys rarely think about getting married and the girls worry that they never will get married. We would've been looked down upon by others if we have *lived in sin* as our parents called it.

I don't need to preach to anyone. I bought my dress at the shop we've just been in Bella, opposite Bea's" she exclaimed. "It's so exclusive that it doesn't even advertise, it doesn't even have its name over the shop" she laughed. "There are probably fewer weddings these days because the cost of them is astronomical. No wonder the shop's going to close and Francine the owner has decided to retire. I can't see many bridal shops being in business in the next five years.

Francine had a very simple white dress in stock. It had lace at the top with short sleeves, an open v at the back with pearl buttons, a long fitted dress with beaded appliques and a small train. Although three months was a tight deadline for her to work with, she only had to make minor alterations. I think it was more difficult for the three of you to co-ordinate your bridesmaid dresses" she said turning to Bea, Vivie and Elle.

"You didn't give us much notice did you Caroline" complained Bea. "It *was* difficult for the three of us to agree on dresses because we're all of varying sizes and have different shapes and colouring" explained Elle.

"We didn't have much opportunity to be together to choose and there was no such thing as the Internet as it wasn't widely used nor were mobile telephones readily available where we could have shared photographs with each other.

We had to buy wedding magazines and try to synchronise how we would look through verbal explanations, by actually having a conversation with each other. Life was much more difficult back then wasn't it?" stated Vivie with irony. "How did you decide what to wear then?" asked Bella. "Hmm, yes, how did we decide? I can't remember" Vivie teased. "Bea do you remember what we did in the end?" said Elle.

Bea looked perplexed and turned to Vivie for support. "I remember it ended up being a very strange year for us all' Vivie said 'because there were three weddings that year" she said mysteriously. "I didn't know that" exclaimed Bella. "Whose?" "Let me finish the tale about my wedding first" said Caroline airily "then you might find out." Caroline turned to Vivie, Bea and Elle with a twinkle in her eye "remind me. How did you choose the bridesmaid dresses at such short notice?"

Bea spoke. "When Caroline returned to Manchester to tell her parents she was getting married to Phillip we travelled with her. Caroline went home and the two of us had arranged to meet up with Elle outside Lewis's on Market Street. The business doesn't exist now. I think that Primark took over their building.

The three of us went to a shop close by called Bride Be Lovely but I don't know why Caroline thought she could trust us to choose suitable bridesmaid dresses. We had the shop assistant in uproar. She asked us if we wanted short, midi or long dresses and we didn't know. She asked us what colour we wanted and we couldn't agree. She asked us the price we were prepared to pay, which wasn't much as Elle wasn't being paid well as a junior doctor and we didn't have loads of money, despite working in London.

The poor shop assistant was so patient but we exhausted all her possibilities.

We tried on halter neck dresses and fell about laughing. We tried on ballerina dresses and cried because we looked ridiculous. We tried on dresses with frills which made us look frumpy. All in all the visit to the shop was a disaster because we didn't have a plan.

At the time my mother was a seamstress for a major retailer. In those days their clothes were made in the UK to the highest standard, before they moved production abroad" she said bitterly "so my mum would have been classed as an expert in her field. When we went home and explained to her what had happened, and that we needed three dresses urgently, she volunteered to make them for us.

My dad drove us, and Caroline, back into Manchester to Lewis's. My mum spent ages with us searching patterns for appropriate bridesmaid dresses and eventually we chose one style which mum thought would suit us. We agreed that pale lemon would be a pretty and neutral colour. Mum suggested that long dresses would be quicker to make. That day, there and then my mum bought the material, buttons and patterns. When we returned to my mum's house later that day she measured us up and was raring to go" explained Bea.

"I think it was a relief for your mum Bea when our parents suggested that they pay for the material and buy our shoes, as repayment to Matilde for her time" stated Caroline. "Yes, my mum was delighted with that gesture" said Bea, "very kind particularly in those difficult days when money was hard to come by."

"Bea" said Elle turning to her friend "your mother worked for hours on those three dresses. I used to pop in from time to time on my way home from work and have a cup of tea with your parents, I mean, Matilde and Robert.

They loved hearing about events at the hospital and always made time for people. I adored trying on my dress so that your mum could check on the progress she was making. While she was adjusting the dress Robert would always enjoy chatting about politics and world events. They are two really wonderful people. I still enjoy it when I visit them both every so often, especially when your dad plays the guitar." Caroline agreed and said "I was delighted when Robert agreed to play music at my wedding."

"Give over, my dad felt really chuffed to be asked" replied Bea. "Your mum was thrilled to be making the dresses. She didn't need to make many alterations when Vivie and Bea returned to Manchester a couple of times for the fittings did she?' asked Elle as she warmed to her theme. "What were the dresses like" asked Bella, "I've never seen any of your wedding photos mum." "They were simple and elegant" replied Elle "made of silk, long and slim fitting. At the top they were off the shoulder, but in the middle was a small knot of fabric. At the back Matilde had added covered buttons to link with the theme of Caroline's dress. All I can say is that they were understated chic."

Bella wished to know whether the bridesmaid dresses still existed. "Yes, we've all kept them" said Elle 'and I can still fit into mine." Bea and Vivie looked at Elle and raised their eyes to the sky "show off" they said with good humour.

"It was an exciting time for all of us. We were looking forward to Caroline's wedding especially as she was having the reception at the Dorchester Hotel in Mayfair' said Vivie mimicking a cut-glass accent. "Very posh" she pointed out needlessly.

"Caroline was happy to pass on all the arrangements to Phillip, who was in his element organising this and arranging that. You did choose the flowers though Caroline didn't you? Those café au lait dahlias in peach ivory were simply beautiful" teased Vivie. "You're making it sound as though I let everything happen around me, which I didn't. It's just that Phillip was so keen to make it a perfect day that I left him to it but kept a close eye on what he was up to, obviously" said Caroline who was slightly wounded by the portrayal. She paused to let Vivie continue speaking. "Let's say it was skilful negotiation on your part Caroline." This time, she was placated.

"What was your wedding day like mum?" queried Bella. "Oh she was in a right dither at first" stated Bea. "We'll all tell you our own bits and you can put them together like a jigsaw" Bea suggested. The other women smiled and Frank pretended to yawn.

"It was a warm September day and the roads were quieter than normal, the tourist season was coming to an end and the usual army of workers were taking a rest that Saturday. The atmosphere in the house was manic. There were people everywhere. All of our parents were staying there, plus us. Two of Bea's friends came to the house to do the hair of eight women. Can you imagine the pandemonium Bella?

We were running up and down the stairs screaming and Robert was playing the guitar. I've never known such a commotion." "I'd arranged for make-up artists to make us look beautiful so they turned up in the middle of all this disorder" said Vivie. "We queued to use the bathrooms. Whose idea was it for us **all** to be there? Bonkers!"

Vivie didn't wait for an answer. "In the midst of all this mayhem the florist arrived with the incorrect order. Caroline cried. Her father went in a taxi to pick up the flowers and returned just in time to walk with Caroline to the church. Caroline cried again thinking that she would be late for her own wedding. That's daft as most brides are late aren't they?"

Elle joined in the conversation "we all drank the champagne that we'd bought from Sainsbury's on Tottenham Court Road to quell our nerves and I'm sure your mother was drunk Caroline before she even left the house." "She was" confirmed Caroline "and drunker still at the Dorchester." Vivie turned to Bea "and through all the commotion Robert kept playing the guitar" she said accusingly. My dad was nervous" retorted Bea in his defence.

"It wasn't far to the church, so we walked. Taxis, buses and cars honked their horns as our wedding party wended its way through the London streets. I suppose it's not every day you see a bride walking through London is it?" exclaimed Vivie. "By the time we arrived, my feet were killing me" stated Caroline "I was thankful to sit down in the church."

"It sounds like a fantastic day with loads of fun" said Bella wistfully "and I won't be having a wedding now."

Caroline got up from her chair and walked round to her daughter. She hugged her tightly and said "that's what life with your father was like. Chaotic and happy." Bella's eyes misted over but she quickly recovered her composure.

Caroline turned to Frank. "I'm sorry Frank, this must be really boring for you." "Despite how I might be portrayed, my head isn't always full of cooking and football y'know. I'm not bored at all" he replied kindly.

Caroline laughed. "We got to the church on time. Just. Phillip was at the altar with Jasper alongside as Best Man. I can remember that the service was beautiful and I didn't want it to end. Robert played a superb solo on his guitar when we went to sign the register at the back of the church. The exquisite sound of Bill Withers' *Lovely Day* reverberated around the church when it was sung by the choir at the end of the service. I couldn't have asked for a better day.

We took a taxi to the Dorchester. It wasn't that far. When we arrived at the hotel the staff really made a fuss of us didn't they even though there were only about fifty people in our party. The Orchid Room, where we had our reception, was light and airy. The white and blue colour scheme on the tables offset our dresses and the mirrors reflected the sparkling lights of the chandeliers. All I can remember after that was dancing and laughing all evening" said Caroline wistfully.

"I think that's what we all did Caroline" said Vivie kindly. "The food was so unusual, and there was plenty of it. The dancing later on was first-rate."

Caroline responded "I was moved that Phillip hired the same DJ who ran the Christmas party we went to in Edinburgh when we first met" said Caroline. "That was typically thoughtful of him" said Bea "and it made for a great evening's dancing and even my dad took a break from playing the guitar." "Thank goodness" joked Elle.

"Where did you go for your honeymoon mum?" asked Bella. "We spent one night at the Dorchester, in a suite which overlooked the courtyard. I wasn't keen to face Hyde Park as there's a really busy road outside the hotel and I thought it would be too noisy if we opened the window.

The room was lovely. It had a seating area, with a writing bureau on which was fresh fruit, and a bottle of champagne. We had a small dressing room where you could get changed away from the bedroom, an enormous marble bathroom and a huge bedroom with a sofa at the foot of the bed and a television screen on the wall. Can you believe we also had a butler who waited on us? Most of the wedding guests had decided to stay at the hotel the night of our wedding as Phillip had managed to negotiate a good rate for them. He was always good at bargaining and very charming.

The morning after our wedding we arranged to meet everyone for brunch in The Grill. When we were younger Bea, Vivie, Elle and I had back-packed in Venice so recognised that the striking hand-blown glass chandelier hanging in the Grill Room was made on the island of Murano.

The room had strange, pivoting wall panels but they did look fabulous against the oak parquet flooring. The flooring reminded me of our house on Gordon Square.

At the brunch we took the chance to catch up with our guests and hear their version of our wedding day. I would like to remind you Elle that you looked rather smitten with that doctor from the Portland Hospital" Caroline teased.

Elle's careworn face lit up. "Yes, Sie was interesting company but unfortunately for me he was also engaged. Inevitable" she said "but yes, we did get on very well. In fact", she said shyly "I met him not so long ago at a conference in Manchester and saw him again this morning".

There was a pause. "And?" questioned Vivie "because there's obviously an and."

"You're right my friend" confessed Elle. "He's divorced now."

Bea, Vivie and Caroline were astonished to hear this and looked quizzically at Elle. "His wife moved in with someone called Linda. There's not much more to tell you. Yet." exclaimed Elle "so please don't ask me for any details." This was like asking night not to turn into day time. As Elle had dedicated her life to the medical profession, Bea, Vivie and Caroline found it impossible not to pass comment.

"There's no way we're leaving this café Elle until we know all the details. Right now I think is a good time for us to have something substantial to eat and then we can interrogate you" said Bea mischievously.

This was Frank's cue to volunteer to make a curry as he knew the women would question Elle mercilessly. As he left the table, Frank looked at her sympathetically.

He recognised that she would be subject to a barrage of questions. "Don't look at me like that. I'm 52 for goodness sake" said Elle. "You sound as though your life is over, when the exciting bit could be just about to start" joked Vivie. "You're speaking to me as if my life has been a drudge for the past thirty years." Bea, Vivie and Caroline glanced at each other and laughed.

"Well it has mostly been work, work, work for you Elle hasn't it? It's possible to put too much of yourself, your emotions into a job so that it can take on more meaning that it should. Your job shouldn't define you as a person. You need to get out more. About time you were a little bit frivolous" said Vivie.

"I have been very frivolous this past year" said Elle defiantly, "I've been on a dating website." For two minutes there was stunned silence. "You haven't" the women shrieked in unison. "What was it like?" they questioned. "I might tell you after we've heard about your honeymoon and eaten" said Elle firmly.

Caroline gave in. "Intriguing" she said. "Ok I'll finish off my tale whilst Frank makes the food. We spent a few days in Madrid. Phillip wanted to take me to watch Real Madrid play football at the Santiago Bernabeu Football Stadium and also to have a tour around Atletico Madrid's stadium, the Vicente Calderon. The Bernabeu is enormous and we sat at the very top of the stadium to watch Real Madrid win their game.

Do you know that it's really warm at the top of the stadium as they have heaters in the roof? You don't even need to wear a coat when you're watching the evening matches.

The atmosphere was fantastic and I couldn't believe that the fans took orchestral instruments into the stadium and played them for the whole match. It was as interesting watching the fans as it was watching the football.

We spent a relaxing day in Retiro Park, hired a rowing boat on the lake and sat watching the world go by as we drank wine with the locals in the park gardens. Later, as we mooched along Gran Via, which has become the main tourist and shopping area, we enjoyed visiting the shabby shops, which I believe are not shabby now, but we didn't buy much. I watched a craftsman hand make a bag but didn't buy it. One day I might go back and buy one just because.

The streets were wide, like boulevards and I was amazed to see botanical gardens in Atocha train station. We spent some time exploring the Museo del Prado which houses the royal art collection including work by Francisco de Goya, whose paintings I thought were very dark, if not a bit scary but Phillip admired them.

One evening we ate at San Miguel Market which is not far from the museum. What a place. It's a fabulous glass and iron structure, is open long hours and all manner of food and drink is sold. I couldn't stop wandering up and down the stalls of fresh fish, meat, vegetables, fruit, tapas and wine bars. The smell, noise and colours were exhilarating and I was intrigued to see all the locals relaxing in such an interesting place, chatting and without being aggressive with each other despite the amount of alcohol that was consumed.

Later on we enjoyed a cup of café con leché at Plaza Mayor and strolled into Puerto del Sol which has a four metre tall bronze sculpture of a Bear and Strawberry Tree.

I rubbed the bear's paw for good luck but Phillip said he didn't believe in such nonsense.

We had a superb time exploring the city because we're not ones for sitting on a beach doing nothing. I've never been back" Caroline said reflectively. "It sounds like a great honeymoon mum" said Bella. Caroline felt as though she owed a great deal of her happiness to Phillip. "Let's eat now" said Caroline quickly "and then cross-question Elle on her love-life."

"Hmm. Eating will give me time to consider the answers I choose to give you" said Elle irreverently.

# Chapter 6 - Is it possible to meet electronically?

In the kitchen Frank began to prepare the food, and banged on the wall adjoining Bea's parents' house, the usual indication that help was needed from next door. He shouted to Bea "your dad's on his way, please will you unlock the door?"

Within five minutes Robert pushed at the black door to open it ¾ of the way "what a miserable day" he said and was taken aback by the crowd of people in the room. "What's going on here? Are you having another tapas event without telling your mum and me?" he asked as he scanned the room.

"Good grief it's Vivie, Elle, Caroline and young Bella. How great to see you all" and he gave each of them a hug. "I didn't know you were having a private function in here today with your friends and we weren't invited" he said accusingly to Bea. "We're not dad. It's impromptu. We're having a chat. About old times" she added and moved her eyes to indicate that he should go to the kitchen.

Recognising the signs when women want some privacy he immediately said "erm I'll go an' help our Frank." Once in the kitchen he asked Frank "what's going on in there?" "Bella has dumped Charlie and they're trying to tell her that he'll get over it" said Frank.

"I'll tell you that's easier said than done"' said Robert sadly "and I should know." "Don't get involved Robert that's my advice" said Frank as he shook his head.
"Please will you help me get this food ready for them?" he implored.

"Yes chef" said Robert cheerily. "Where do you want me to begin?" "If you can dice the onions, that would be a great help and then set the tables, or the other way round, whichever you prefer." "I'll do the onions first, then whilst I'm setting the tables I can find out what's happening." "You're incorrigible" said Frank and Robert laughed.

"Will Matilde be ok on her own as I think that we're in for quite a storm?" queried Frank. "I'll knock on the wall if it gets any worse" replied Robert. "Shall I go and get my guitar?" he asked. "NO" shouted Frank.

Within ten minutes Robert was placing fresh tablecloths and cutlery on the tables in the Hub. "How're things?" he asked genially. "They're helping me Robert by explaining that life has its ups and downs. I've called off my wedding to Charlie and everyone is worried there will be repercussions" said Bella calmly.

"Oh Bella love, I'm sorry to hear that. Charlie's a good lad. These things happen. I've been married to Matilde for fifty seven years. They've been fantastic years but when we were courting, she broke my heart by finishing with me."

"I didn't know that dad" said a surprised Bea. "It's not something us men talk about is it, having your heart broken? It's hard for us men" said Robert. "What happened?" asked Bea.

"D'yer know, I still don't know Bea. All I know is that she said she didn't want to see me anymore. When she said that, every evening for ten days solid I stood outside her house for hours waiting for her to come out. She never did unless she sneaked out the back." "You stalked mum until she gave in, is that it dad?" joked Bea. "Something like that. I just knew that I didn't want to spend my life with anyone else and the past fifty seven years have been, at times, brilliant" confessed Robert. "Matilde was worth pursuing" he said cheerfully.

"Do you think Charlie will find someone else Robert?" asked Bella. "You've only just broken his heart love so I don't know. Feelings are funny things aren't they? Who knows what motivates people or what that special something is between them" said Robert sagaciously. "Even at my old age I still don't know what it is." Bea thought her father looked old and frail. She watched him as he looked away and he said "Frank's giving me the look that says *stop talking* so I'd better get back to the kitchen." Affairs of the heart, he thought were very difficult to comprehend.

Bea thought it was time that Vivie contacted her husband and son in case they were worried about her, particularly as she'd been away from home for some time. "Text your Tom and Ben to ask them to come to the café" she told Vivie gently. "Frank'll prepare enough food to feed us all for a whole week. I'm sure they'll both be worried about you not going home."

"Ok I'll text, but I'd be surprised if Frank hasn't already contacted Tom. Frank, did you ask Tom to come over here?" shouted Vivie. From the kitchen the reply came "yes and I've knocked on the wall for Matilde as well." Bea and Vivie smiled at each other.

Their families had been good friends during the years. "We'd better look out for them because if they have to wait for the door to open they'll get soaked. Just look at the rain swirling around out there. It's like a monsoon. When did we last have one of those in Manchester?" said Vivie with irony. "Wasn't that yesterday?" kidded Bea.

"It's a violent storm isn't it? We'll be lucky if we're not swept away. I think that our weather is so unpredictable and changeable. Wish we had warm bright sunshine." As Bea and Vivie peered out of the window at a purple sky, a flash of lightning lit up the road followed almost immediately by a loud roar of thunder. In the streets, grids were not coping with the amount of rain hammering on their surface and puddles were collecting rapidly.

"It's grim out there" stated Vivie. "I hope that Tom can manage to drive here safely. Perhaps we shouldn't have invited him and Ben." Vivie's face turned white with anxiety. "Can't you ring him?" asked Bella. "I don't want to disturb his concentration when he's driving. Let's wait a while longer before I allow myself to panic" replied Vivie. Her head was thumping. Her heart pounding with ominiscity.

Looking out of the café window, Bea spied Matilde pointlessly gripping an open umbrella and struggling to shut her garden gate. She wrestled with the howling wind to pull the gate closed.

Bea unlocked the café door, and using all of her strength dragged it open as wide as she could which just would not budge beyond ¾ opening.

The raging wind almost lifted Matilde off her feet as she tried to enter the Hub so Bea grabbed Matilde's arm and heaved her inside, a bedraggled mess. "I could hardly breathe in this weather. Did you see me? I was nearly blown into the road. The weather's that bad that I just saw one of those saplings the council planted earlier in the year ripped out of the ground and slammed onto the pavement. It's appalling out there. I'm glad I'm not driving" said Matilde slowly.

"Here Matilde, come and sit by me" invited Bella "at least it's warm and cosy in here and we're about to be fed." "What's going on? I didn't know all the girls were coming round" Matilde questioned Bea as she noticed the friends sat around the tables. "It's an unexpected surprise mum and Frank's making curry for us all. We're just waiting for Tom and Ben to turn up."

"Tom's not driving is he?" asked Matilde "I don't think he should be driving in this weather. That's ludicrous. Have you seen it out there?" she said with apprehension in her voice. Vivie's face paled and her heart felt as though it had plummeted to her feet.

Bea pulled up the window blinds as the group shifted the tables and chairs further away from the window and glass door. This was partly to be able to watch out for Tom's car but also to avoid being too close to the glass should it shatter.

Vivie could feel her heart thudding rapidly in her chest and the blood throbbing around her veins. Bea could see that Vivie was beginning to panic so made her a coffee and added a large splash of brandy to the drink.

Vivie's hands shook as she sipped the hot liquid and she wasn't sure that mixing alcohol with a headache was a good idea. Throwing caution to the wind, so to speak, she swigged down the hot coffee. As fifteen minutes ticked by the group strained to see out of the café window which bulged as if in conflict with the wind and driving rain. Every headlight they saw presented hope that Tom's car would turn up soon. Vivie offered up silent prayers as she paced up and down the tiny café, becoming more and more agitated with every passing minute.

Suddenly, in the distance she spotted the distinctive, feline shaped headlights of Tom's car stealthily creeping towards the café. Despite the obvious danger, Vivie pushed her face against the café window and noticed a huge hole on the passenger's side of the back screen on Tom's car. She watched the car purr slowly as Tom maneuvered to park around the corner of the café.

Bea tugged open the café door to enable Tom followed closely by Ben, to run inside. "Sorry we're late" breezed Tom. "A bloody branch has just shot through the back window and onto the passenger seat. It's a good thing that Ben was in the front seat, not the back, otherwise he would've been hurt very badly." He spoke calmly as if nothing untoward had happened.

Vivie hugged him and then Ben, saying "I saw the car in a poor state. Thank goodness you're ok. I was so worried about you both." Vivie sat down as Tom said "now, the first thing I need to do is to cover up the car Vivie before there's any more damage to it." He shouted into the kitchen "Frank, have you got any strong plastic bags that I could use to protect the car mate?" Frank's head appeared at the kitchen door.

"Hi Tom, Ben. Yes, just give me a minute, I'll put my coat on and help you."

"I'll help too" said Ben.

After hauling a huge oilcloth canvas from the store cupboard, Frank and Tom opened the front door and were almost lugged out of the café by the greedy grasp of the wind. Once outside, they had to shout to each other to be heard above the noise of the storm. Both men battled against the wind to cover the car with tarpaulin. As each held the cover in place on either side of the car, Ben joined them and tried to throw a rope across the top of it, which was a futile attempt. His actions were rendered ineffective by the wind which seemed to be playing a game by throwing the rope back to him.

Ben returned to the café, stood near to the closed door and shouted for help. Within moments Bella had put on Bea's raincoat and was outside trying to assist. Bella stood on one side of the car gripping the rope and Ben fought against the wind to move himself to the opposite side.

Once the rope was over the top of the car, he threw the end of the rope underneath the car for Bella to grasp. On her knees on the pavement Bella had to feel beneath the car, in cold, swirling puddles to try to seize the rope. Her hands were freezing as she rummaged around. At first her efforts were ineffectual but after what felt like an age, she finally grasped the rope and, hands shaking, tied the two pieces together as tightly as she could. The second time she and Ben repeated this exercise by trying to tie the canvas over the bonnet of the car.

The wind howled louder and tugged at the tarpaulin. The rain lashed harder and it was tricky to manipulate the rope.

Bella was shaking with cold, and she could barely clasp the rope. Frank and Tom were holding on to the canvas as solidly as they could as the wind whipped around them. Like Ben and Bella, both were bedraggled and drenched.

Finally, Bella was able to find the second piece of rope beneath the car and tie it around the canvas. Soggy and cold, feet soaking wet, the four of them waded through puddles back to the café. Bea unlocked the door and the four sodden bodies entered the warmth of the room.

"C'mon upstairs" said Bea as she steered the saturated group to the staircase at the back of the Hub. "I'll take you to the bathrooms so that you can shower, and dry off. While you do that I'll cobble together a change of clothes for you all. It won't be anything fancy. Just tracksuit bottoms and oversized t-shirts but at least the clothes will be dry and you'll have the chance to get warm."

Bea and Frank led the sodden group to their apartment above the café. In this large Victorian building the spacious living accommodation was spread over two floors. The first spindle staircase led to a double sized reception room, a study, a huge dining kitchen and a utility room. The top floor housed four double bedrooms each with an en-suite bathroom. Bea sprinted down the staircase to the utility room, grabbed a pile of clothing for each person and placed the garments on each bed before anyone had finished showering.

She went downstairs, stirred the curry and waited for Frank, Tom, Ben and Bella to join the rest of the group. As she entered the café she said "this has turned out to be quite a day hasn't it?

Poor Bella, she looked like a drowned rat on this horrible day. I guess she didn't expect to be tying rope around a car in typhoon-like weather, today of all days." "No, but thanks to all of you for trying to help her feel better. I really appreciate your kindness" said Caroline.

"That has always been the wonderful thing about all of you, the fact that you make time for other people and always have. I'd better stop all this mushy talk before they all arrive back" she said hastily. The four friends hugged each other and then embraced Matilde. As they sat back down at the table Vivie raised her glass and said "let's make a toast. Thanks to each of you for always being there no matter what."

Eventually when most of the group were seated, Robert brought a stack of poppadoms, chutney, chopped onion and four naan breads to the pushed together tables, then received a cheer for his efforts. Everyone sat down passing food to each other as if they were at a large family gathering. A family of friends.

Once they had finished their starters, Frank placed a huge round stoneware red terrine on the table, resplendent with lid. He made an enormous fuss of lifting the lid to display his home-made curry, the ingredients of which were a closely guarded family secret. Frank's father had worked in India for many years and garnered the recipe during his stay overseas. It had always been a family tradition to eat *dad's curry* as it was called, on special occasions.

Despite his dour demeanour, Frank enjoyed the company of others and worked hard to make people feel welcome. A custom he followed from his own family upbringing.

The raising of the lid brought with it another cheer from the group which produced a smile on Frank's face. Bea looked at him with pride. Sometimes he could be an infuriating man; at other times he was a superb partner. Bea realised she was lucky and smiled at him when he caught her eye.

"Now Bea" said Frank, "I was wondering whether we were going to hear about how you ended up with Jasper or if Elle would tell us about the adventures of Internet dating. Which is it to be?" Frank said brazenly. Elle looked at Bea. Bea remained silent so Elle volunteered quickly "I'll tell you about my escapades, but I'm not sure where to begin."

"As none of us knew that you'd ever done that kind of thing, perhaps it would be wise to start at the beginning" Vivie said sardonically. "What possessed you to try that dark art?" exclaimed Bea. "You're in the dark ages you lot if you think that people don't use the Internet to find a potential partner" Elle stated. "The majority of people these days meet using dating apps. Where else would you be able to meet someone?" she asked briskly. "I think you need to move into the 21st Century."

"I think their husbands" said Caroline pointing at Bea and Vivie "would have a lot to say if those two knew how to use dating apps." "Good comeback Caroline' said Elle approvingly. "I knew you lot'd be difficult about this. Why do you think I haven't told any of you in the first place, but now you know, I might as well spill the beans" she said brusquely. "Sorry Elle" said a chastened Vivie.

"You'll probably be pleased to know that it's mostly been disastrous anyway" said Elle abruptly.

"I made the mistake of just going on a general dating app. I went for a meal with the first man I met – to McDonalds. Not a very romantic setting but I agreed because I was happy to meet in a very public place.

When he turned up he looked a bit awkward. Perhaps, I thought, it was because he had a black contraption wedged in his ear with a little antennae sticking out.

For the whole date I shouted at him thinking he was deaf. From time to time the device flashed so I thought that indicated it was working properly and picking up sound. It turned out he had an ear piece for a mobile telephone in his ear. That was Mr. Headset. An idiot.

The second person, let's call him Mr. Colonic Irrigation, spent the whole evening describing a medical procedure he had recently experienced. I never saw him again. The third person I met was a man who, when he encountered me, was dressed as an alien. Let's not talk about that event.

I almost gave up hope of meeting anyone but agreed to meet man number four who seemed to be fine. We had a couple of dates which went ok and were going to meet again when I found out who he really was. I was walking along the canal tow path in Manchester city centre one Sunday afternoon when I passed a barge and spotted my bloke on it. He became known as Mr. Wife and Three Children I Didn't Know About Until That Moment. All in all it's been a disaster!"

Following those very negative experiences, one of my colleagues at work persuaded me to join an exclusive online dating agency.

She recommended it by saying that this UK based agency provided professional help by offering expert advice about their client list. They're based in Northern Quarter so I felt a bit more secure signing up with a company whose address I knew. The minimum fee was £15,000 which I paid up front. Their success rate is supposed to be high and their client list ranges from doctors, lawyers, self-made people, A List celebrities and very wealthy people.

I've been on a couple of dates using this company. The first man was a property tycoon who was too keen to flash his cash, as if I would be impressed by that. The second man was very pleasant but we didn't have any kind of spark.

Just when I was at the point that I thought I'd never meet anyone, I went to a conference in Manchester to present a paper about pregnancies. I literally bumped into Phillip's friend whom I met at your wedding. Remember Sie Patel?" "How could we forget that handsome man?" exclaimed Caroline. "I have seen him from time to time but we've not really had the opportunity for a proper conversation."

Elle gave a wry smile. "I told you that he's now divorced" said Elle. "He's moved to Manchester to work as a Consultant at the city centre hospital. He was standing at the buffet table at a conference and I had my back to him as I gossiped to a friend when Sie inadvertently, he said, backed into me. As I turned round we recognised each other straightaway, started chatting and I thought no more about it. Well, that's not entirely true.

During the afternoon I thought of nothing else but him, about your wedding Caroline and the wonderful time I spent with him, albeit briefly. I kissed him more than once at your wedding y'know." "You're a wild woman Elle" teased Caroline. Elle rolled her eyes and carried on. "At the end of the conference I couldn't believe it when he sought me out and invited me to dinner." "Not sure why you couldn't believe it" said Vivie "you're an interesting, vivacious, intelligent, kind and funny woman Elle, why wouldn't he ask you out?" Elle blushed. She was too self-effacing.

"We've been on a few dates, including a trip to watch the Grand Prix at Silverstone. We went in a helicopter" she said giddily. There was a squeal of delight from Vivie. "That's one hell of a date" she said, "already I'm impressed with Sie. Not the cinema or McDonalds for him. Bit ostentatious though isn't it?" "Yes and no" replied Elle. "His brother is a pilot who has his own helicopter. He and his wife were going to Silverstone anyway and had two spare seats so we were lucky enough to get a lift. I was absolutely terrified. Those helicopters are incredibly noisy y'know. As the helicopter hovered over Silverstone we could see hundreds of people camping in fields around the place just because they wanted to be close to the track. I can't blame them.

When I saw the queues of traffic waiting to get into the car parks I realised we would have been stuck for hours if we had driven. Sie had been to Silverstone before and knew that a helicopter to the Grand Prix was a bit like most people catching a scheduled flight on their holidays. You should've seen the number of helicopters landing and taking off every few minutes. That was as exciting as watching the Grand Prix."

"Bloody hell Elle you're lucky to get to go to watch the Grand Prix. All of my life I've just watched formula one racing on the telly" stated Tom enviously. "What was it like?" he asked Elle. "Like nothing I've ever been to before" said Elle. "I couldn't believe how the noise of the roaring engines could be heard everywhere, the rumble from the cars was deafening and reverberated around the stand we were in. At the end we were lucky enough to be able to get down onto the track side in a hospitality suite and there was palpable excitement when the drivers appeared. I surprised myself by how much I enjoyed it.

Sie and I were able to wander around and watch the drivers being interviewed at close hand. I'm sure if you looked closely enough when Damon Hill was interviewing Lewis Hamilton for Sky TV you would've been able to see the two of us in the background. At that moment I had to force myself not to wave as I was trying to be sophisticated when really I wanted to be giddy. I didn't see much of the race when we stood track side, we found that it was better to watch it on the giant television screen in the hospitality pavilion.

It's difficult to fathom the speeds these men drive at until you see the cars whizzing past you. Hamilton is an unbelievable driver. He's amazing and so tiny. Going to the Grand Prix is an experience you don't have every day. The people in the arena went wild when Hamilton won. There's a young driver called Verstappen. I think he's only about eighteen years old. His driving style was exciting to watch but he passed other cars so closely that I thought he would crash." "He came second in that race" said Tom "and yes, at times, he makes risky manoeuvres. He's definitely one to watch. I predict that he and Hamilton will have some amazing tussles" said Tom sagely.

"I think, given the chance, I'd like to go to the Monaco Grand Prix" he said longingly. "Perhaps one day … in your dreams" replied his wife Vivie who made a mental note to save up and take him one day.

"Maybe one day Tom you'll get to go to Monaco" said Elle kindly. "It's early days yet for my relationship with Sie but he does seem genuinely disappointed when I can't see him.

I'm even thinking of cutting back on my work commitments so that I can spend more time with him. My house is paid for. I've slogged my guts out ever since I went to that awful convent, so I think it's about time that I started to be kinder to myself." "Quite right Elle" said a sagacious Matilde. "Seize the moment" she shouted. "Congratulations Elle. You were brave to use a dating app. I wouldn't have the nerve to do such a thing" said Caroline and she shuddered at the thought. "I wonder what your parents will think" said Vivie.

"About dating over the Internet or about dating someone who isn't a Catholic?" asked Elle. "Both" replied Vivie and Bea in unison. They can think whatever they like" stated a defiant Elle. "I think I'm old enough to make my own decisions. I'm sure they'll be pleased for me."

"We're pleased for you Elle, and he's certainly put a smile on your face" stated Bea. "Perhaps we could all go to the Grand Prix sometime" suggested Tom. "Great idea" re-joined Frank.

"Do you fancy organising it Tom, for next year?" asked Bella "to give us something to look forward to." "I will. Yes, I'll look it to it" said Tom. Suddenly a quiet harmony descended the café until Frank spoke. "Now Bea, you've put us off for long enough. Tell us all about Jasper." Bea looked at Caroline as if willing her to speak. After a brief pause she said, "I think Caroline and I will probably end up telling that story together."

# Chapter 7 - What happens when the lights go out?

The day continued in its shadowy hue. Lightning split through the damson coloured clouds which hung below the charcoal sky. A wallop of thunder shook the shop. Instantaneously the Hub was plunged into darkness except for the gentle flickering of the table candles. Bea, who was near the window, peeped through the blinds but could see nothing. Slowly her eyes began to adjust to the darkness. She could distinguish only the outline of buildings across the road cast in gloom because the orange street lights had been snuffed.

"Looks like there's a power cut" she announced to the group. "I'll get some more candles" volunteered Frank. "Bea please will you get some blankets for us all as it'll get cold very quickly" he asked. "I'll help" said Vivie. "What about the food in your fridges and freezers?" Elle queried to Frank "won't they start to de-frost and warm up?" "I'm not too worried about those because we have a back-up battery powered generator for them. We made that investment a few years ago because it'd be disastrous for the business if we lost all the food in there."

"Right Vivie, let's take a couple of candles and we'll go upstairs for the blankets. The weather's so bad, it's not safe for anyone to travel home yet is it?" asked Bea to no-one in particular. "No" answered Tom.

"The lashing rain made it tough to see what was in front of me when I drove over and the weather seems to be getting worse. There were puddles on the roads, torrents of water gushing in streams along the pavements and trees swaying ominously.

Branches were flying everywhere. The state of my car showed you that it's not safe to be out in this didn't it? When I was driving, I clenched the steering wheel just to keep the car moving in a straight line, the windscreen wipers were on full blast and I still couldn't see very well. It'd be daft to go out in this weather."

"You're right" said Frank. "We'll batten down the hatches here. Let's stay in the Hub for a little longer. We can always go up to the apartment later on if the storm doesn't pass through." Following this brief exchange Vivie and Bea walked ponderously, feeling their way through the dimly lit café.

Cautiously they ascended the first flight of steps and were distracted by their shadows dancing along the walls. "It's eerie living by candlelight isn't it and the wind seems to be screaming which is quite scary" said Vivie nervously.

"I'm glad we live in the age of electricity, where power is available at the flick of a switch" replied Bea. Imagine living life without electric lights, a washing machine, a tumble dryer or central heating. We're really lucky aren't we and I suppose we usually take all this for granted" stated Vivie.

"You're right. When the others were soaking wet I'm sure they didn't think twice about having their clothes put into the tumble dryer to dry them, or about having hot water for the shower at the press of a button" Bea said.

"Flipping heck if we think about what your mother must've endured Bea, she'll have seen lots of dramatic changes during her lifetime and we've probably never taken the time to ask her about them" uttered Vivie.

"No, we've never thought to ask any of our parents about what life was like for them when they were growing up and the changes they've experienced. Perhaps we should ask Robert and Matilde about *the old days* when we get back downstairs. They'll be delighted to reminisce" assured Bea.

In the semi-darkness Bea led Vivie to the utility room where spare bedding was kept in a cupboard. "I think five large blankets should be enough for the ten of us" Bea said as she counted out the covers. "We're going to have to be careful now not to fall if we're carrying all this stuff, especially holding the candles as well" pronounced Vivie. "It'll probably be better if I carry the candles and you carry the blankets. I can light up the way as we walk" replied Bea.

"Good idea Bea, let's go but don't walk too fast or too far ahead of me. I'm a bit scared up here in the dark. The two women stepped deliberately along the first floor towards the stairs. "Can you see where you're going Vivie?" asked Bea anxiously. "I hope I don't fall, 'cos if I do I'll land on you and send you flying" joked Vivie. "Let's walk very slowly then and I'll count out the stairs for you so that you know when you're at the bottom Vivie."

Bea held the two candles in front of her to light the way; Vivie followed but could barely see above the five blankets she was carrying. They arrived at the top of the stairs and were about to descend when Frank yelled "Everything ok up there?" The noise in the darkness startled Vivie because she screamed and dropped the blankets.

This shouting and sudden movement surprised Bea who dropped the two candles on the stairs. The fall extinguished the flame of one candle but the other was still alight. Apart from the small flickering light of a candle half-way down the stairs the stairway was thrown into darkness.

Both Vivie and Bea screamed. They caught the sound of concerned voices coming from the café and heard footsteps, which they assumed belonged to Frank, as he ran up the steps towards the flickering candle. Within a moment he stood on the dancing flame and crushed it. For a few seconds Frank, Bea and Vivie were in complete darkness.

At the bottom of the stairs, the shadow of Tom holding a candle emerged from the café which threw a little light upon the scene. Frank grabbed Bea and hugged her. Tom shouted "Vivie, are you ok?" "Yes thank you" mumbled Vivie as she, Frank and Bea bent down to pick up the blankets. "We're all fine thanks to Frank's quick thinking" she said generously.

She thought that the blankets wouldn't have fallen if Frank hadn't shouted in the first place. "I'll hold up the candle so that you can see the steps" shouted Tom. Frank grabbed all of the blankets, and the three of them made their way to the bottom of the stairs.

"What a day" sighed Vivie as Tom continued to hold up the candle to light the way back into the cafe. As they emerged into brighter light Matilde asked for a full explanation of events, which a very relieved Bea and Vivie recounted, describing Frank as a hero.

"He'll be moaning at me tomorrow though when he sees a big hole in the stair carpet" wailed Bea. "Somehow it's bound to be my fault even though it was caused by him shouting" cried Bea. "You're right" exclaimed Frank "I'm never wrong."

Whilst Bea and Vivie had been away, Frank had placed two bowls of desserts on the table in the café. As she sat at the table, Vivie noticed home-made tiramisu and home-made trifle and knew that both would have been made with lashings of sherry. Frank and Bea certainly knew how to look after people.

The group settled at the table once again, but this time their legs were covered by the warmth of shared blankets "brought despite death staring us in the face" maintained Vivie dramatically, to which everyone cheered and raised their glasses.

Frank and Bea served dessert, pleased to observe that everyone had two helpings each. Bea thought that this had turned out to be a lovely day shared with friends, despite the sad news of Bella's abortive attempts at buying a wedding gown and calling off her wedding. Being with people she cared about meant a lot to Bea but she wasn't too sure that Frank, who enjoyed his own company, was as enamoured with entertaining people. She noted that he stayed with the group, so assumed that he was happy to carry on otherwise he would've gone up to the apartment and stayed there alone. Sometimes he liked to be a solitary man.

"Mum" said Bea to Matilde, "Vivie and I were wondering what do you and dad think are the most startling changes you've both seen over the past seventy years?" Matilde looked surprised at the question.

"Gosh, there's been a lot of change that we've had to contend with. What do you think Robert?" she asked, turning to her husband.

Robert pondered for a moment, then spoke. "I started work at 14 and now my grandchildren can't leave school 'til they're 18 so that's a big change.

There's an assumption that most young people go off to university but in my day, we didn't even know that university existed. We didn't move in those circles where it was an expectation to get a degree. I remember in my first job having to push a barrow down Chapel Street across Manchester to Oldham Street to do plumbing jobs. We didn't have a van so we had to walk everywhere. That was hard work and long hours for very little pay."

"I remember helping my mother with the washing every Monday" added Matilde. "We didn't have automatic washing machines and tumble dryers. We had a machine which we called a top loader. Mum and I put the clothes into the top of the machine, filled it with water, a cup of washing powder then turned it on. When the washing cycle had finished, as mum took out the clothes one by one she passed each item to me and I fed it through a wringer. It had a handle which I had to push and if the clothes were very thick, both of us pushed at the handle because it could be difficult to manoeuvre.

In the summer the washing was hung on the washing line outside. On damp or wet days the clothes were put on a clothes horse in the house.

Our clothes dryer had six wooden laths suspended between two cast iron rack ends and worked on a pulley system. The clothes rack could be raised and lowered by a rope and the clothes would dangle just below the ceiling in our kitchen. We've still got one in our house next door. As kids we broke the pulley more than once because we used to try and hoist each other off the floor to see how high we could dangle.

The fun we used to have with simple things. We also used to tipple over down the stairs using the stair rods to help us along and we used to slide down the bannister" Matilde smiled at this memory.

"D'you remember our dryer Bea? You were always ashamed of us having a clothes horse in our house, when your friends all had mod cons in theirs?" "Yes" nodded Bea "I was very embarrassed." "You daft thing" said her mother kindly.

"When Matilde and I got married" began Robert "we had a coal fire which barely kept a room warm, never mind the house. At times we would have to go to bed and put coats over us because the bedrooms were so cold that you could touch the ice on the inside of the windows. When we got central heating and were able to have a bath in a warm room that was luxurious to us.

Then we got really up-market and bought double glazing which meant that I didn't have to paint the outside of the house any longer. The house was lovely and warm which was also a positive move." Matilde nodded in agreement with Robert's reminiscences. "We never had a car when the kids were little though.

The young ones think it's the end of the world if they don't have their own car as soon as they pass their test at 17. Your eldest two", Matilde said turning to Frank and Bea, "both got a car when they reached 17. Even though we didn't have a car we used to go on our holidays on the train to the Lake District or to Wales. We went camping because we couldn't afford bed and breakfast.

Do you remember Bea that everyone had their own little job of being responsible for carrying something for the holiday?" asked Robert. "I do dad, because I left the camping stove on the train one year didn't I?" asked Bea raising her eyes to the sky. "Luckily for us the train was still in the station when you noticed I hadn't got the stove. You jumped on the train to rescue the stove and I remember crying when the train set off and dad was still on it. Mum was crying with laughter. You always see the positive side of things don't you mum?" asked Bea.

"Mum just said, 'your dad knows where we'll be, he'll catch us up eventually' and proceeded to walk to the camp site."

Robert took up the story. "I had no ticket so had to explain to the conductor what had happened. Luckily enough he was a good sort and put me on the next train back but he had to explain to the conductor of the other train what had happened before I could travel. I didn't get to the camp site 'til late in the evening. All the family had pulled together to set up the tents, sleeping bags and make things comfy. When I got back you were eating sandwiches that Matilde had prepared and were drinking lemonade. You all thought it was hilarious and I must admit, I quite enjoyed my mini adventure" giggled Robert.

"We were really daring and went camping in Scotland once didn't we mum?" asked Bea cheekily. "Yes and I was nervous that we would be arrested when we crossed the border because we didn't have any passports as I supposed we were going to a foreign country" replied Matilde.

"No-one we knew had passports in our younger days" said Robert "because foreign travel was out of our reach. It was only for rich people. Nowadays you young ones go on holiday abroad about four times a year and consider it to be routine."

"I thought that learning French in school with Sister Georgina was almost the biggest waste of my time because I never dreamt that I would travel outside of Britain" explained Bea. "'I would like you all to know that the biggest waste of my time was studying Physics" she paused then added for no particular reason "actually going to school was my biggest irrelevance." Robert shook his head. "A clever girl like you not liking school. Sinful it is.

In the '70s Sir Freddie Laker, bless him, pioneered cheap air travel. That was marvellous. We queued up for air tickets at Manchester Airport and went to America for £59 each. We thought it was wonderful. We took packed lunches on the 'plane because food wasn't included in the cost of the ticket. It was terrible what happened to Laker's company though. The big boys in the airline industry seemed to put him out of business and I think he was given £6 million compensation because of it. On reflection, his entrepreneurial spirit opened the door to you all being able to afford air travel" reported Robert. "Laker was a man to be admired. Not good at school but very industrious when he started work.

I wonder whether we need school at all, except as an expensive child minding service for people who work. Anyway don't get me started on that. Matilde and I think that travel has changed a lot don't we love?"  Matilde nodded in agreement.

"The biggest change surely has been the ability to access money" said Matilde. "The relaxation of the rules on borrowing money to make it easier for ordinary working people to buy things on credit, must be up there as an important step mustn't it?" she asked of the group.

"When we were first married, I stayed at home and looked after the children.  Robert had two jobs so that we had enough money to pay our bills.  You didn't buy things on tick like you young ones do.  We saved up for what we needed and appreciated what we had.

When I go to your house Bea the three kids must have at least six pairs of shoes each.  We were lucky to have one pair of shoes, and those we bought from Tommy Ball's warehouse.  Do you remember Robert that the shoes were hung on racks by pieces of string holding a pair of shoes together?"

"It's got to be better now Matilde" said Robert. 'If you have access to money it gives you a degree of freedom to get what you want, not just what you need to get by. Living hand to mouth like we used to do was not a pleasure was it?

C'mon love, things have improved for us all" said Matilde.  "Remember my granny?  When my grandad died she had to bring up five kids and couldn't afford to do it.  The youngest two, one of them being my father, had to go away and live at that boarding school in Manchester 'cos my granny had no money to look after them.

I've got some papers about it that I managed to get from the school's archivist. I'll nip next door and show them to you" said Matilde. "Don't be daft woman, I'll go" interposed Frank "I know where you keep all of your precious documents Matilde"  with that Frank moved into the kitchen which was lit by candle light and lifted a key off the wall which was there for the purpose of what Matilde called, *eventualities.*

He knew this meant that if ever anything happened to Robert and Matilde he and Bea would have a key to get into their house.  Frank quickly put on his coat and slipped quietly out of the back door.

Fighting for breath against the raging wind and bitingly cold rain he tugged open the back gate and, pitching his weight against the wind, managed to get to next door and open the rattling gate.

He thought that he could see the outline of a man lurking in the shadows at the back of one of the buildings a little way down. Frank paused, peered into the darkness but was blinded by the driving rain.  If there was somebody there, they had hidden out of sight.

With his heart racing, he ran through the back yard and reached his neighbours' back door within seconds. He heard someone shuffling about in the alleyway behind the house.  He looked around, he was sure it was a man, but convinced himself that no-one would be out on a night like this, unless they were mad, or thinking of rooting for Matilde's valuables!

Frank felt for the keyhole and managed, after three attempts, to open the back door.  He was shaking.  "Must be the cold" he thought.  On entering the house he waited for his eyes to acclimatise to the murkiness.

Through the shadows Frank could see the outline of the oak bureau where Matilde kept her treasured possessions, links to her past. He opened the top door of this piece of antique furniture and in the dim light saw the light green envelope which contained documents relating to Bea's grandfather which Matilde had shown him years before. Frank opened his coat, grasped the envelope and hugged it tightly against his chest before zipping up his coat again.

Despite the breath-taking wind and hammering rain, Frank managed to hold tightly to Matilde's precious document. Adroitly he opened the back door, slowly scrutinised the darkness seeking out anyone lurking in the shadows before nimbly setting off on the short journey to the café.

As he opened the back gate, he scanned the dark alleyway. Glittering in the darkness were two eyes, staring wildly at Frank. He jumped backwards as a small figure emitted an ear piercing screech and ran away. Frank withdrew into the yard, banging shut the gate. 'It was only a cat' he convinced himself, but he wasn't too sure about that.

As he waited for a few moments Frank cursed as the wind whipped his whole body and rain blasted at his coat. Softly he opened the back gate and peered behind him then ran into the Hub like a whippet. Frank entered the kitchen, hung up the key for *eventualities,* took off his coat as his sodden hair dripped coldly down his back.

He heard a noise in the backyard and peeped into the darkness. No-one there he assured himself. "Oh Frank, you're a good 'un" said Matilde. She got up, opened a drawer and passed him a small tea towel.

Vigorously Frank rubbed his hair, face and hands, mostly to get his circulation moving again. He was freezing cold, his teeth were chattering, his heart pounding then he heard Matilde ask "please will you tell everyone what the documents say about my father?" He smiled and felt honoured. He knew how painful this would be for her. Frank took a deep breath in an attempt to slow down his heart rate and read aloud.

"The contents are about Douglas, Matilde's father" he said. "The first document is a petition for admission into the hospital, which was an historic term for a boarding school, for a poor boy from the town or township of Manchester dated February 1920. The application for admission states:

*Particular attention is called to the following regulations.*

*1. Boys eligible for election must be resident in the Town or Township of Manchester, Salford, Droylsden, Crumpsall, Bolton-le-Moors or Turton **and not elsewhere**.*

*2. They must be over 6 and under 10 years of age on the day of election.*

*3. They must be the children of honest, industrious, and painful parents, and not of wandering or idle beggars or rogues, and must not be bastards, nor lame, infirm or diseased.*

*4. This Petition must be accompanied by the following Certificates:*

*i. of the marriage of the boy's parents*
*ii. of the boy's birth*
*iii. of the boy's baptism*
*iv. of the parents' death (if deceased)*

*5. This Petition should be correctly filled up and returned to the House Governor, Manchester*

*N.B. If it should afterwards be discovered that the Governors have been deceived in any of the particulars contained in this Petition, the Boy received under such misrepresentations will be immediately returned to his parents or friends.*

There are details on a separate piece of paper about the income Matilde's mother Mary received from taking in washing at home. Her earnings were 49d. Her son Edward was a bread boy and received £1.20 as a wage. The document states that Mary's husband died of bronchitis.

There is a separate petition which asks if Douglas, who was aged nine at the time could be accepted into the *hospital.* It looks as though this petition had to be signed by a clergyman to vouch that Douglas was from Manchester. He also had to be certified through a medical examination which I will read out to you.

*I hereby certify that I have this 12th October, 1920 examined Douglas and find him free from any Scrofulus Disorder, and of Sound Constitution; he is exempt from Deformity, and all serious defects, both physical and mental. There exists in him, at present, no infectious disease. He also had to be vaccinated.*

*We the undersigned being acquainted with the Petitioner, believe the statements in the foregoing Petition to be correct, and beg to recommend the case to the favourable consideration of the Governors.*

The petition was signed by a local farrier, school teacher, store keeper, insurance agent, foreman, and two other names which are too lightly written for me to see" stated Frank.

"Thanks Frank" said an emotional Matilde.

My father told me that his school day began at 6 in the morning and he either picked up litter, cleaned the toilets or stoked the boiler until 7.30 then he'd have breakfast.

His mother and his three brothers were able to visit each term and on his birthday. Every day from 8.30 in the morning until 5 at night, except on Thursdays and Saturdays when lessons finished at midday, he studied an hour of prayers, arithmetic, grammar, the classics, shorthand and office skills.

I know that he was able to write to my grandmother once a month as she kept all of his letters. My grandmother said that the regime at the school was severe. I don't know what severe meant but it was harsh when we went to school too but not as bad as he endured. My father tried to hide the shadow of cruelty from us.

He was delighted to be given an apprenticeship working at the ship canal at the age of fourteen and moved back home. The separation was heart-breaking for my grandmother who never got over it. Robert and I have always lived in dread of not being able to pay our bills" said Matilde quietly "and of not being able to look after our family."

"No" burst out Robert "I think that being able to borrow money, if you can pay it back in instalments, is mostly a good thing.

Some people though go bonkers don't they? For some it's spend, spend, spend with no regard for tomorrow." "Trouble is" stated Matilde "almost anybody can have a credit card even if they can't afford to pay off the debt. You're right Robert. We didn't have anything unless we saved up for it.
Nowadays people borrow money for all kinds of things and are living in debt that they might struggle to pay off. I wonder how they get help when there is a downward spiral of mounting debt" she asked sadly.

Robert thought for a moment, then said "it must be a living nightmare, especially if they have no-one to turn to for guidance.  People will struggle if interest rates go up the way they did in the 1980s.  At one time we were looking at interest rates hitting 20% which would have been a disaster for us as mortgage holders.  Now the interest rate is about 5% which makes a huge difference on mortgage repayments" said Robert.

"Let's hope interest rates don't go that high again" said Bea "otherwise we'll all be in the workhouse."  Robert and Matilde shuddered at the thought.  "I think that young people should be taught money management in school by people in the banking industry, not teachers" said Robert "and I'm going to write to Mark Carney, the Governor of the Bank of England to suggest it."  "Good plan" said Frank supportively.

"One thing we do struggle to understand is technology.  We grappled with learning how to use the computer, didn't we Robert?" asked Matilde.

"That must have been the biggest change we've had to contend with.  Oh my goodness when our Bea and Frank bought us a tablet last Christmas Robert and I looked at each other 'cos we had no idea what it was.  When they told us they'd bought us a tablet we thought it was medication, a machine that we had to have strapped to us.
Bea's always warning us about eating too much sugar which will lead to diabetes and telling us our blood pressure might be high.  We thought the tablet was some kind of health monitor.  We didn't like to ask Bea or Frank what we were supposed to do with this tablet machine."

The group laughed. "It's all right for you lot" said Robert "you've adapted and we haven't. Most things you have to do online and we didn't have a clue what that meant. Even when we asked Bea and Frank for help and they showed us they went – click this, that and the other. There, now it's done. I looked at Matilde and she looked at me. We used to say 'oh right thanks' and still had no idea what to do. We even hatched a plan. I'd ask Frank, he'd explain it to me, Matilde was supposed to watch what Frank did then when he went she was meant to tell me what he'd done. The problem was, she'd forget what he'd done. This computer lark is completely foreign to us" lamented Robert.

"When Frank said click the mouse on the screen, Matilde screamed thinking we'd got a mouse. When he told us to scroll up and down, how did he think we would know what to do? Technology is the one thing we haven't ever got to grips with isn't it Matilde?" asked Robert. Matilde nodded. "A computer is a bit like us old 'uns, because it always seems to have memory problems" Matilde commented.

"Once the computer wouldn't turn on. We knocked on the wall for Frank. When he came round he looked at us, looked at the computer, said just a minute, plugged in the computer, switched it on and it worked. We felt like complete idiots. When the grandchildren spoke to us about needing extra microchips, when we went shopping we spent ages looking for microchips in the freezer cabinet at Tesco.

We feel like we've been left behind in a world full of technology" stated Robert.

"I'll give you a couple of examples of what I mean. We've had this new boiler installed in the house. It's called a combination boiler which we'd not heard about before. When we turn on any hot water tap, the water runs and only takes a few seconds before it gets boiling hot. No need to use an immersion heater anymore so it reduces the cost of our bills.

It's magic this new contraption but last week Matilde and I sat in the freezing cold for two days because our heating wasn't working. I checked the boiler, it was switched on and when I turned on the hot water the water came out of the tap boiling hot but the radiators stayed cold. It was like the olden days, when we had to sit in the house in our coats because the rooms were so cold. When the two of us spoke, we could see our breath in the air. All the windows were full of condensation so Matilde had to wipe down every single window to dry them. That's not easy at our age. When I watched her working so hard, I felt exhausted."

Bea smiled at the irony. "Anyway, Frank happened to pop in to check we were ok, which we weren't. Frank's organised it so that our new boiler links to an app on my mobile 'phone which sends signals to the boiler through wi-fi to turn the heating on and off at certain times.

Don't ask me how it works, it's like a modern day mystery to me. Anyway, for some reason the boiler wasn't receiving a signal from the wi-fi so that's why we had no heating for two days. We had to rely on Frank to sort it out because we didn't have a clue what to do.

That's what we mean, it's difficult to keep up-to-date with this modern technology and I wouldn't have known how to explain what was wrong to the heating people if I had rung them. Left to our own devices, we might have frozen to death" said Robert sadly.

"Don't be daft Robert" said Frank. "You've got people popping in to see you regularly." "I know that Frank, but what about people who are on their own and don't have a family. Who checks on them?" Robert asked.

"You're right Robert" agreed Bella "there are lots of vulnerable people who could do with regular support and I suppose for some of them, they rely on strangers to offer a life-line. Or have no help" she said sadly. "Or come to the Hub" said Matilde kindly.

Matilde and Robert were in their element with a captive audience. "There's another problem for older people too isn't there Robert to do with paying for things. We've managed to work out how to use a debit card, but it's hard to keep track of our money when we pay with a card. In the old days we used to have cash and when it had gone, we knew where we were up to. A debit card can be confusing.

We're encouraged not to use cheques too and Bea had to help me out last week" confessed Matilde. "I was writing a cheque when Bea happened to call in. She told me that I wasn't writing a cheque at all, I was writing on a paying-in slip. When she looked through my cheque book she saw that I'd already paid two bills using paying-in slips. What a to-do. I was so frightened that I'd be arrested for fraud.

Bea laughed when I told her that. She had to take me to the bank to explain what I had done. I had to take my passport, cheque book and bank statements to prove who I was.

In the old days, everyone knew who you were because you used the same bank, the same gas shop, the same food shop. Now people shop in different places to where they live so we've become a society of strangers.

When Bea took me to the bank there was a policeman outside. For a split second I thought he'd come to get me but Bea made a joke about things and I felt a bit better. The bank teller smiled when Bea explained what I had done but I got a bit frightened in case I was starting with dementia. Bea said it was an easy mistake to make as the last cheque I wrote was four years ago and I couldn't be expected to remember how to do something I'd not done for four years. I felt a bit reassured.

Then we went to the post office because I'd paid my 'phone bill using a paying-in slip. The post office assistant was really kind and she said I would have received a final demand before my 'phone would have been cut off. A final demand! Fancy that. We've never paid a bill late in all our lives have we Robert?" probed Matilde.

Robert smiled "no love, we haven't. You've always made sure of that." Matilde continued "the other bill I paid was, would you believe it, insurance for the boiler in case it broke down.

When Bea checked our paperwork for the boiler, she said we're already covered for two years so I didn't need to pay any bill. It's just that I got a letter from a gas supplier saying that I could insure my boiler. I thought it was a good idea so paid £126.

Thankfully, I'd paid on a paying-in slip so the lady at the bank said that if it was presented it would be rejected by the bank anyway. So really my mistake made me £126 better off." Robert laughed. "You daft thing, you weren't supposed to spend £126 so you're not better off." "In my mind I am" retorted Matilde.

After listening to their mishaps Bella asked Robert and Matilde "would you not consider moving out of next door and into a retirement home? They're smaller, so less expensive to run. There's a warden on duty part of the time in case you need any help. I've seen that our local retirement home has a lovely shared lounge where you can meet up with other people?

Everything is on one level so you wouldn't have to struggle with stairs."

There was an audible gasp from Bea and she tried to make eye contact with Bella to indicate that she should steer away from this channel of questioning, but it was too late.

Using as much dignity as she could muster Matilde said "those places are for old people and we're not old. Robert's 79 and I'm 77. There's plenty of life left in us yet and we can manage in our own home. We're going nowhere" she stated firmly. With that, this line of conversation ceased immediately.

"Ok Bea. We've had a trip down memory lane with your parents. Now are you going to tell us how you ended up with Jasper?" asked Frank in a determined manner.

# Chapter 8 - Reminiscing

Bella was laughing at one of Robert's jokes when Bea glanced at her. At that moment, as if she sensed that she was being observed, Bella looked up and spoke to Bea "I was wondering, when you left the Convent Bea, what made you move to London with Vivie and my mum?"

"She did really well at a very posh place, didn't you Bea? Fitted in like a dream she did. We're so proud of her" interrupted Matilde. "Ok thanks mum. It was odd really because although I passed the entrance exam for the convent I found that I never really enjoyed writing and thought I wasn't very clever. We did so much writing, copying notes from a board, writing some more and working in silence at school that I didn't like being there.

Once in an English lesson, when the class had an essay to write of 1,000 words at the end of every line I counted the number of words I'd written. As soon as I reached 1,000 words I finished writing, mid-sentence with no proper ending. My teacher went berserk; she shouted so much at me. She called me a lazy brat. Little did she realise how much effort it actually took me to write that story.

Teachers can really influence you can't they? For good or bad. The things I got into the most trouble for at school, such as chatting to people and being an independent thinker, are the things that have served me well during my working life. I enjoyed making things but that didn't seem to be valued at school so I couldn't wait to leave.

Vivie felt the same. I suppose we were both clever but in ways that weren't recognised at our school.

We were what you might call *divergent thinkers* and teachers generally don't like answers that aren't in a book. We just didn't like being constrained.

In my final year of school my last exam was in June but it really was a waste of everyone's time me even taking exams as I'd never done any work for them. I wanted a job where I didn't need to do much reading or writing and I was lucky enough to find one.

Apart from being with your mum, Vivie and Elle, the best bit of my school life was when I met up with Frank every day after school. We did that for years. I thought he would always be there to chat to and discuss things with. He seemed to share my distaste of being imprisoned in an education system which didn't much care for the use of imagination.

We would share each other's daily joys and worries so I was devastated on the day he told me that he was going to work on a cruise liner. I stormed off and didn't look back. I was very frightened that I'd never see him again and it took me ages to resign myself to the fact that he was very likely to meet some girl whilst he was abroad whom he would marry and be with forever.

The day he told me he was leaving I flounced off, stormed into the house, ran up to my room and sobbed.

After a few hours of lying on the bed sobbing I remember my parents coming in to my bedroom to ask me what was wrong. I wept so much I felt as though my heart would break. My parents were really worried about me. It was my dad who said that I needed to let Frank go and not to let him know that I was sad about him leaving.

My dad said that it was never a good thing to stand in the way of a young man. For weeks I avoided meeting up with Frank. I stopped eating properly and moped around pining for Frank's company.

Eventually my mother told me that Frank had left for New York, and he was delighted to be working on a cruise liner. She said that I couldn't rely on someone else to make me happy, that I would have to be responsible for my own happiness through hard work and enterprise. The heartache of a first love is a very difficult thing to deal with.

For months I thought that I could see Frank in the distance and I ached just to hear how he was. My mother must've understood this. She was, and still is, a great communicator. She made it her business to find out information on how Frank was faring at sea. To my ears it sounded as though he was having a wonderful time so eventually, I gave up hope of ever seeing him again. Until tonight, I never knew he'd visited my parents just before I married Jasper." Bea looked lovingly at Frank.

"Robert and I had seen the effect that Frank leaving had on you" said Matilde "the light had gone out and there was nothing we could do to help. We saw that our lovely daughter who'd been sad for such a long time began to exude joy when you were with Jasper. We didn't want to cause any upset by telling you that Frank had called so decided it was better not to tell you. We hope that you think it was the right decision at the time. You barely ate anything when Frank left and we were worried when you lost so much weight. When Jasper appeared on the scene you were almost back to your usual self."

Bea looked at her mother. "I understand now. I'm not sure I would've understood then though. Things are different when you're younger. Everything feels so much more intense. Nursing a broken heart, on the day of my last exam I caught the train into Manchester.

I decided I never wanted to be limited, ever, and that I would never care about a boy again.

I sauntered from Piccadilly Station and avoided Piccadilly Gardens, which were quite scary at that time as they're were loads of druggies there. It bothered me to think that life was so desperate for these people but I had no idea how to offer help and I was full of thoughts about my own misery to take too much action.

I meandered down Market Street through throngs of people and stopped in Meng and Ecker, a café that used to be at the end of the passageway which links St. Ann's Square with King Street. King Street used to be posh in those days. I bought myself a cup of tea, sat beside the window for ages and, at the ripe old age of 16, pondered what I could do with my life.

As I sat there on my own two girls, probably in their early twenties, came into the café and chose to sit at a table near to me. I noticed them because they looked fashionable. I knew that the clothes they wore were from Elle and Fiorucci which were designer clothes shops on King Street. As I wanted a distraction from my own thoughts, I decided to eavesdrop their conversation.

The two young women chatted about their work. I realised they were from Verbier's, a hair dressing salon round the corner on King Street.

They talked about their clients, who sounded exciting and the outrageous haircuts that they were encouraged to create. The life they talked about seemed right up my street.

I decided there and then that I was going to go into Verbier's and ask to become an apprentice hairdresser, just like that. I didn't have a plan, I hadn't researched the company and I'd never worked in a hairdressing salon before so had no experience. On the positive side I was able to hold a conversation with people, enjoyed being creative and was looking for a challenge.

Filled with the courage of the ignorant, I drank my tea, walked out of the café and onto King Street. As I turned right and tottered down the cobbled street I saw the smoky brown glass of the salon on the ground floor. I stopped and stood on the opposite side of the street gazing up at the building. On the first floor were three life-size portraits of models displaying unconventional hairstyles. This use of imagination and inventiveness appealed to me after years of being inhibited at school.

My initial audacity deserted me. I must have paced up and down King Street until I wore down the heel of my shoes on the cobblestones. I desperately wanted a job but couldn't think how to phrase my approach and lost the courage to go into the shop. I thought that everyone who worked there would be snooty.

I can still remember how I felt my heart thumping as I finally forced myself to open the door to the salon. Immediately in front of me, slightly to the left hand side, was the large, black reception desk behind which sat two glamorous ladies.

The receptionist who spoke to me was a woman in her early thirties. Her short black hair was immaculately presented, she looked chic and her smile shone brightly. She wore a name tag, Hazel and asked if I had an appointment, I said no and that I was looking for a job as an apprentice hairdresser.

Hazel didn't laugh at me, as I'd expected, instead she gave me a pen, some lined paper and an envelope, sat me at a huge black and white striped chair in the reception area beside a glass and silver table full of fashion and hair magazines, and instructed me to write a letter of application.

She gave me guidance about how to present the letter, what to include and even the name of the director of the salon so that my letter was addressed to a named person.

Hazel said that it was important to send a letter to a named person otherwise the correspondence could be ignored easily. Even at the time I recognised that this lady was being extremely kind to me. When I had written the letter, I handed it to Hazel who promised to deliver it.

I walked out of the shop as if I were walking on air. In my mind I'd been given the job and I imagined myself working in places like London, Paris, Munich and New York. All places I had never visited before but had seen on telly. I almost danced through St. Ann's Square, up Market Street, passed Piccadilly Gardens, on my way back to Piccadilly train station.

I kept glimpsing myself in the shop windows and imagined that I was going to be a famous international hairdresser. When I got off the train I skipped all the way home, along the High Street.

I couldn't wait to tell Matilde and Robert about what I'd done. Once home, my parents were so excited.

Mum said that I was brazen. At least she didn't say I was a brazen brat like the teacher had said on more than one occasion. I never understood why she chose to use that term. The next days were filled with trepidation. Every morning I ran to get the post, searching for a letter from Verbier's and by the end of the week my nerves were knotted. A whole ten days went by and finally on the Saturday morning I received a letter addressed to me in a brown envelope which bore the name *Verbier's* embossed on the front.

I hardly dared open the letter. If it contained bad news I would've been crushed as I was already downhearted. I took the post to my room and held the envelope for a long time.

My hands trembled when I cut open the envelope with my mum's crystal letter opener which she got from my dad for their fifteenth wedding anniversary. I skimmed the page really staring hard at the words waiting to be disappointed, but I wasn't. I'd been invited to an interview the following Tuesday. I ran downstairs and into the living room to tell my parents. They were delighted and spent the whole weekend with me shopping for clothes that my mother thought would be suitable and I considered to be trendy.

Robert kept giving me mock interviews and asking ridiculous questions such as *where do you see yourself in five years?* As if anyone would be able to plan so far in advance what they were going to do in this chaotic life.

How could I possibly have a grasp of what would happen in the future? How could I possibly plan my life? The only thing I knew I could plan with an amount of certainty was my journey to the interview.

My parents gave me money to buy a drink so that I could sit in a café in case I was too early, and money for my lunch. They must've been disappointed with my lack of effort at school but they never showed it. They were always supportive of me" said Bea as she smiled at Robert and Matilde.

"Together the three of us worked out how much money I would need to earn if I got the job as my wages would need to cover the cost of my lunches every day. We agreed that £30 a week would be a good payment and that I could give my parents £10 a week towards my board and lodgings. This meant that I would have to negotiate with an adult for my salary."

"You gave money from your salary to your parents?" asked Bella with incredulity. "Yes. Don't young people do that these days? It was what had to be done to help pay the bills at home which was why I would never have been able to stay on at school beyond 16 and do A Levels or go to university" retorted Bea. "I never realised that" replied Bella.

"It never even occurred to me to do that for my mum" she said shame-faced. "I've been saving up my spare money towards buying a house. That's really selfish of me isn't it?" she asked of Caroline.

Her reply was that she didn't want her daughter to worry "I don't want any money from you Bella. I was glad that you were saving towards a house.

The price of property in this country is absolutely ridiculous. Nowadays a two-bedroomed terraced house can cost £250,000 and you need a 10% deposit to be able to get onto the housing market. What young person can do that without help?"

"Do you want to hear this story or not?" asked Bea impatiently. "Come on Bea, we've waited long enough" answered a disingenuous Frank and so finally, Bea told her story.

"At 8.30 a.m. exactly I pushed open the brown smoky front door of Verbier's. The place was abuzz with the animated chatter of hairdressers and receptionists. I spotted Hazel's black hair, made my way over to her, and told her that I had an interview at 9.00 o'clock, she looked delighted for me as though she had been expecting to see me again.

On this visit Hazel led me upstairs to the first floor of the salon. I walked slowly up the wooden staircase, along a brightly lit room which housed twenty hairdressing stations, where black leather adjustable chairs were placed opposite floor to ceiling mirrors.

I felt a tingle of excitement ripple through me. At the furthest end of the room was an oak door which Hazel opened. I was taken aback by the bright orange colour of the carpeted floor set against a backdrop of black walls. The room was lit by two black chandeliers, there were two leather sofas with orange and black cushions set at right angles to each other.

On one of the sofas sat the director of the salon who stood up and introduced herself as Gill. She had closely cropped blonde hair, piercing blue eyes and an elfin face.

She greeted me with a warm smile, and shook my hand. I wasn't sure how to shake someone's hand as I'd never done that before.

I should've practised that with my dad. As I looked at the clothes Gill was wearing, I knew that my mother, the seamstress, would've approved of the black dress and jacket as they appeared to be hand-crafted by a bespoke tailor. I had expected nothing less. Gill's shoes drew my attention as they were red, suede court shoes with black polka dots at the front. The low chunky heel was in black leather with red polka dots and, despite appearing trendy, looked very comfortable. I suppose they needed to be comfortable as she would probably be standing all day for her job. Sorry, I'm digressing" apologised Bea.

"The interview went well. Gill gave me different scenarios which tested how I might deal with customer complaints.

My father had prepared me to answer interview questions by relating my answers to high levels of customer service.

The discussion with Gill lasted for exactly thirty minutes. At the end Gill said that that salary would be £40 a week, staff were entitled to a 50% discount off hair products and haircuts were free. She told me that I could start work at the salon the following Monday, if I were interested.

Interested? I was ecstatic. At the ripe old age of 16, I had landed my very first job. I couldn't wait to get home to tell my parents.

They were thrilled, especially when they heard that I would undergo a formal training programme at the Verbier Academy to become a qualified hairdresser. Gill had said that there were opportunities to work in London, Paris, Munich and New York so I was determined that I would work harder than any other apprentice they had ever employed.

The following Monday I was terrified. My dad walked with me to Deansgate at 7.30 in the morning so that I'd be early for my first day of work. It was a bit out of the way to his own workplace, but I was thankful for the company whilst walking through Manchester. I was anxious to arrive on time.

When Robert stopped walking, there were no coffee shops open as there would be now. In those days, apart from newsagent shops, other places didn't open until 9.00 o'clock at the earliest. There was no 24 hour shop opening back then. I walked around the streets looking for a café where I could have a cup of tea and while away an hour. I timed my walk so that I would know how long it would take me to get to Verbier's.

I kept looking at my watch. Time passed by so slowly. When it got to 8.10 a.m. I decided to go directly to the salon.

My parents had bought me a beautiful outfit from Fiorucci. It was a pale blue short-sleeved dress with an elasticated waist and I had a pair of light blue, flat heeled suede shoes to match. I wore a dark denim Fiorucci jacket over the top and thought I looked amazing.

I desperately wanted to fit in at such a vogueish place.

During the first month I followed an induction programme. This introduced me to the company, its history, culture and administrative procedures. I spent time working with the receptionists, answering the telephone and dealing face to face with customers. I shadowed the administration manager to understand how to manage invoices, and deal with the inventory of stock. All of this was done before I joined the hairdressing staff.

That part of my induction gave me a clear idea of different roles within the company and how they interlinked. After four weeks I finished working with the ancillary staff and moved onto the hairdressing side of the business. I was assigned as a trainee to four stylists and my role was to help them. I had to do lots of jobs such as sweeping the floor, cleaning individual rollers with a toothbrush until they shone, cleaning and unblocking sinks when they became clogged with hair.

To most people in the salon I was invisible, but I had a plan to rise to the top. After months of unremarkable jobs, I was promoted to cut rolls of foil for the stylists, mix different colours for the colourists, manage the timing of hair heaters, wash clients' hair, and go to the shop to buy lunch for the senior staff. It really wasn't as glamorous as I had hoped but during that time I was able to speak with customers, get to know how to manage people effectively and begin to glean a small understanding of the workings of an international business. It's an approach which formed an excellent basis for the whole of my working life.

I was keen to learn and willing to undertake the routine jobs needed to help around the salon. I never moaned because, on days when I was tired and despairing of ever moving away from the mundane, I remembered my plan.

To move on up. During the day I worked in the salon and then one evening a week for a year I attended evening classes to learn how to become a counsellor.

Being in the salon made me realise that people discussed all kinds of problems with their hairdresser and the people I thought had perfect lives, often didn't. Those who were rich seemed to have no-one they could rely upon to offer truthful advice. One of the important things I recognised was the need to build trust with people.

Over time I was allowed to work with models to style and cut their hair, I even had a few of my own clients, but not many. We used to enter competitions to demonstrate our creativity and I was delighted when I won a few of them. After five years of working as an apprentice hairdresser, with Gill as my mentor, she asked if I would be interested in going to London for a couple of years to work in the Bond Street salon. Wow, I thought, first London, next Paris where I could learn French, then Munich where I could learn German and then wend my way to New York by the time I was thirty and sophisticated!

It was then that I wished I'd been more scholarly during my French lessons at school. Sister Georgina, the nun who taught me French, told me I never paid attention during lessons, at least, that's what I think she said. I realised what a wonderful opportunity going to London would be and I was going to grasp it with both hands.

Obviously during this time I had kept in touch with Caroline and Elle.

Vivie and I used to meet up each week. We would write letters to the two 'university bods' as we called them, describing what was happening in our lives. We didn't have mobile telephones in those days. When Caroline wrote and invited me to Edinburgh for the weekend I was ready for a break and to experience some fun. My endeavour had paid off at work and I was prepared to celebrate.

Going to Edinburgh was a marvellous chance to relay the news to Caroline that I'd been chosen to work at Verbier's salon in London the following summer. I intended to let my hair down, no pun intended, at Caroline's Christmas party.

Caroline and I were assigned to sit with Phillip and Jasper for the meal that evening. The two men were great fun, really good company and, to our young eyes, extremely sophisticated. Phillip was more serious than Jasper, perhaps because he was a lot older and had more responsibility as he owned the company.

As Phillip chatted to Caroline, this offered the chance for Jasper and me to find out about each other. He was fashion-conscious, stylish, and appeared to be interested in the hairdressing business. I wanted to discover what it was like to live in London as he'd graduated from a university there and had lived in central London for six years.

He had a lot to tell me about life in the capital city. We got on really well and had a lot in common. When the meal had ended, we danced together all evening. At the end of the night we joined a group of people who'd chosen to walk through the hotel garden but we talked only to each other and laughed until we cried.

Jasper didn't kiss me at the party and the following morning he and Phillip had left the hotel before Caroline and I went for breakfast. Caroline and I were disappointed they hadn't stayed to have breakfast with us. I thought I would never see him again, but I was wrong.

In February, two months after the Edinburgh party, on a particularly busy day at the salon, I received a 'phone call from Hazel who was manning the reception desk. She said that there was a handsome stranger in reception who wanted to see me but wouldn't give a name. I remember being in a tizzy as I had no idea who would pop in to the salon to see me other than my father and Hazel had met my father. I'm not sure she'd call him handsome.

Fleetingly I wondered if it was Frank but that thought didn't stay long in my mind. I wasn't sure if the stranger was a man or a woman but I assumed it was a man as Hazel had said handsome and not beautiful. I had to stay with my client for fifteen minutes until I could break away without appearing ill-mannered but I'm sure that I became quite agitated during that time.

Eventually, as I walked from the first floor, down the wooden stairway, I spotted Jasper sat on one of the black and white striped chairs in the reception area. He was chatting unconcernedly with Hazel but looked up when I appeared on the steps. His vivid green eyes met mine and I swear that my face burned an intense red.

As he flashed a smile showing brilliant white teeth, I was flustered and wondered how on earth I would greet him. As I approached him slowly, with each deliberate step I noticed more about him.

Under his unbuttoned overcoat, he wore a navy suit and pale blue shirt without a tie. His brown curly hair looked unkempt but his shoes shone as if they had been polished by a military man. I smiled when I spotted the tartan laces in his blue shoes and he noticed this involuntary reaction. He stood up and came towards me.

I wondered how to greet him, but need not have worried. He clasped me in a bear hug and kissed my burning cheek. As he pushed me back, he looked intently at me and invited me to dinner after work that evening. He arranged to collect me at the salon at 7 o'clock. My heart felt as if it would burst. When Jasper left the salon Hazel turned to me, pursed her lips and said 'wow, great catch Bea'. I became even more discomfited."

"You little rat Bea" said Caroline good naturedly. "I never knew that you'd been meeting up with Jasper before we moved to London. No wonder Jasper and Phillip knew where to find us in the local bar when we first started living there."

"Don't be cross with me Caroline" pleaded Bea. "I thought he'd disappear the way Frank did. I didn't know whether anything would come of it. I kept meaning to tell you but I was frightened Jasper would get bored and our relationship would fizzle out. Then, as time went on and we moved to London, it felt as if I'd been hiding a huge part of my life from you. Then I thought you'd be hurt by that, so it was easier to say nothing at all."

After a few moments of uncomfortable silence, Bella urged Bea to go on with her story.

"Thankfully I kept one set of spare clothes at the salon in case we ever went out after work, but actually, we seldom did this. By luck I was able to change at the end of the day into a brown suede suit of shorts and a jacket which I teamed with a white t-shirt and little brown ankle boots bought from the shop named Elle, not my friend named Elle.

I had to be trendy didn't I working at Verbier's? When I told Gill that I had a date, bless her, she volunteered to style my hair before I went out for the evening."

"We must make you look like you represent the finest hair salon in Manchester Bea", said Gill "we can't have you looking less than amazing can we? You've never mentioned a young man before." "Gill was true to her word. When she changed my hairstyle, I felt incredible. She had created little barrel curls with my hair and pinned them around my head with tiny crystals. They weren't real crystals, just plastic hair grips made to sparkle.

Earlier in the afternoon, during my break, I had already persuaded one of the beauticians in Kendals to do my make-up for free. I was so excited for the evening ahead and wasn't disappointed.

Jasper collected me promptly from the salon. We walked arm in arm up King Street, over Cross Street and ambled towards China Town. He was in Manchester on business and decided to pop into the salon to see if I still worked there as he'd remembered discussing the hairdressing business with me in Edinburgh.

Conversation with him was easy. Despite being a Londoner, he followed Manchester United and was keen to discuss football with me. Ron Atkinson was the manager at the time.

My father is a huge fan of Manchester United so I've been brought up talking about football. We ate at the Ying San in China Town, which was supposed to be posh. When we'd finished, we sauntered down towards Albert Square and, as Jasper had heard about the Hendo, which was a nightclub at that time, he decided that this might be an interesting place to visit.

The Hendo nightclub was in a remarkable building at the bottom of Deansgate near to the train station. If you were deemed trendy enough by the bouncers, you'd be allowed to enter the club through large metal doors.

The interior was very industrial, with steel girders, glass, iron and wood which was an unusual style back then, it's probably a little more common these days. Jasper and I must've looked the part because we were allowed into the club and spent a couple of hours in there listening to electro funk. The SOS Band's song *Just be Good to Me* always reminds me of that date but surprisingly I never ever returned to the Hendo.

At the end of the evening we ambled up Peter Street together, holding hands. Jasper was staying at the Midland Hotel, which is opposite to one of the most unusual buildings in Manchester, as it's cylindrical, y'know, Central Library. As we stood outside the library we kissed, just once.

Immediately afterwards, Jasper hailed a taxi and instructed the driver to take me home to my parents' house. Obviously I gave the taxi driver the address as Jasper wouldn't have known it. As I got into the taxi my emotions were in a turmoil.

When the car drove away from the library I looked back at Jasper. I was determined that my heart would not be broken. He was standing in the street watching me leave. For a second time I thought I'd never see Jasper again." "This is like a bloody love story" complained Frank.

Like a portent of doom, or *ominiscity* as Vivie called it, a loud thunder-clap overhead shook the building and everybody jumped. Echoing around the Hub was the sound of roof tiles being dashed to the ground by the railing wind, as if made furious by something. Bea, Caroline and Bella exchanged frightened glances which Frank and Vivie noticed. Immediately Vivie took charge as she knew that now would be a good time to change the subject, especially for Frank.

"Let me tell you about how Tom and I ended up together' she said, pointing at her husband. "I hope this isn't too embarrassing for you Ben." Bella glanced at Ben's handsome face. As their eyes met, she blushed.

"Every day is an embarrassment with you and dad" Ben joked.

"Let's hear your love story then mum" chuckled Ben.

# Chapter 9 - A quirk of fate?

"I'll start by apologising to you Caroline" stated Vivie. "Why the need to apologise?" quizzed Caroline. "You'll find out soon enough" replied Vivie "when you hear this story" and she grimaced. "It started with Bea" began Vivie as she pointed at Bea. "Bea" exclaimed Frank turning to his wife "you always seem to be in the middle of things." "Not on purpose" she protested. Frank shook his head and looked at Vivie. "Go on" he said theatrically, "as I'm intrigued". Vivie had the good grace to look embarrassed as she regarded Bea.

"It's not my fault we're all trapped here. Blame the weather" exclaimed Vivie. Robert and Matilde laughed. "You girls, can't help yourselves can you? Always getting each other into trouble of one kind or another. You were hard work when you were younger, particularly at school.

We're not surprised by anything you lot've done" scorned Robert. "They could've been a lot worse, it was just silliness really, nothing serious, and you know it" defended Matilde. "Look how they've turned out. They're lovely. All of them."

Elle, Bea, Caroline and Vivie beamed with delight at Matilde. It meant a lot to each of them that she was protective of them. Vivie turned to Frank and said condescendingly "See. Despite what you might think, we're absolutely delightful in the eyes of other people." Frank snorted.

"I'll start again" she said in determined voice. It began with Bea. She returned home to Manchester immediately after the Edinburgh jaunt and was in raptures about Jasper.

She'd only met him for one evening and couldn't stop talking about him. You've always been a romantic Bea" said Vivie who paused for a moment and looked at Bea as if seeking her permission to carry on. As Bea did not interject, Vivie continued "when he turned up at the salon she was over-joyed. I suppose I'd better give some background to this story so that you understand how Bea's story led to my meeting with Tom.

As Bea already told you all, she and I finished school at 16. Bea was lucky enough to be taken on at Verbier's to follow a hairdressing career but I had no idea what I wanted to do when I left school.

My mother was really annoyed that I hadn't worked hard and was determined to ensure that I got a job of any description. As far as she was concerned, I needed to bring money into the household. When I asked her if I could stay at school and go into the Sixth Form to study for A Levels she laughed mirthlessly. My mother said that I needed to make money to help pay the bills and that I could forget qualifications when I'd messed up my O Levels. She thought that qualifications were pointless anyway. She said that people like us should know our place. I didn't understand what she meant by that.

Money had always been tight at home so I knew from the outset when I joined the Convent at eleven that there was only one path for me – I had to go to work to earn some money to help pay our bills as soon as I reached sixteen. My father had left home when I was much younger. He'd 'run off with another woman' as my mother put it. For a Catholic family, that was the height of humiliation. Divorce was almost unheard of in those days and we never discussed this chasm that suddenly appeared in our lives.

It wouldn't have done any good anyway to constantly re-live things that caused unhappiness. That would have kept them at the forefront of my mind.

I decided a long time ago that I was going to try to be positive about my life. My mother earned a meagre salary working part-time and her money was allocated very carefully. By Wednesday of each week the funds had almost gone and our evening meal was an egg. At least we got one each!

My escape from the reality of a silent, empty home life was through reading. Every Saturday I would go to the library and spend all morning there. I would read anything and usually was the last to leave when the library closed.

I enjoyed Saturdays but thought that Sunday was the most hellish day of the week. No pun intended. No shops open, no library to go to, no friends to speak to on the telephone, nothing good to watch on one of the four television channels we had.

I should've woken up and realised that a good education was a way out of poverty, but I was too young to grasp this and trusted my mother and the nuns when they said that I was too much of a dreamer to amount to anything. Negativity can be believable and powerfully suffocating.

As I've grown older, I refuse to surround myself with people who don't have a positive attitude to life. This is why, my dear friends" said Vivie looking around the table "I have stuck close to you all. You're great and I hardly ever tell any of you how pleased I am that we are still friends after all these years.

Anyway enough of this. The reality is that I knew, when the results would be published in August, that I would've failed my exams. My mother took me to the local Job Centre the day after my last school exam.

Luckily for me there was a job on offer as an Office Junior in Manchester. The lady at the Job Centre arranged for me to have an interview. I felt very grown up having my first ever job interview in Manchester no less. My mother lent me her clothes to wear for this important event. I must've looked sixteen going on forty and was totally unprepared for what I should expect at an interview.

I arrived in the plush six storey building where the reception area was manned by a concierge who was kind and offered me a drink as I must've looked very nervous. I heard the concierge speak to someone on the telephone and mention my name. I looked around me at the beautifully ornate building and watched people going into and getting out of a wooden lift. I observed as the floor numbers were highlighted on the dial in the lobby whenever the lift reached a floor.

After about ten minutes a small, dishevelled man stepped out of the lift. He looked straight ahead and took tiny steps towards me. When he eventually arrived at the seating area of the reception he introduced himself as Roy Rodgers, can you believe that? He wasn't wearing a cowboy hat, nor did he burst into song and I couldn't see Trigger waiting patiently in the car park. The first things I noticed were that the few teeth this man had were yellow, he smelled as if he smoked cigarettes incessantly and his clothes were crumpled. It was as if he, or anyone else had never cared about him or his appearance.

Roy turned out to be an anxious man but by the end of the interview it had become obvious that he was an incredibly kind man. He explained that I would have to do a battery of psychometric tests, a bit like the 11+ exam he said. I felt at ease as I knew I'd passed my 11+ with flying colours even though I let my education slide after that.

The tests were easy, then my interview followed. My mother had told me to ask about career progression opportunities and for once, I'd listened to her advice. Following my interview, Roy said that my test scores were very high. He offered me a job, and said the thing that had tipped in my favour was the fact that I had expressed an interest in developing myself. Great. Thanks to me listening to my mother's advice, I got the job.

The following week I began life as an Office Junior working in a posh office block in the centre of Manchester. One of my main duties was pulling a shopping trolley laden with post from one end of the building to the other, over six floors. Not glamorous, but it was a start.

I found that working was like unmitigated freedom. I didn't have to ask to go to the toilet like I did at school! Work was refreshing, stimulating and interesting. A complete contrast to school for me.

Like Bea I was determined to rise to dizzy heights at work. I was motivated to learn and keen to understand the business from the bottom up. I went on courses to acquire the skills about how to use the photocopiers and became the chief photocopying operator whenever the machine broke down.

When computers were introduced, shortly after I joined, I put my name down to be taught how to use spreadsheet, word processing and database software. Most of the other workers were afraid of technology but I embraced it and discovered as much as I could. By listening and watching carefully, over five years I amassed a wealth of knowledge and skills.

There was a management hierarchy pinned on the wall of the main reception area at work and I planned how I would move up the career ladder.

When Bea spoke to me about signing up for her night school classes to study counselling, I enrolled to learn business skills. Bea and I helped each other to study. By this time I had guessed that Bea might be dyslexic. It's quite a common learning difficulty which is recognised these days but wasn't when we were younger.

By collaborating with each other, I realised that using word processing software supported Bea when she was learning as we could use spell-checker and highlight mistakes. In an odd way this aided me by enabling an understanding of Bea's difficulties. By the age of 18 I'd amassed enough qualifications in office practice to be asked to train other people at work.

Slowly, over time, I was promoted but I was a long way off having my name on the office hierarchy sheet on the wall, which was my goal back then. It was rare for a woman to be in a managerial position. So motivated was I to carry on learning that I decided to study part-time for a degree at night school. That was such hard work. At times I had to run from the office, as I often had to work late, and go straight to university across Manchester. Sometimes I hadn't even eaten.

I did this for three years and graduated with an honours degree at the age of twenty-one. At home I was rewarded by my mother asking me why I had bothered with such 'crap'. People at work were more positive. My boss presented me with two first class return train tickets from Manchester to London with overnight accommodation at the Hilton Hotel in Mayfair in recognition of my hard work. I was thrilled.

As Bea and I had supported each other during our learning, I thought that it would be fun for the two of us to have an adventure in London. Elle and Caroline were busy studying for their important exams.

We planned our trip to be in March which gave us time to save up money from our salaries so that we could afford to treat ourselves. By this time we knew that Bea and Caroline would be working in London later that year, so we called this our *reconnaissance trip.* I too wanted to live in London and was trying to percolate a plan which would help me to achieve this goal, but wasn't sure what I wanted to do as a job.

When the date of our trip to London arrived in March, Bea's parents went with us to Piccadilly train station. We could barely contain our excitement and we giggled like two naughty schoolgirls.

Robert and Matilde walked to the platform with us and made sure that we sat in the correct seats reserved for us in the First Class carriage. As he turned to leave us, Robert pressed £50 in Bea's hand which he told her was for the two of us to spend. 'Make sure you treat yourselves in London and be careful' he instructed as he left the carriage.

Both he and Matilde stood waving on the platform until we were out of sight. The train glided over the tracks, as we hurtled closer and closer to London, and breakfast was served in the Pullman carriage. We ate as much as our tiny stomachs could hold so that we'd not need to eat until much later in the day.

When breakfast was cleared away we planned our short journey on the underground train from Euston to Green Park which was the closest tube station to our hotel. We decided that our first exploration would be to walk up Bond Street. We were perfectly well aware where all the so-called *high class* shops were because we often read old editions of Vogue which Bea brought home from the hair salon. We couldn't wait to arrive in London and have the freedom of the city.

Euston Station appeared to be awash with suitcases accompanied by their intrepid owners. We had to be deft negotiators to wend our way past the melee of people who were scurrying around the station purposefully, confident of reaching their desired destination. Unlike us, timid in this unfamiliar environment.

Cautiously we made our way to the down escalator and headed for the tube. We bobbled along like rabbits, as we ventured through a labyrinth of tunnels in a warren and ran to get on the tube train which had just arrived at Euston station. We changed at the aptly named Warren Street onto the Piccadilly Line heading towards Green Park. It was hot in the carriage and the stench of perspiration hung in the air but the journey was smooth and quicker than we imagined.

You won't believe what remarkable event happened as we left the tube at Green Park.

Bea and I were tugging our suitcases behind us, fearful that we may not be in the correct place as we joined the up escalator to get out of the station at Green Park. We obliged instructions by standing on the right hand side.

As the escalator moved slowly upwards I heard a man shouting Bea's name. We both looked across at the escalator which was moving down towards Green Park underground line as we slowly ascended on our escalator. I noticed that the voice belonged to a young man with brown curly hair. 'Bea' he bellowed 'wait for me at the top of the escalator.'

Bea gasped in surprise." Her first words were "Oh my goodness Vivie it's that Jasper I've been telling you about." "At the top of the escalator, Bea and I waited for Jasper to join us. I could tell that Bea was nervous as she swayed gently from side to side.

When he joined us, Jasper practically leapt off the top step of the escalator and almost landed in Bea's arms. He hugged Bea as if she were a long-lost friend. He kissed her cheek and I watched her blush.

I stood awkwardly to the side of Bea. As the two of them exchanged pleasantries, Jasper's friend who was with him introduced himself to me as Tom.

I too blushed. In a dither Bea explained to Jasper why she and I were in London. He seemed to be delighted to see her and insisted that the four of us walk to the Hilton Hotel 'it's not far' he assured us.

Jasper and Bea chatted animatedly as they walked in front of Tom and me.

I was embarrassed and not very good at making small talk with a stranger, particularly one with deep brown eyes, a tanned complexion, Scandinavian blond hair and almost a foot taller than me.

Tom and I were silent as we walked away from Green Park, along Piccadilly through the back streets. We stopped at Shepherd Market for a drink. I wished myself to be a million miles away. I was sure that Tom must've felt the same way."

"I didn't" interjected Tom as he shook his head. "I'd heard about Bea from Jasper. He was obviously smitten by her as he talked non-stop about this girl he'd met in Edinburgh and then taken out in Manchester. He didn't want to have a long distance relationship. He thought that wouldn't work so that's why he was reticent at first with Bea."

As they reminisced, Tom turned to look at Vivie. "When we met at Green Park Station, and you blushed then lifted up your face to look at me I couldn't think of anything sensible to say. I thought you were gorgeous but, had I said that, you would have assumed I was weird as we'd only just met."

"Of course I would've thought you were weird. Every girl hates to hear those words" said Vivie with irony "so instead, you didn't speak for ages and when eventually you did, you preferred to ridicule everything about me. You led me to believe you didn't like me at all" blurted Vivie.

"Yes" nodded Tom, smiling sardonically "I've always been an idiot. See how effective that was? It was all part of my master plan."

"I don't think so Tom" retorted Bea, "you were scared that Vivie wasn't interested in you at all. That's what you said to me when she went to the loo."

I ll tell you all how it was" stated Vivie emphatically. "We had a drink together. We stood for an hour whilst Bea and Jasper chatted on and on and on. Tom and I stuttered our way through stilted conversation, before Jasper guided us to our hotel.

We arranged to meet Jasper and Tom later that day outside Harrods in Knightsbridge. Jasper had told us to meet at the first entrance we came to as we walked down Brompton Road. I felt a bit downhearted. I feared that my celebratory weekend would end up with me playing gooseberry to Bea and searching for things to say to Jasper's gorgeous but silent and dull friend.

I didn't allow my gloom to last for long. When we arrived at the Hilton the hotel room was spacious and we felt very sophisticated to be staying in London. The location was perfect, so close to the places we wished to visit. We unpacked quickly and set off to explore London. We made our way up Bond Street and paid our first, but not last visit to Fenwick's department store, marvelling at the prices some people could afford to pay for clothes and handbags.

As I enjoy all things stationery, I spent ages musing around Smythson's and even bought myself one pack of Bond Street blue woven writing paper with matching envelopes which I still have tucked into a drawer. It's a memento of my first trip to London.

We looked into the windows of the exclusive jewellery shops including Cartier and imagined what it might be like to be able to buy anything we fancied.

My teachers were right when they said I was a dreamer. We tried to be nonchalant as we strolled past the Verbier salon, but Bea couldn't help making a fuss that she would be working there later that year. She did that non-stop as we made our way back down Bond Street until we reached the promenade of shops enveloped in Burlington Arcade. The roof of the Arcade was glazed which allowed light to shower through and each shop had a projecting window to display the wares on offer. It was like going back a hundred years, if we'd been rich. We probably wouldn't have been allowed into Burlington Arcade a hundred years ago had we been poor.

We drifted from one window to another before descending steps into Piccadilly. As we crossed the main road we spotted the distinctive Fortnum and Mason store resplendent in jade green. Once there Bea purchased a tin of Explorers' Biscuits for her parents in the company's branded green tin. Matilde you still use that tin don't you?" asked Vivie as she turned to Bea's mother.

"I bought a china mug for my mother which she never used. In the pursuit of more gifts we continued to wander around Piccadilly and stopped at Prestat in Princes Arcade where we'd been instructed to buy Gin Truffles for Caroline's parents and Champagne Truffles for Elle's parents. We took our goodies back to the hotel before we ventured through Green Park on our way to Buckingham Palace.

Buckingham Palace was enormous and grand. We marvelled at how so few people could live in such a gigantic building. As we stood outside it was evident that the Queen was in residence as the Royal Standard was wafting in the gentle breeze. We pretended that we could see her peeping out of one of the windows at the front of the Palace.

We decided to walk to Knightsbridge but it wasn't easy dodging the traffic at Hyde Park Corner and we realised that catching a bus would have been stress-free and safer. As we walked along Brompton Road we stared in the windows of shops which sold Persian carpets, wondering who on earth had the poor sense to buy those and laughing mercilessly at their bad taste.

We arrived early for our rendezvous with Jasper and Tom. I imagined that when they arrived we would be taken to afternoon tea in one of the posh restaurants, perhaps even into Harrods so allowed myself to get a little excited. I was keen to experience something new and considered by me to be a treat. That was fanciful thinking.

When Jasper and Tom arrived, they guided us across the road from Harrods to a place called Wendy's. This café was akin to a McDonalds café that we know these days. We sat in Wendy's and each of us ate a portion of American burger and chips for the very first time in our lives. It turned out to be fun and different. The food was better than I thought originally. Bea and Jasper couldn't stop talking but I did feel a bit like a gooseberry."

"You've always known how to treat the ladies dad haven't you?" questioned Ben "taking mum to Wendy's on your first date. Wild." He laughed and winked at Bella.

His father Tom merely smiled. "Tom was awful at making small talk" said Vivie. "I found him really difficult to get to know and in the end I gave up speaking to him. In fact, I thought he was a little bit arrogant especially when he poked fun at my Manchester accent.

The food was tasty and it was pleasing to see Bea so happy to be in Jasper's company." "Tom was shy Vivie" explained Bea. "I didn't know that at the time Bea did I?" protested Vivie. "I thought he was snobby." "Please let me tell them what happened next" begged Bea. "Go on" responded Vivie "I'm embarrassed to tell this part anyway."

"As the four of us left Wendy's café a little git snatched Vivie's handbag. She screamed and in an instant Tom was running after the thief who crossed Brompton Road. In hot pursuit Tom ran into the road, grabbed the bag back and was hit by a car. The thief got away empty handed."

"Blood hell, never mind the thief, what happened to my dad?" asked a shocked Ben who'd never heard about this incident. "In those days we didn't have mobile 'phones so your mum ran back into Wendy's and asked the staff to call for an ambulance.

Brompton Road is very busy so it took a while for the ambulance to get through. I stood at the side of the road because I didn't want to see any blood" explained Bea. "I thought he was dead. Jasper went to your father, who had rolled over the bonnet of the car. All I could see was a shoeless foot."

For a moment there was silence then Bella asked in amazement. "What, his foot had come off? Tom's got a false foot? I have noticed your limp but didn't know it was because of that."

Tom laughed. "No Bella. My shoe had come off but all Bea could see was my foot. It was still attached to my leg." Vivie explained "when I came out of the café after asking a waitress to ring for an ambulance Bea was stood at the side of the road crying.

The traffic had come to a standstill. I walked with trepidation around the car which had hit Tom. The driver, who was out of his car, was distraught. It wasn't his fault, Tom had run straight into the road and the driver had no opportunity to stop. I saw Tom lying face down on the floor with blood seeping out of his head. He was clutching my handbag and I didn't have the heart to take it.

Tom was unconscious with Jasper crouched beside him, kneeling on the floor, telling him to be strong and that everything would be fine. Jasper was calm but when I saw how tangled Tom's legs were I felt sick. Jasper and I stayed by Tom until the ambulance arrived. He was cold and pale so I put my coat over Tom to keep him warm and I felt his wrist to check that he still had a pulse. He did.

Neither of us tried to move him in case we caused any more harm. It felt like a really long time before the ambulance appeared. When the paramedics did turn up they took charge immediately and we stood to the side. They checked that Tom was breathing, fixed an oxygen mask over his nose and mouth, placed a brace around his neck and secured splints to his legs before they moved him on to a stretcher. He was still unconscious.

Tom went in the ambulance with Jasper and a taxi driver, who'd stopped at the scene, took Bea and me to St. Thomas's Hospital. The taxi driver didn't even charge us.

It was a good job because Tom had been taken to University College Hospital which meant that we had to travel from Westminster across London to the hospital which is near to Euston train station.

I'm amazed that we managed to find our way around the tube so successfully on our first visit" exclaimed Vivie. "Needs must" retorted Bea.

"When we finally arrived at the hospital, Tom was in the operating theatre. He had multiple breaks to his legs, and a deep cut on his forehead. His parents were out of the country on holiday at the time so Jasper, Bea and I were the only people he had to care about him. We spent Saturday evening waiting to hear news about the success of the operation. When the orthopaedic surgeon who operated on him approached us I felt so guilty. It was my fault that Tom was in this mess.

We were told that the bones in his legs had been fixed with metal plates and that an external frame had been attached to both legs with metal pins to keep his legs in place. His forehead needed six stitches and he had been heavily sedated. The surgeon said that it would take up to six months for Tom's legs to heal and that his injuries might be life changing. I just cried. Jasper went white. Bea tried to placate us both.

When we were allowed into the ward to see Tom, he was in a side room on his own, asleep and linked to different machines. We sat with him for about an hour and then went to eat a small snack, very late, in the hospital café. We sat in silence. Jasper insisted on taking us back to our hotel and we arranged to meet the following afternoon in Green Park so that we could visit Tom again.

The following morning was warm, bright and sunny. We decided to pass the time until we could visit Tom by seeing some of the sights even though our hearts weren't really in it but we wanted to be in the fresh air and try to clear out the horrible images of the accident.

Immediately after breakfast, which we barely ate, we followed our tourist map which guided us down Regent Street towards Piccadilly Circus. The area was quiet as few shops were open so we sat for a short while on the steps of the Eros statue watching people wander aimlessly as red buses navigated the roads around the circular sculpture.

We decided to explore as much of London as we could so that we had something to tell my mum, Matilde and Robert. We knew that we had five hours to kill before we could see Tom at the hospital so we strolled along Piccadilly, into Leicester Square and on to Trafalgar Square. We stayed there for a while, feeding the pigeons and wondered about the kind of people who would be lucky enough to attend Central Saint Martins, the world famous art college.

When we had finished deliberating we ventured along cobbled streets to Covent Garden Market which appeared before us in a functional and unadorned design. Looking at the artisan wares and roaming around the stalls we were beleaguered by market traders of all description. We bought a jar of bee pollen each and I bought a hand-knitted jumper which was unique. In fact, I've still got that jumper somewhere as it's stood the test of time. Nowadays the stall holders just let you mooch, maybe have a short conversation with you.

Back then there was so much noise in the market as stall owners were trying to grasp our attention by telling jokes to us as we passed: *'I haven't spoken a word to my husband in years. He hates to be interrupted'* shouted one; another said *'my friend's a pessimist he's always saying things can't get any worse. I'm an optimist so I told him, of course they can.*

---

Bea and I still tell those jokes when we go to functions with people we don't know. Surprised we're invited back.

We bought a couple of little things at Covent Garden including some fruit for Tom and drank tea at the Punch and Judy bar.

We wanted to see Big Ben and the Houses of Parliament so we zigzagged through The Strand and onwards to the most iconic buildings in London. We would have plenty to talk about when we got to see Tom later that day. We caught the tube from Westminster using the Jubilee Line for only one stop before we arrived at Green Park for our meeting with Jasper.

I made an excuse to Bea and visited Fortnum and Mason so that she could see Jasper on her own for a while. We arranged to meet an hour later outside the store. See Ben and Bella, things were more difficult to organise in those days. Without mobile 'phones all we could do was arrange a time and place to meet. If someone was delayed, we wouldn't know until they didn't turn up at the allocated time.

When the three of us met up we walked towards Green Park and together we caught the tube on the Victoria Line to Warren Street. Luckily for us this was close to Euston train station so we could stay with Tom for quite some time before we had to head home to Manchester.

I was really anxious when we arrived at University College Hospital and concerned that Tom would blame me for his predicament. Well, it was my fault wasn't it? Robert had warned us to be careful and I hadn't been vigilant enough to stop a thief. I was the last of our little group to enter Tom's room.

I held back at the door in case he asked me to leave but, as I peeped around Jasper, Tom spotted me and smiled.

The first thing I said to him was *what's a nice man like you doing in a place like this?"* "Couldn't you think of anything more original to say mother?" scoffed Ben. "You've got to remember that he was almost a stranger to me. I did make a huge effort to chat to Tom and be more pleasant than I had been the previous day" remonstrated Vivie.

"He looked terrible" said Bea "all battered and bruised. He also looked uncomfortable because he couldn't move at all." "It was pretty grim" agreed Tom "but I had plenty of ladies making a fuss of me, which I liked." He smiled. He still had a gorgeous smile thought Vivie. "I bought Tom a present from Fortnum and Mason" divulged Vivie. "A small box of violet and rose cream chocolates. It was a tiny gesture to apologise and thank him at the same time, for being my hero.

When Bea and Jasper left the room to get drinks for the four of us, I gave him the small box and a kiss on the cheek. To break the silence I read articles to Tom from a newspaper I'd bought on the way in to the hospital. When he was thirsty I lifted a glass to his lips and held his head so that he wouldn't choke."

"When Jasper and I returned to the hospital room we made a list of all the things that Tom might need during his lengthy stay" interjected Bea. "Luckily we were able to go to the shops around the corner on Tottenham Court Road and bought what we could" she said. "We were trying to make him as comfortable as possible which of course, was virtually impossible."

"Eventually we had to leave the hospital to catch our train to Manchester. Before I left I promised Tom that I'd go back to see him the following weekend" stated Vivie. Turning to Caroline she said "that's why I needed to apologise to you because Bea and I haven't told you any of this until tonight." Caroline was dignified in her silence.

# Chapter 10 - Unchartered territory

Vivie noticed that Caroline looked nonplussed. "What's the matter Caroline?" Bea asked. For a moment she said nothing but picked up her glass of wine, from which she sipped slowly. "Please ignore me. I'm just trying to absorb all of this information and piece it together" said Caroline who seemed distracted. She turned to Vivie and said gently "sorry Vivie, go on, tell us all the rest of the story."

With a huge intake of breath Vivie began to speak. "On the train back to Manchester Bea was talkative about the weekend and the time she'd spent with Jasper. She was enthusiastic about returning to London the following weekend. Bea usually worked every Saturday but had to take her holiday allocation before the end of March so taking the following weekend off would fit in with the salon.

During the journey home we asked the ticket collector if there were any inexpensive weekend train ticket deals we could look out for and he gave us good advice. Bea had already spoken with Jasper and arranged for the two of us to stay at his apartment in Bloomsbury which he shared with Tom, so we only had to find money for our train fare which turned out to be quite inexpensive.

As we returned home, I have to admit that I only half-listened to Bea as she spoke about Jasper. Sorry Bea. I was mulling over what to do next. I felt that I'd caused Tom to be so terribly injured and knew that I had to make it up to him somehow.

The only thing I could think about was visiting him again, but that wasn't the only thing on my mind. I'd got a university degree and needed to plan what I wanted to do next but there wasn't great careers advice around and my mother wouldn't have been able to guide me.

Seeing Tom so poorly made me realise that life could change in an instant. I think the accident made me a little more reflective and when I returned to work the following day I contacted the Human Resources department to find out about career options. The manager of the department, Justin Thyme made an appointment for me to see him later that week.

When I met him, Justin told me that my colleagues thought that I was a great tutor, and he advised me to apply for a job in the Human Resources Training Department at work. I agreed to consider this as an option but I knew that it wasn't really the role I wanted.

Bea and I didn't talk with anyone else about what had happened in London. Bea didn't want people to know that she was going to see Jasper and I didn't want to re-live Tom's awful accident.

I told my mother that I was going to be spending the next few weekends in London helping Bea to find suitable accommodation for when she moved in the summer. I hoped she wouldn't find out about Caroline's family offering the house share in London. I told her that we'd managed to get cheap train tickets, which we had, and she seemed satisfied with that.

The following weekend we set off to London, but this time Jasper met us at Euston station.

We jumped on a bus outside Euston to his apartment which, although in Bloomsbury, was at the Holborn end of town, just a bit too far for us to walk.

Their home was a typical lad pad. It was on the third floor of a large building with stair and lift access. When we arrived the lift wasn't working so we had to climb about one hundred steps to get to the apartment. Bless him, Jasper dragged our bags behind him and lugged them up the stairs.

I noticed that the living room had a triple bay sash window and an ornate fireplace, nothing like my home. This apartment was enormous. The kitchen was amazing, with black units and black quartz worktops. See what I mean about it being a lad pad? The kitchen was large enough to eat in which I thought was unheard of in London. There were three bedrooms, so that overcame any embarrassment we may have had about the sleeping arrangements as we all had our own bedroom. I got Tom's room."

Vivie thought for a moment and then continued. "Bea and Jasper agreed that I should see Tom on my own so I decided to walk the twenty minute journey to the hospital. I had no idea what I would say to Tom or how he would be with me now that the medication had worn off. I went into the hospital with great trepidation.

When I saw Tom I became hot and uncomfortable not knowing what to say. He spotted me peering hesitantly around the door and smiled. The bruising on his face had abated a little and he looked somewhat smaller than I remembered. I felt like an idiot and I must have acted like one because the first thing I said was *don't come running to me with your problems*, as he lay there strapped up with two broken legs."

Ben and Bella laughed. "I'm glad you two laughed because Tom did too. It broke the ice between the two of us. I spent time telling him about my week, asking him what treatment he'd been given and I read aloud news articles. He said the main problem with being in hospital was boredom. I decided that when I returned to Manchester I'd write him a letter or send him a card each day so that he had something to look forward to. No text, Instagram or Twitter in those days." "I've still got those letters and cards in an old tin" admitted Tom and Vivie beamed. "It's not a tin from Fortnum and Mason is it?" she asked and Tom winked.

Vivie stopped for a moment, took a sip of water and sat back in the chair to relieve the physical pain she was experiencing in her back. Tom took up the story. "I was worried that I might lose my job as I knew that I'd be off work for at least three months if not longer.

Jasper had spoken to my boss and explained what'd happened to me. My boss was amazing. He arranged for me to be paid full salary and my colleagues from work visited me at least twice a week. It was a great relief to know that I was supported during what was a very difficult time."

Vivie joined in. "During that weekend Bea and Jasper would pop in at different times, but I stayed with Tom all day each day. We began to get on well and I liked his sense of humour. I was still in a state of flux about what to do next as a job and had plenty of time to think during my visit to London. I talked things over with Tom. He suggested that I looked at studying to become a secondary school teacher and at first I thought he was insane.

On the way home to Manchester I was able to discuss this as a possibility with Bea. She suggested that I move to London in September, live with her and Caroline, and study there. A terrible sense of anxiety came over me and I wondered where my reckless-self had gone. In contrast, Bea's face was red with excitement and I had to admit that the possibility of a change and living in a different vibrant city with my friends, particularly in close proximity to Tom, did invigorate me.

Over the following months when I saw Tom there were times when he experienced a very low mood, when he despaired of ever being able to walk again. I was terrified. Fear would sicken my stomach and my heart wrung for him. Occasionally when we were together we contemplated that his future life might be very different to his previous existence.

We faced the reality that he may be consigned to be wheelchair bound for his remaining days. Tom may tell a different tale, but I think that our choice of deciding not to look too far ahead was the correct one. It helped Tom to avoid plunging into a deep depression. Low, black moods I could help Tom deal with, but real depression would've been a much more difficult problem to tackle. The reports from the doctors were positive as the bones began to heal, but they were unsure Tom would ever be able to walk unaided.

The idea of teaching was beginning to filter into my mind, becoming more acceptable as each week passed. From his hospital bed Tom'd made a few enquiries about teacher training. The nurses were kind and advised us to visit some of the fabulous libraries around University College Hospital.

When Tom felt well enough, during my weekend visits, I would wheel Tom to the university library on Gower Street to research what I needed to do to apply to become a teacher.

There was no Internet then, so it was very difficult to find out a wide range of information. There were some colleges which offered bursaries for people to join the teaching profession. Although it wasn't much money, it would help me to pay the bills. Tom enjoyed being out and about even if it was in a wheelchair, and having something to think about. He's great at researching and noticing the minutiae which most people ignore. Together we found a course which I could attend in London and we both mulled over the implications of this for a few weeks.

By this time Jasper and Bea were either seeing each other in Manchester or in London at the weekend, but they still didn't want Phillip or Caroline to know they were a couple. Neither of us spoke about boyfriends to anyone else. When I travelled to London to see Tom, I was always able to stay at Tom and Jasper's apartment. Jasper was incredibly kind and generous.

Eventually I garnered the courage to apply to become a teacher. Tom and I waited eagerly to find out whether I'd been successful. I was invited to an interview where I was asked to give a ten minute presentation on a topic of my choice. I decided to speak about the tobacco industry as this topic, even then, always provoked a reaction from people. I've never smoked, but it was an accepted and huge part of society back then. My application for teacher training was successful. In retrospect, going in to teaching was not the best decision I've ever made" said a wretched Vivie.

"Surely it's a good job" queried Bella. "Depends what you mean by a good job" replied Vivie. "It's probably a recession-proof job with good holidays but there are lots of negatives about it too. My first teaching practice was in a school deemed to be 'difficult'. To be candid, most of the children weren't interested in learning. Also, the staff appeared to be very demotivated because of implementing one initiative after another.

On my first day of teaching practice I noticed that a piece of broken glass was sticking out of a fire alarm. As the fire alarm box was at face height I was concerned that someone might catch their face on the glass. I didn't realise that when I took the piece of broken glass out that it would set off the fire alarm and resulted in the whole building being evacuated. I didn't know what to do so I stood with the piece of broken glass in my hand next to the fire alarm whilst everyone else left the building.

Suddenly this massive hulk of a school caretaker approached me and bellowed down at me 'who broke that glass?' In a very meek voice I confessed that it was me as I hadn't realised that it would set off the fire alarm. When he heard this, the caretaker bent down to my tiny frame and barked 'this is your first day at this school and it's probably going to be your last'. I was terrified and humiliated.

That was my introduction to teaching. I should've realised that it wasn't just children who bullied each other, it was adults too."

Bella, with her effervescence, lifted the mood in the room. "Did you hear about the student who studied in an aeroplane because she wanted higher education?" Her mother and Ben laughed.

With great enthusiasm she raised herself from the wooden chair and said "I'm going to make a milk shake" she paused then said "by scaring it. Does anyone else want one?"

The heavy atmosphere which suspended the air in the café had been shattered. Ben too stood up and walked into the kitchen behind Bella. Bea bellowed "you two know where everything is don't you?" "No, but we'll rummage around thank you" Bella and Ben shouted in return.

Tucked away in the kitchen, out of sight of the others, against a background of gentle laughter and affable conversation, Ben put his arms around Bella as they kissed.

After what seemed like an inordinately long time, ten glasses containing variations of milkshake flavours, were delivered to the table by Bella and Ben. Each person grabbed the flavour of their choice as the two youngest members of the group took their respective place at the table.

There was a warmth in the air which ignored the glorious storm outside. It was noticeable to the group that Vivie's pale pallor had brightened which indicated that her pain had abated. She decided to take up her tale once more.

"After about four months of being in hospital, Tom's two casts were removed. He worked with a physiotherapist to learn how to walk with crutches. Walking up and down stairs was a challenge and getting onto and off a bus was a veritable nightmare.

It took weeks before Tom was able to walk properly with crutches and he had to do exercises every day which appeared to be very painful. He needed to strengthen the muscles in his legs as they'd become terribly skinny, and was very sensible about the amount of weight he bore. He needed ultrasound stimulation to help to improve his muscles and massages on his scars.

After what seemed like a lifetime, Tom was allowed to move back into his apartment. It was great in one way as the living accommodation was on one level, but proved to be a pain when the lift wasn't working. Over time, Tom did learn to walk, but it soon became evident that his range of motion would be limited permanently.

The five months I'd spent visiting him in the hospital meant that we'd forged a great friendship which developed into something more. Once I'd been offered a place on the teacher training course I chatted to my mother about it. I asked if she would mind if I moved to London. I explained that Caroline and Bea would be living there, in Caroline's grandparents' old house and that I could live with them for very little rent thanks to her parents' generosity.

With effort my mother calmed herself and, without pleasure, replied that it was my life. I took that to mean, yes and, in great raptures, moved to share the house with Caroline and Bea. The story of how I ended up in London."

Outside the restless wind howled in misery as though despising its isolation. Had they pulled back the blinds, the group would have spotted scurrying clouds trying to avoid the wind's spite.

Tenaciously, the wind continued to wail and its grief could be heard throughout Manchester. Happy to be inside the Hub, part of this caring group, sheltered from the confusion of the storm, Bella said cheerily "What's the story of how you married Tom? How did that come about Vivie?"

"Hmm. Even when we moved to London we didn't tell Caroline and Elle that I'd been seeing Tom and that Bea had been dating Jasper. Somehow, as time went by, it became more and more embarrassing to own up. The three of us moved to London in August and started our new lives. In September Caroline went to work at the stock-broking company, I started teacher training and Bea took up her contract at Verbier.

One evening Bea and I arranged to meet Jasper and Tom in a bar after work. We persuaded Caroline that she'd enjoy being with us and Jasper convinced Phillip to join him. You might say that we engineered for Caroline and Phillip to get together." "Oh" cried Caroline "I never knew that. So you tricked me?"

Dampened by Caroline's outburst, Vivie looked pale and nervous. Thankfully Bea, ebullient as ever, interceded. "It was for your own good Caroline. You'd spent years at the convent studying hard, and years of your youth slaving over your studies at university so we wanted you to have some fun. We knew, from what Jasper had said about his brother, that you two had loads in common. We contrived your coming together which led to your happiness. What's wrong with that?"

"I don't believe in messing with fate" said Caroline simply. "We didn't mess with fate, you idiot. Don't be daft. Surely it was fate that brought us all together in the first place" exclaimed a surprised Bea.

"That's the most nonsense I've heard today, talking about fate interrupted Frank "and I've listened to some bloody things today" he said solemnly. There was a momentary silence.

Vivie was crest-fallen. Elle was dumb-founded. Caroline's black eyes flashed angrily. The wind and rain pounded on the café door and window in spitefulness. Bea said "Caroline, I know that you might be angry with us right now, but marrying Phillip was the best thing that ever happened to you wasn't it?" Bea beseeched the group. "No-one can argue with that can they? What we did may be misinterpreted. We wanted the best for you Caroline, and we all thought that Phillip was it. In fact, he definitely was the best thing ever."

Caroline was silent for many minutes. Bella fidgeted in her seat as she looked intently at her mother. Then Caroline answered calmly. "You're right Bea. Phillip and Bella have given me the best time ever, and so have all of you. I've been luckier than most people but I need a strong drink."

She was shaking. Frank and Bea jumped up. "Alcohol, a soft or hot drink anyone?" asked Frank. Various drink orders were placed. Ben and Bella offered to help Frank and Bea as they followed the couple into the kitchen. The quartet busied themselves with an unfathomable air of tense emotion clamouring around them.

Drinks were made, carried into the Hub and dispensed with aplomb. Bea had seen Vivie taking more medication. She was worried about her friend who seemed in great discomfort.

Frank too had noticed that Vivie, although enjoying the camaraderie, was physically uncomfortable. When Vivie was distracted by Bea, he found a moment to speak to his friend Tom who, it turned out, was also very concerned about Vivie's health. "There's nothing we can do at the moment though Frank, so let's enjoy today and being together in this group" whispered Tom.

"Vivie" said Frank gently "tell us about how you and Tom ended up getting married?" "I'd love to take that trip down memory lane Frank" answered Vivie, her voice quavering. Tom gently rubbed her arm. "The teacher training in inner city London was like a baptism of fire. Some nights I came home and cried because of the behaviour and attitude of some of the students. Had it not been for Tom encouraging and believing in me, I would've given up.

Slowly though I found how to be me, as a teacher. I could never be a teacher who shouted or threatened. I was unobtrusive, and I found that this quiet, steely determination mixed with kindness and the ability to listen to others worked well for me and my students.

People often seem surprised when I tell them I'm a teacher. Goodness knows why. I think they expect a harridan, but I wanted to be the kind of teacher I never had throughout my school days, the type of teachers I had heard others speak of fondly.

Sadly in my year of teacher training, my mother died suddenly. She had pneumonia. I received a telephone call in London, but by the time I'd got to the hospital in Manchester, she was gone.

Her passing affected me deeply. It made me realise that choosing a partner could be a good or bad decision for life. It made me unhappy that my mother had endured such sadness in her life, particularly through her marriage and subsequent divorce.

I saw the joy that Robert and Matilde shared as partners and the happy homes that my friends belonged to and wished so much that my mother had met someone who could've made her sparkle. Instead, any cherished hopes and dreams she had, lay lifeless. I was engulfed by gloom, overcome by an over-whelming desire to cry and never stop.

Somewhere in my distant memory I can remember the gentle tones of Tom, who was incredibly supportive as he quietly and efficiently organised my mother's funeral. I remember that we had a harpist and a heart-rending choir. We held the funeral reception at a beautiful country hotel not far from my family home so my mother had a send-off of which she would have approved.

As the only child I inherited the house but sold it a few months later. It held no happy memories for me. I returned to London and carried on with my training. Strangely, this experience made me acutely aware that some of the young people I taught had difficulties which made them desperately unhappy every day and some carried this burden into school. Sometimes, in the mad rush to help students acquire examination grades, we may forget that they need emotional support. That their well-being is of utmost importance.

I worked incredibly hard to be a good student-teacher which was difficult as I had no personal experience to draw upon as I'd never been taught by an inspirational teacher.

I passed my Post Graduate teaching examination but chose not to go to the graduation ceremony. It would've pressed home to me that my mother had gone and couldn't share in my success.

I chose not to apply for a permanent teaching job in that first year, instead I joined a supply agency with the aim of gaining experience of a range of different schools in London. This choice turned out to be fortuitous for me.

On the evening before Caroline's wedding Tom suggested that the two of us had a picnic in Green Park. We met after work outside Fortnum and Mason, went inside and bought a small bottle of champagne, some pies and a large tin of violet and rose cream chocolates. With our bag of goodies we made our way down Piccadilly, past the Ritz Hotel and into Green Park.

We sat on a bench, unpacked our picnic, opened the champagne and Tom poured it into two plastic cups we'd brought with us. As we munched our way through the pies, followed by lots of chocolate Tom asked me if he thought we should get married. He explained that he hadn't presumed to buy an engagement ring in case we didn't share the same feelings. I looked at his ardent face. This decent, hard-working, determined, kind and funny man that I'd grown to love, had asked me to be his wife.

I almost exploded with joy. I nodded imperceptibly and cried a little. I told him that I didn't want an engagement ring. A wedding ring would be enough for me. I wanted to know what had prompted him to ask me. It turned out that Tom was transferring to New York for two years at Christmas and wanted me to be with him. In the space of a few months, my life had turned on a sixpence.

I never did get an engagement ring. Instead, I chose a wedding ring with two diamonds in it. We didn't want too much of a fuss either, particularly as I was an orphan to all intents and purposes.

Tom and I planned to get married in London, the place which I'd adopted as my home. That exciting, exotic, cosmopolitan mix of cultures where it truly felt that I was a global citizen.

We married in October, a month after Caroline. Those pale lemon, simple and elegant off the shoulder bridesmaid dresses, made of silk, with covered back buttons came in handy" joked Vivie. "What" exclaimed Bella "mum's bridesmaid dresses were worn again to your wedding?" "Ha" cried Vivie "that surprised you didn't it? Of course they were worn again, waste not want not!"

"I'm surprised" replied Bella. "What did you do about the third dress? Don't tell me. Matilde made another one." "Yes" laughed Matilde. "I did. I made one for Caroline and I made Vivie's wedding dress too" she said proudly. "You're simply an amazing woman Matilde" said Bella, impressed by Matilde's creativity. "We didn't tell anyone that we were going to get married until a few days after Caroline's wedding.

We chose to have the ceremony at a registry office on the Kings Road in Chelsea. The day of the wedding was great fun. The sun sparkled, the sky was blue and the air was warm. I couldn't have asked for better weather. My dress was a beautiful form-fitting gown in silk crepe and lace with cap sleeves and a lace neckline. I wore red shoes, and we all carried red flowers in deference to Manchester United.

My bouquet had classic roses and red peonies, the bridesmaids' flowers were roses, anemones, berries and loads of greenery. We had very few guests. Tom's parents came, Jasper and Bea, Matilde and Robert, Caroline and Phillip, Caroline's parents, Elle and her parents. That was it. Small and simple. Just fifteen of us. We had an absolute ball and I was thrilled that Robert gave me away.

After the wedding we walked up the Kings Road to a small restaurant where Tom had booked a table. We ate the most amazing food and spent the whole afternoon in animated conversation, a bit like today really.

For a laugh, instead of getting taxis, the whole wedding party caught the number 19 bus from Sloane Square. We left our group on the bus when we jumped off at Hyde Park Corner to stay at the Lanesborough Hotel. I think the doormen were flabbergasted to see a bride and groom get off a red bus and enter the hotel, as their guests usually arrive in a Rolls Royce! We did chuckle at that. The rest of our guests said they were heading back to Bloomsbury but instead they went out again and partied all night."

Vivie's pallor had brightened again as she reminisced. "Shortly after we arrived at the hotel we received a telephone message. It was from you girls" she pointed in the direction of Caroline, Bea and Elle, "asking if we wanted to join everybody, which we did about an hour after we'd left you. Tom and I only stayed for a couple of hours though and left when Robert went back to the house to get his guitar. No offence Robert, but we knew that it would turn out to be an all-night event for you all" confessed Vivie. Tom laughed.

Caroline took up the narrative. "The following afternoon, when we finally woke up, there were bottles all over the downstairs rooms of my grandparents' house. It took ages for the whole gang to clear up. We all ended up going out for our evening meal that day as we had nothing left in the cupboards or fridge.

Your wedding was a weekend party for all of us. What a great time we all had" she laughed. Her unhappiness had lifted. "The excitement didn't end there did it?" she said mischievously. "Are you talking about when my twin sister and I were born?" asked Ben optimistically. "No. Don't be silly" said Caroline simply. "Although, without doubt that was an electrifyingly terrifying time."

"How is Jo?" enquired Bella, referring to Ben's twin. "I've been so busy with my own wedding that I've lost touch with what's been going on lately." Silence permeated the air. Vivie's pallor was grey, Tom looked uncomfortable and Ben took a deep breath.

# Chapter 11 - An explanation

"We were going to tell you after your wedding Bella" said Ben, his face wretched. "Tell me what?" asked Bella as an ebony knot grew in her stomach. At the side of her, Ben balked. "We were going to tell you about Jo." Bella stared at Vivie whose pale face was shrouded in fear. Her eyes turned to Tom whose head dropped with the burden of despondency. Finally she looked at Ben. His handsome face and gentle eyes returned her gaze.

"What about Jo?" cried Bella. She'd been so busy with her wedding plans of late that she'd definitely neglected her long-standing friendship with Ben's twin sister Jo. She'd intended to contact her to organise the bridesmaid dress but had wanted to wait until Caroline had helped her narrow down the choice of wedding gowns. 'Once I've decided upon my wedding gown, everything else will fall into place' Bella had thought.

Being reminded of her wedding cultivated the knot. As she sat with her hands by her side gripping the chair, Ben stealthily slid his hand over hers and surreptitiously squeezed her fingers. The contact felt comforting to them both.

"I had a telephone call at work a few weeks ago from Jo's boyfriend, Sergio." Bella turned to look at Ben. She could see despair in his eyes. "And?" she prompted. Ben looked around the room, all eyes were upon him. "There's something we need to share with you all" said Ben hesitantly. Bella felt the spasmodic movement of Ben's hand and watched as he looked at his parents. They nodded almost imperceptibly, both remained mute.

"Jo found a lump in her breast. She thought it was a swollen gland and that it'd go away. She looked up the symptoms for breast cancer which were nothing like her symptoms so she ignored the lump. Whenever she went shopping into town she would pass the pop-up breast clinic then, after seven months of indecision, she gave way to a tiny nagging doubt that she had and last week made an appointment for a breast examination.

The doctor on duty examined her, said she thought it unlikely, in her early twenties for it to be anything other than a benign lump so Jo gave it no further thought when she was referred to the local hospital's breast clinic. The doctor at the breast clinic reassured Jo that the lump was likely to be benign but, to be cautious, carried out several tests including an ultrasound scan and a biopsy just as a double-check. Jo was told that it would take a week for the results to be ready and gave it no further thought. She said that she wasn't really worried as she thought herself too young to have breast cancer.

Two days after the ultrasound scan and the biopsy Jo received a 'phone call at work from a nurse at the hospital. She was asked to go to the hospital the following day to collect her results. Even though she'd heard from the hospital earlier than the time they specified, she wasn't too worried.

She and Sergio went to the hospital intending to go to work once they'd heard the results but what they were told, changed everything. Jo said that she remembered hearing the words breast cancer and her boyfriend grabbing hold of her hand very tightly. She said that she felt everything seemed to happen in slow motion. She could tell by her Sergio's face that he was extremely upset but Jo said she felt very numb, as though this wasn't really happening to her.

Jo told me that her only thought was about losing her lovely long hair. During the appointment the doctor talked to her, telling her about the treatment she would face. She felt completely lost amongst the news and the information about what was ahead of her. She thought they were talking about another girl, not her. The doctor told Jo that she wouldn't be able to leave the hospital that morning as she needed to have further tests. Thankfully Sergio stayed with her.

When he rang me I knew something was wrong otherwise Jo would've spoken to me. When he told me that Jo had breast cancer, I rang mum and dad who were both working. They immediately left work, came for me and the three of us headed to the hospital. My heart was pounding and I felt light headed. Goodness knows what my parents were feeling." At this point Bella gave Ben's hand a tight squeeze. "That day, within the space of a few hours, Jo discovered that she had cancer and she'd have to stop her beloved teaching job immediately. We are all optimistic that it's only for a short time."

"Oh Vivie and Tom, how on earth have you coped with this news?" asked a distraught Elle. "We're trying to be very positive" replied Tom stoically "because we can't afford to be any other way." Ben inhaled then exhaled slowly. Bella could feel the movement of his arm close to hers. She sensed his anxiety and longed to hug him. Instead, she willed him to speak.

"Jo's chosen to have treatment at her local hospital rather than the Teenage Cancer Trust unit because she wanted to go to an adult unit and be close enough to go home whenever she could. I think she was thankful to be put in touch with this charity, even though she didn't use them, because they were able to give her other advice.

They put her in touch with a Youth Support Co-ordinator who's given her enormous encouragement and helped her to get involved in activities such as Chomp and Chat and Feel Good, Look Good.  This meant that she's been able to meet other young people with cancer and not feel so isolated.

As her brother I feel helpless knowing that she's going to have to fight every inch of the way and there's nothing I can do.  I wish that I could take her place but was delighted Jo accepted my offer to pay for her long hair to be cut and styled to shoulder-length.  The hair she had cut was sent off to be used as wigs for young children.

It's overwhelming standing on the side-lines and not being able to take away any of Jo's discomfort so I was glad to be of practical help."  It was obvious to the group that Ben wished to help and protect his beloved sister.

"She'll have to complete six cycles of chemotherapy and has already begun to lose her hair.  Can you believe that her Sergio shaved off his hair too, as a gesture of solidarity?  We've visited her a couple of times.  The side effects of the treatment appear to be endless; nausea, insomnia, tiredness and struggling to stand up for any length of time because her whole body aches.

Our vivacious Jo is exhausted doing anything.  We do talk about her being diagnosed with breast cancer at such a young age.  Jo said that before she was diagnosed, she was quite naïve about the long-term side effects of the treatment.

We're all just focused on the here and now, dealing with the daily problems but for Jo, at her age, the long-term effects are difficult to comprehend and deal with."

Ben's voice strained. Vivie looked at him with pride, his father moved slightly in his chair. "One of Jo's main concerns about the cancer treatment has been the effect the chemotherapy will have on her fertility. She wasn't even aware initially that this could be an issue.

Cancer is not something we young people give much thought to, I always thought it was older people who suffered with it, not people my own age. Jo was told that chemotherapy could leave her with a 20-30% chance of not being able to have children. We all know that having a family was something she'd always dreamed of, and unless you're told otherwise, you always think that having children will happen when the time is right.

She's been having Zoladex injections to put her ovaries into hibernation and induce a temporary menopause with the hope that this will lessen the chance of infertility to 10-15%. Although this is a massive worry, for now she's trying not to think about it and is focusing on becoming happy and healthy again.

With all the side effects and things on her mind, our independent Jo has accepted that she needs help. We've told her that it's fine to have bad days. She still faces radiotherapy and an operation but is remaining positive and focused on returning to work.

The Head Teacher at her school has been amazing. Jo didn't realise that she'd have to worry about how long this treatment would last. No-one told her that the school would need to record her sickness absence, which includes submitting a sick note from the doctor. She didn't even know what a sick note was!

After 100 working days her salary will reduce to half pay. She was worried about how to pay the bills and anxious not to put too much financial strain on Sergio as they've just moved into their own apartment. We did some research, have told her that we're happy to help her financially and that she'll be eligible for Employment Support Allowance.

Thankfully she's in a union and her Union Rep will be able to advise her too, as these people have experience of dealing with this sort of thing. Jo didn't know anything about long-term illness at work. She says she's lucky that she has a family that can help and knows that we're here for her every step of the way. Some people don't have that support do they?

It's ironic really because last year she sat in her classroom teaching teenagers about the signs and symptoms of cancer in young people without realising at the time that she'd soon develop cancer. During that lesson, she said it became very clear that every person in the classroom had been affected by the disease in some way. She said that her class were extremely mature and there were some sensible questions and responses.

You all know how dynamic and energetic Jo is. When she's well again, she says she's planning to go onto a course to be able to teach students in her school properly about cancer in young people. She's very keen to get across the message that it's important if someone is concerned about a change in their body, even at a young age, they should seek medical advice.

In hindsight, at the time she was diagnosed she said she did feel absolutely exhausted and couldn't put her finger on what was wrong.

She thought it was because she was over-worked. Jo now realises that it's important to listen to your body. She's amazing and says she's feeling very optimistic about her experience. Although it's been the hardest few weeks of her life, the amount of support she's had from her us, Sergio and colleagues has been fantastic.

She still has the same ambitions to buy her own house, travel and have a family. For now, she says she's concentrating on the little things, like spending time with the people she cares about. I don't agree with her that spending time with people you care about is a little thing" he said with a smile.

Bella was at a loss about what to say or do. She simply hung her head. An overpowering silence fell upon the group punctuated only by the sound of the raging wind and battering rain outside. Eventually Caroline said "we're all so sorry to hear that Jo has to fight this battle, but she will fight it. She has such a vivacious personality that I'm sure she will turn this into something positive. Is there any practical support that any of us can offer?"

Elle, who was more used to dealing with illness than the others said "you know that we all want to help, but don't want to say or do the wrong thing." "You are all so kind" said Vivie gently. "Just be around. It's going to be a long road back to good health, but we're trying to be upbeat and positive. Jo certainly is facing this stoically so we have to do the same."

Unable to cope with the news Bella excused herself from the table and retreated into the kitchen. Ben followed her.

As she wept silently at the news of her friend's difficult challenge, Ben held Bella tightly. Presently Bea and Frank joined the couple in the kitchen. "Come on" said Bea kindly. "You two are excellent at helping out in the kitchen. Let's get to work and prepare some sustenance for our guests."

Ben kissed the top of Bella's head, hugged her and whispered something inarticulate. This tiny gesture of comfort left her motionless momentarily. She looked attentively into Ben's watery eyes and smiled feebly. Somehow, he made her feel secure and protected despite the stark news on this strange day. Bella trembled, reached up and kissed Ben's cheek.

She smiled and said "C'mon, let's help out Frank and Bea." Under their keen direction, Bella and Ben helped Frank and Bea prepare yet more food for their guests.

After a long while of toing and froing Ben said "I wonder what your mother meant when she said that the excitement didn't end with Vivie's wedding?" "I've absolutely no idea. Today's been full of surprises. Not all of them welcome, but I'll ask her" declared Bella "when we've served this food."

# Chapter 12 - Was there a third wedding?

The storm raged around the café, and the icy, knobbly fingers of cold were angrily prodding the air in the Hub. The five blankets which covered the group provided some protection from the chill.

Bustling out of the kitchen Frank placed a huge pan of mushy green peas on the table in front of his guests. He was joined boisterously by Bea who was carrying hot, home-made cheese and onion pasties whilst Bella and Ben were both armed with hot potato pasties. Those great Manchester delicacies.

Hands clambered at the pasties as Frank served the accompanying mushy green peas on to individual plates. "Manchester caviar" Frank said. The smell of freshly baked, hot pastry permeated the café. "It's a long time since I've had pasties" stated Elle "and they're as tasty as I remember them to be. It's true. Good fortune never comes alone does it?" she reflected. "Tuck in" ordered Bea.

"Are we ever going to hear the tale of Jasper?" asked Frank somewhat testily. No-one's eyes met his. Only Elle was brave enough to look up and peruse the room. There was silence.

Elle decided to quell Frank's impatience by directing her attention to Ben and Bella. "You asked about the excitement which followed Tom and Vivie's wedding" she said lightly. "I'd be happy to tell the tale if there are no objections?" Her eyes scanned Bea's face. Hush flourished. Elle took this as her cue to speak.

"Tom asked Jasper if he would video the wedding as a memento and gift for Vivie.  As Jasper loved technology he bought a new portable video camera just for that purpose.  Nowadays you can video on your mobile 'phone but in those days we had to use a purpose built, hand-held video recorder.  Jasper was thrilled to be asked.

In the few weeks leading up to Vivie and Tom's wedding, Jasper asked individual members of the group if he could rehearse using the video recorder by filming each of us separately.  As part of his preparation he'd asked each person to hold up one letter, which was typed on A4 paper, each letter was printed in a huge font.  It seemed odd, but none of us questioned what he was doing.  He even got Matilde and Robert to hold up individual letters too when they turned up for the wedding.

Jasper commandeered Robert and got him to play a solo on the guitar whilst he captured the performance on video.  We were all amused that he was taking things so seriously.  His attention to detail was obsessive.  Mind you, it was understandable as Jasper and Tom had been friends since they were five years old.  Two days before the big day, the two men invited us all to their apartment for a meal on the basis that it would be chaotic at the house where Vivie, Caroline and Bea lived.  Jasper said that he wanted us all to watch the pre-wedding film so that we could give him filming tips before the big day.

When we arrived for the *big viewing*, it was obvious that Jasper had gone to a lot of trouble for what he dubbed the 'pre-wedding event'.  He'd laid on champagne, and prepared Severn and Wye Smoked Salmon, Chestnut and Wild Mushroom Tortelli, Spinach and Sweet Potato.

For dessert we had Eton Mess which was delicious, and he served coffee with petit fours. A really unusual treat, so much that we were all bamboozled by his behaviour.

His plan for the evening was that we'd eat, watch the video, then go out to celebrate the forthcoming wedding of Tom and Vivie. All of this he'd done with the support of Tom but not Vivie as she knew nothing of the detail.

We all settled down around the television and Tom gave Vivie a box with a huge red question mark stencilled on top. When she opened the box, inside was a video. By this time, we were all intrigued. Vivie placed the video into a machine which was attached to the television and the film began to play. You were really intrigued Vivie weren't you?" asked Elle.

"I was really surprised and wondered what was on the video" agreed Vivie. "I was a bit apprehensive in case it was some kind of joke that the two of them had conjured up between themselves. I was totally unprepared for what happened next though" she said.

"Now I'm riveted" exclaimed Ben. "Me too" stated Bella. "What was on it?" she demanded as she looked at Tom and Vivie who both shrugged as they glanced first at Elle, then at Bea. Frank looked morose. His black eyes watched Bea keenly but she was calm and resolute.

"Go on, tell them Elle. You tell them what was on the video" said Bea. Elle did as requested. "The video began with a speech by Tom which explained to Vivie that Jasper was going to video their wedding.

The next scene showed Tom passing over the microphone to Jasper who explained that the video was a rehearsal in preparation for Vivie's wedding day. The following scenes were a little bit surreal as we didn't understand the significance of the places that were featured.

It showed the Balmoral Hotel in Edinburgh, then the scene shifted slowly to Manchester's St. Ann's Square. We thought that it was because Vivie is a Manchester girl. Then it showed inside the Verbier salon in Manchester, panned along King Street, before the scene moved to the majestic Town Hall, then showed Central Manchester Library as a backdrop. Most of us were dumbstruck as we didn't know what to make of it.

We knew that Bea had worked at the Verbier salon in Manchester but didn't know why the other places were included. In the background accompanying the video was the sound of Robert's guitar playing the Oasis tune, 'Wonderwall'.

I distinctly remember an audible gasp from Bea and then, one by one we saw ourselves appearing on the television screen holding up a different letter. We remembered that Jasper had asked each of us to hold up an A4 typed single letter when he was preparing the video but none of us had taken much notice of the letters. We never asked Jasper what was the purpose of it all. Anyway, I'll tell you what each letter was, and then you can tell me what you think.

willyoumarrymebea?'

For a few moments, Ben and Bella were dumbstruck, then realisation prompted Bella to speak.

"What? Tom was asking Bea to marry him through a video intended for Vivie? I'm bemused." "You're right. You are bemused" answered Elle. "Think about it. Jasper made the video for Bea. It was Jasper who asked Bea to marry him and none of us realised what he was doing until the night he showed us all the video. At the closing scene of the video Jasper bent down on one knee, held an engagement ring up to the screen. It was his way of asking Bea to marry him."

"Oh, even I've fallen in love with Jasper now" claimed Bella "that's so romantic." "What did you do Bea?" probed Ben. "I did the dignified thing" replied Bea quietly, "I just cried." "After all these years, now I understand the significance of the different buildings in Manchester and why they were in the video" stated Caroline "it was thoughtful of Jasper."

"You must've said yes" stated Bella at the same time as Frank said "you deserve to be treated well Bea." He got up from his chair, bent over Bea and kissed her head gently. In a cordial voice, though his face was pale, he said "let's hear the next saga then." Bea suspected he might be more irritated than he showed.

Bea struggled to speak, so Elle intercepted. "Let me" she said, turning to Bea who nodded subtly. "When it finally dawned on us all what was happening, that Jasper was asking Bea to marry him we all shrieked and danced around the apartment.

Robert sat on the brown leather sofa, in the middle of the living room, got out his guitar, and played a few tunes whilst we all sang along. We finally persuaded Matilde to sing.

I don't know why she didn't turn professional because she has a beautiful voice.  She gave us a rendition of *Que Sera, Sera* by Doris Day and another couple of songs, but I can't remember the names of them."

Elle turned to Matilde who helped by saying *Bewitched, Bothered and Bewildered* and *When I Fall in Love*'. "It was a brilliant evening.  Matilde, please will you sing *The Way We Were*?" pleaded Elle.  All eyes turned to Matilde. "My voice isn't what it used to be" replied Matilde "it's not strong anymore."

"That doesn't matter mum" cajoled Bea "we can all join in and help you along.  It'll be like old times.  Please." Robert turned to Matilde and kissed her "go on, be brave." Matilde stood up.  She had a sparkle in her eyes and her face shone with delight.  "Right, here goes" she said as if on a mission to Mars, "but I'd like you all to dance please. I'll close my eyes and imagine the old days when my bones weren't so achy and my memory was razor-sharp. Days when I put the milk in the fridge instead of the oven. Days when I didn't find slices of buttered bread in our cutlery drawer!"

Frank, Tom and Ben moved the tables and chairs to the side of the café in preparation for a rendition of *The Way We Were* courtesy of Matilde.  Dance partners were sought. Frank and Bea, Robert and Elle, Vivie and Tom, Ben asked Bella and Caroline to join him in a dance as the soft sound of a love song resonated around the café.  Frank held Bea tighter than he would normally.  She looked into his coal coloured eyes.  It was always difficult to read his emotion. He looked down at her, smiled and kissed her lips.  She held him tightly.

When the song ended, everyone clapped and shouted for another. Matilde was flushed with pride. She carried on and sang *Que Sera, Sera* whilst the others danced. No-one sat down, as they wanted more. Matilde, who was tired, stepped down and joined Robert and Elle. Bella stood up, called Elle to join her and replaced Matilde as the singer.

The haunting tune of *My Tears Dry On Their Own* by Amy Winehouse belted out of Bella's tiny frame as she emulated the original singer's smoky delivery and Elle joined in on the chorus.

The group danced. When the song had ended, Elle asked Bella to sing *Don't Be So Hard On Yourself* by Jess Glynne which lightened the mood considerably. Robert insisted on giving a rendition of Frank Sinatra's *I've Got You Under My Skin,* followed by *Fly Me To The Moon* and he finished with *Strangers In The Night.* As Robert sang the last song, Ben moved across the floor to dance with Bella.

He found that the smell of her perfume and the feel of her soft hair upon his cheek pierced the barrier he had been hiding behind for the past year. For the first time in a long time, he was irresolute. He didn't know how to react. It took a moment for Ben to compose himself. He looked tenderly at Bella and smiled.

"I'm so sorry that things have turned out badly for you Bella." "Shush" she implored and closed her eyes "right now, I'm happy." "The sun always comes up. Even following a bleak day" he whispered. Almost imperceptibly Bella kissed Ben's cheek. They continued to dance even though Robert had long since stopped singing.

After a while, Frank approached the couple and prodded Ben. "Please will you help me to move back the tables?" he asked gently. Bella helped too and when they were ready, the two young ones sat down beside each other.

Caroline involuntarily viewed Ben, as the torrential wind and rain hammered at the Hub window and door. She watched as he wrapped a blanket first around Bella, ensuring that she was comfortable, before he covered his own legs.

On the café tables, the candles flickered as the wind battered, finding its way into nooks and crannies in the Hub.

Caroline caught a glimpse of Ben's eyes, her face blanched as if she'd seen a ghost. Hope and sorrow flittered across her expression. She took a moment to compose herself, turned to Vivie and said "that was a brilliant reminder of a fabulous evening in London." Vivie patted her hand.

Inside the Hub became silent as a graveyard, except for the rattling door, the wailing wind and the sobbing tear-drops of rain pattering against the window. Ben directed his attention to Bea and asked "are we ever going to hear your story?" From her expression, he knew something had happened and was intrigued to find out what it was.

All eyes turned to Bea. She looked around at eager faces. Shadowy shapes fell upon individuals as the warm candlelit glow danced at the table. Bea blinked away dark shadows and tried to recollect a bright time which once existed all those years ago when she moved to London. Momentarily she was grave.

If an onlooker had scrutinised Bea's face they might have noticed a slight shake of her head and then observed her face light up the room as her disposition changed to its usual genial gaze. She gulped and attempted to embody her memories.

"I was young and unsure what to do when Jasper proposed. We were surrounded by our friends, had been to Caroline's wedding and were planning Vivie's wedding.

We were all swept away by romantic notions and the excitement of something new" she said by way of explanation. "I was shocked that Jasper had proposed to me. I hadn't expected that. I agreed to marry him and everyone went wild. It just seemed the right thing for me to do at that time.

He had an engagement ring made for me by Hancocks, one of the long established jewellers in Manchester. The ring had a large diamond in the centre with a smaller diamond at each side, 'to represent the two children we will have' Jasper said."

Bea looked down at the ring on her right hand which matched exactly her description. As she looked up, her face revealed a lurid shade. Frank poured her a glass of water and silently pushed it in front of her. Bea thanked Frank, took a sip and gently caressed his face. Frank welcomed this embrace.

The ice cold water provided relief to Bea's parched throat. "Robert and Matilde were elated weren't you? I knew that they'd been worried about me since Frank had left town and despaired that I would ever get over him. Mum offered to make my wedding dress.

Elle, Caroline and Vivie were excited and suggested they wear the same bridesmaid dresses that had been worn twice before.

Fleetingly I thought this must be a good omen, so agreed. As I'd always envisaged a winter wedding, the date was set for the Saturday immediately following Boxing Day.

The weather that December was generally unsettled, incredibly wet and extremely windy. I worried that my guests who were travelling from Manchester might be unable to make the journey to London. Today's weather is not unlike some of the weather we endured that year so is probably not as unusual in Britain as we tend to think.

Jasper and I were both eager to be married in London. We arranged to be married by our local parish priest at the church of Our Lady of the Assumption and St. Gregory, on Golden Square not far from where I lived in London.

We particularly liked the strong musical tradition it had then. Matilde and Robert were thrilled as it meant they could belt out the tunes in the church. It's still got a unique character and is in a strange position in London, surrounded by extremes of wealth and poverty. Remember when Vivie and I met Jasper and Tom by accident, or fate as Vivie would say, at Green Park?

The church is very near to that park so it was a particularly poignant place to choose. If you look at the church from the outside it's quite unremarkable, with its plain red brick façade. Inside is amazing with gentle light blue coloured walls, huge arched windows flooding it with light and golden mosaic paintings.

I still pop in whenever I go to London. It gives me a sense of peace probably a little bit how you felt Bella at St. Pat's cathedral in New York.

The weeks before our wedding seemed to rush by. We had to choose cars and decided upon a trio of cream coloured Rolls Royce limousines to take us to the church. Elle, Caroline, Vivie and I agreed that cobalt blue would be a vivid colour in winter so the flowers we chose were Aquileia Winky blue and white. We'd never even heard of them before.

Caroline made the wedding cake, iced it and created tiny blue and white flowers for each of the three tiers. She's always been very creative. We arranged for the reception to be at Dartmouth House which is a beautiful Georgian mansion, right in the heart of Mayfair. It had a really elegant enclosed, marble lined courtyard with a fountain as a centrepiece where guests could enjoy champagne and canapes.

The rooms we planned to use had beautiful painted ceilings, walnut panelling, crystal chandeliers and the place even had a sweeping French staircase. Gorgeous.

Jasper had asked Tom to be his best man and the two of them arranged to travel from their apartment and meet Jasper's brother Phillip at the church. It was organised that I'd be collected from the house on Gordon Square with my dad; the three bridesmaids would go first with my mum.

I suppose you'll want to have a description of my dress?" Bea asked looking straight at Bella who grinned and nodded. "It was a high-neck white silk sleeveless dress with a fitted top.

Across my waist was a silk ribbon made of white and cobalt blue, tied into a large bow at the front. The skirt was a ball-gown style made of white silk but with a piece of cobalt blue in the middle, at the back of the skirt. Mum and I went to Harrods to pinch ideas for the wedding dress before she made it for me.

Christmas was manic that year because we were organising the wedding too. The wedding day arrived really quickly. My mentor Gill from the Verbier salon in Manchester was invited to the wedding and she arrived that morning to create different hairstyles for everyone. I chose not to wear a veil. Instead Gill wove tiny, fake crystals into my hair the way she'd done when Jasper and I went on our first date in Manchester.

We were all so excited. The first two cars arrived at the house and whisked away mum, Caroline, Vivie and Elle taking them to the church in plenty of time. I sat quietly with dad and tried so hard not to cry when he told me how much he and mum loved me and how much joy I'd brought into their lives.

He talked about the wonderful friends I had and asked me if I felt that I was making the right decision." She turned to Robert and said "I can remember dad you asking me if I ever thought about Frank.

I told you that I did, but that I'd moved on and could marry Jasper knowing that he was a good man. That seemed to satisfy you." "Yes, it did love. I wanted to know that you were marrying Jasper for the right reasons, not because you felt swept away by the romance of it all" said Robert sagely.

"I clearly remember walking out of the house and looking up at the damp, grey sky. The sharp wind pulled at my skirt as if it were trying to pull me back into the house. Dad helped me into the limousine. The drive to the little church seemed to take ages, as if we were buying time, which seemed strange.

When we eventually arrived Phillip was waiting outside the church. He looked a little agitated but smiled broadly at me. Dad got out of the car, and I stayed inside whilst he spoke with Phillip. I never for one moment thought that there was anything wrong. As I watched Phillip speaking I could see the pallor of dad's face change. He went pale and walked slowly back to the car."

Frank poured Bea another glass of water, from which she took a refreshing sip. "To my amazement, dad got back into the car. He told the chauffeur to drive around for a little while.

Dad told me that Jasper and Tom had been inexplicably delayed. As the car prowled around Mayfair and Knightsbridge, I sat and stared out of the window. I think my eyes looked at, but didn't really see Green Park.

I knew in the distance stood the majestic building of Buckingham Palace and I wondered what kind of Christmas it'd been for the Royal family. The car powered into Knightsbridge and passed Harrods. I looked to the right at Wendy's café where we'd our afternoon meal on the day of Tom's accident.

I felt a claw digging at my stomach where terror lay menacingly. The car turned into Beauchamp Place and the purring engine stopped.

The driver turned to dad to ask him what to do. I sat in the car, dressed in my wedding garb, waiting to enjoy the best day of my life, still wondering what was happening.

When dad told me that Jasper was not at the church I needed fresh air and got out of the car. The pavement was damp so I lifted my skirt a little and wandered along slowly. Luckily the street was almost deserted.

I must've looked strange, walking up and down Beauchamp Place with my dad by my side, heading nowhere in particular. I wondered if I looked like the jilted bride I was." "No" exclaimed Bella. Ben gasped. "What? Jasper didn't turn up to the church?" he exclaimed. "The git." Bea looked at Ben and smiled.

"Things were so different in those days. We didn't have your wonderful communication methods. We didn't have mobile 'phones. It was really difficult to contact someone when they were away from the office or their home because we mostly relied on land lines for our telephone conversations. All anyone knew was that Jasper and Tom hadn't turned up at the church.

Phillip had told dad that the priest wouldn't be able to wait for longer than 45 minutes as he had another wedding that day. Dad persuaded me to get back into the car. He said that we could drive past the church and that Phillip would wait outside to let us know if Jasper had arrived. I felt humiliated but surprised myself as I didn't cry. The car purred its way through the London streets.

Phillip was outside the church looking morose. The chauffeur manoeuvred the car to a halt. Phillip looked directly at me and shook his head.

I wound down the window. Phillip opened the door and got into the car. He apologised to me that Jasper hadn't turned up. He said that the priest would wait for another 15 minutes in case Jasper arrived, but not a minute longer. Phillip then hailed a taxi and left us to go to the apartment to try to find his brother.

Ten minutes passed, then fifteen as dad and I sat outside the unremarkable church. Dad left me in the car, entered the church and spoke to the priest. The wedding had to be called off. Dad explained to the congregation that Jasper had been inexplicably delayed. He invited everyone to Dartmouth House to celebrate the non-marriage of his daughter.

He tried to make light of it whilst I sat in the car mortified as my guests trooped past me. I knew that their pitying eyes would be upon me. I sat immobile until dad returned to the car. We sat together and waited for Phillip to return. Every second seemed like a minute and every minute passed like an hour. My heart thudded until my ears felt as though they'd pop. My head throbbed.

Dad opened a champagne bottle which was in the car, poured a huge glass for each of us and we both gulped as if it were water. I heard the car door open and turned to see Jasper's face. His skin was ashen coloured, his brown curly hair was unkempt and his green eyes were wild. His muscular hand grabbed mine.

His words tumbled out. 'I'm so very sorry Bea. I left the apartment early. I was eager to get to the church. Tom and I decided to take the lift for the sake of speed. I know that the apartment is only three floors up but I thought that taking the lift would be quicker than walking down the stairs.

We got into the lift and as it approached floor two, the machine came to a shuddering halt. All the lights went out.

We were trapped in a tin box, in total darkness, between floors three and two. I pressed the emergency button at least one hundred times, but nothing happened. I tried to prise open the lift doors but they wouldn't budge. Tom and I banged on the tin walls but no-one heard us. I've been stuck in the bloody lift for two hours and have missed the most important event of my life. Oh Bea, I'm so sorry what must you think?" Jasper was distraught.

"I'd feared that Jasper would leave me the way Frank had done. Relief swamped me. The black desolation which had gripped me began to disappear." "Come on" I heard a distant voice shout. "The priest will marry you now if you hurry up. The other wedding's finished" shouted Phillip.

Tom ran to tell the guests and they traipsed away from the wedding reception. I'm sure most of them were drunk by that time. Within minutes the guests staggered into the church looking slightly unkempt. One by one they entered the church, dad followed them as he walked me down the aisle. Our wedding ceremony lasted a mere fifteen minutes. I clung to Jasper as we left the church as husband and wife. 'Til death do us part" said Bea as painful memories darkened her face.

Elle saw sadness in Bea's countenance. "I'm sure the caterers didn't know what to expect when we all trooped back into Dartmouth House" Elle interjected.

Jasper and Bea were taken hastily to the reception room, announced as Mr and Mrs Jasper Butler and the partying continued where it had left off but this time with a lighter air. It all seemed surreal somehow that one minute we were miserable because there wasn't a wedding, then the next minute, we were gleeful as there was one. How life can change in a moment!" Elle exclaimed.

A flash of lightning lit up the café despite the closed blinds. A melancholy thunderclap resonated around the building as the spiteful rain spat at the café windows and glass door in tormented vexation. Frank's demeanour was one of wretchedness as his frame shrivelled into his chair.

Tom lifted himself up with an awkwardness rendered by his misaligned leg. "I'd like to propose a toast" he whispered "to the good friends who are here, and those who are no longer with us but always remembered." Outside, the wind screamed its wordless song. Bea managed to hold back her own salty tears but noticed Caroline's involuntary sob. The sisters-in-law shared a brief hug.

Gently Bea passed Caroline a tissue which was received with a watery smile. She looked at Caroline and marvelled at how resolute and resilient she appeared to be when she had been through more than most people. Bea thought about her beloved niece Bella and wondered how she'd manage the difficulties she'd encountered today. "Yes" thought Bea "life changes quickly for bad and for good."

## Chapter 13 - New beginnings

Ben broke the silence. "What happened with Jasper and Phillip?" he asked. "I've never known." Caroline felt her heart sink and she looked at Bea thoughtfully. The atmosphere in the Hub became awkward which Bella didn't sense. "Yes mum" interjected Bella as she turned her head to look into her mother's deep brown eyes, "what did happen?"

Caroline had known for a long time that at some point she would need to have a conversation with Bella about Phillip. There had been plenty of opportunity for thinking things through, and practising what to say thought Caroline, but now the time was upon her she felt nervous, she could feel her heart pounding. Caroline glanced around the room. Knowing that she was surrounded by people who cared about her and Bella, seemed to offer the support she needed.

"When Phillip and I married we moved into a house in John Street, Bloomsbury" began Caroline and her beautiful countenance lit up at the memory. "Oh describe it mum so that I can try and remember it" implored Bella. Her mother looked at her. "I loved that house. It was gorgeous.

We spent a long time making it into our home. It was a five bedroomed town house made of red brick, with a white colonnade around an imposing shiny, black front door. An entrance which promised a feast of excitement and mystery within. There were five floors if you count the basement and it was a devil of a place to keep warm.

We decided to dedicate a year at a time to redecorating each floor. This was going to be our forever home, full of laughter and a safe haven from the rest of the world. We knew we were taking on a huge project. Phillip and I made a conscious effort to use local workmen and bought everything from independent traders. Remember we were married during a recession in Britain, except in London where times weren't so difficult, so we tried to buy goods from various businesses based around the country whenever we could.

We wanted the kitchen to be the real heart of our home, an enormous space with plenty of room for cooking, eating and relaxing. At the weekends we made casseroles and soups to take to the homeless shelter. Phillip was really passionate about giving people a helping hand and a second chance.

At times he caused me anxiety because he was a very trusting man and found it difficult to turn away from people who needed help. I worried that he may become a target to unscrupulous people who would try to take advantage of him but I soon found out that he was streetwise and nobody's fool. He seemed to sense if someone was lying to him.

His piercing green eyes seemed to see into your soul somehow. He believed in helping people to find the power to help themselves.

Aside from the kitchen, another part of the house which I enjoyed being in was the living room because Phillip and I spent time in there together just relaxing or talking about day to day events.

I recall Phillip was determined to have real fires in the house and we spent a few weekends traipsing around looking for old fires and fire places. There was no Internet search for us back then. After much rummaging around reclamation yards Phillip came across some very simple black, iron fire surrounds and black iron fireplaces which had been retrieved from an old hall. When they were fitted in our home and working, they looked fantastic and gave out loads of warmth but they were such hard work to maintain and clean.

The ceilings in every room were very high but Phillip said that I knew how to create rooms which had a real cosiness to them. In the living room we placed two sofas opposite each other, both distinctly different which seemed to match our personalities. One sofa was purple, my choice and the other was a cream and gold checked material, Phillip's more conservative choice.

It sounds awful now when I'm describing it to you but at the time I thought it looked stunning. There was a gold coloured rug on the floor in between the two sofas and I loved rubbing my bare feet over it. Having the furniture set out like that meant that we could look at each other and discuss things more easily.

Phillip and I would sit together most evenings in the winter with the fire burning and make time for each other by chatting about ordinary, small, every day matters. An ocean away from the worries of the business he shared with Jasper which caused him endless angst. When the weather was pleasant, we'd often stroll to Green Park, sit on a bench and observe London's busy people as they skittered to and fro.

At home we had the space to create an office which we both shared. It was a light and airy room, but really Phillip used it the most.

He particularly liked the two huge Georgian windows because the sunrays streamed in and light danced around the room. In our office, we placed a similar fireplace to the one in the living room and put a cream coloured chair in one of the alcoves with a matching footstool. Sometimes, when Phillip was thinking very deeply, or had a huge problem to deal with, he would sit and ponder in his chair. When he sat there, I knew not to disturb him.

The office was quite sparsely furnished as the only other pieces of furniture it had were a huge walnut desk and two leather, adjustable black chairs a bit like the ones at Verbier's I suppose, where Bea worked. Above the fireplace Phillip had placed two enlarged photographs of Banksy's street art. Phillip had taken the photos during one of his many trips. The pieces satirised oppression and hypocrisy. One showed a man sticking a red banner over the words *follow your dream*. The red banner had the word *cancelled* pasted across *follow your dream*. The other photograph depicted a young man climbing a wall. Beside him was a quote in bright red which stated *if we wash our hands of the conflict between the powerful and the powerless we side with the powerful – we don't remain neutral.*

I know that Phillip considered it important to be reasonable and fair with everyone. He really epitomised that it doesn't need to be dichotomous; having money and understanding the difficulties faced by people who don't have access to much money. He used his resources wisely, to help and instil power in others, particularly through training, education and offering work."

Caroline looked sad and her head hung low, but within moments she composed herself. She sighed. "Our bedroom was on the third floor and here we indulged in having a four-poster bed. It was definitely ostentatious I know but we decided to be silly one day when we saw it in a tiny shop in the Cotswolds.

We speculated wildly about how the shop-keeper had ever got the bed through the shop door. The delivery men had a hell of a job to get it into our house and up the stairs. We really liked that bed because it was whimsical, something that we very rarely were. At the bottom of the bed was a gold coloured sofa and two armchairs. We had a separate dressing room, a walk in wardrobe and an en-suite bathroom. That should give you some idea of the size of the room.

It took us five years to turn the house into our home but we made great use of it and the place felt as though it was never empty. The view from the roof garden, over the city of London, was amazing. We both enjoyed standing on the roof terrace and we never stopped being impressed when stood at the top of the house and looked out to see the Post Office tower and sparkling lights across London city in the evening. Even the construction cranes looked exotic and full of promise in the nightfall as they glowed with their flashing red lights. A bit like Manchester looks now; full of exciting opportunities and the edginess of change.

Phillip was extremely ambitious for the company he shared with Jasper. I worked there for almost twenty years and helped it to grow although Phillip had to shoulder a huge burden of responsibility and accountability as the overall boss.

He built up a large workforce operating from three offices, one in Manchester, one in Edinburgh and the other in London. The three of us, Jasper, Phillip and I, spent a lot of time travelling between the offices. At least I did for the first seven years of our marriage. It was an exciting time.

We had meetings, made plans, discussed business problems and managed to resolve most of them. Except we couldn't resolve one very large personal problem that we had. I couldn't become pregnant."

Bella blushed. Her stomach churned. Hundreds of questions lurched around her mind. Was she not really Caroline and Phillip's daughter? Was she adopted? Was she the daughter of a surrogate mother? She dared not ask. Instead she bowed her head to avoid her mother's scrutiny and she missed the look of fondness that Caroline gave to her daughter as she carried on her tale.

"In desperation I contacted Elle. If anyone could advise me, I knew that she would be able to. I felt that speaking to her would not be as embarrassing as discussing this problem with a doctor who was a stranger to me. Elle proved to be so perceptive and arranged to meet me in London so that we could go shopping, have some lunch and catch up. We met in a café which had private booths so that I could pour out my troubles to my beloved friend.

Elle was really calm, knowledgeable and supportive. She explained that it was likely I had damaged fallopian tubes and then discussed a new process called IVF which had recently been pioneered. As Elle spoke I thought that it sounded like a gruelling process.

The IVF treatment would begin with me having a course of hormone therapy to stimulate the development of follicles in my ovary. The follicles would be collected as eggs which would then be fertilised in a test-tube. Did you know that's where the term in-vitro comes from? Several embryos would be created by this method. Within two to five days of being in an incubator, one, two or three of these embryos would be implanted.

It sounded straightforward but Elle warned me that it was an arduous process. She said there may be no follicle development or too much stimulation which would produce an unusually large number of eggs, such as more than fifteen.

She told me that egg collection could be very uncomfortable and that I might need a local anaesthetic. It also meant that Phillip would have to agree to go through this clinical method and the quality of his semen would be scrutinised. He was such a private person that I doubted he would ever agree to this. Even if he did, Elle cautioned me that not every embryo implanted would lead to a pregnancy and that any hopes Phillip and I had of having a baby could be raised, and dashed, on a number of occasions.

We would have to be emotionally secure to cope with great sadness as the success rate was around fifty percent on each try. Elle warned me that it was also possible that the hormones may stimulate the ovaries too much and that could lead to multiple pregnancies which brought extra possibilities of danger to the embryos and to me. Elle questioned me about being emotionally strong enough to cope, not only with my own disappointment but with Phillip's too.

Counselling, she said, was an important factor in this type of treatment. Right at that moment I felt as if life could be very complicated. I was amazed that anyone had ever been born. It sounded like IVF was not a decision to be entered into lightly.

When Elle hailed a taxi to take her to Euston Station, I walked away from our meeting in Knightsbridge in a daze. In the distance I could see Hyde Park and decided to walk through it to get some peace and clear my mind. Well, that didn't work at all. Everywhere I looked I seemed to see mothers with their children, or nannies with other people's children.

I felt bereft, disappointed, bewildered and a failure. How could I possibly put Phillip through all this? He had a business to run. Lots of people depending on him for their livelihood. This was one extra pressure which he just did not need. I felt selfish for hoping that I could have it all. I gave myself a good talking to and went for a coffee at a tiny café just off Oxford Street and bemoaned my body. I found that telling myself off was no good at all.

The late afternoon turned into early evening. I wandered around Oxford Street, down Regent Street and into Piccadilly Circus. London was teeming with people. People with families. Babies in buggies. Toddlers holding on to prams. Hundreds of mums and hundreds of children. I thought I was going out of my mind.

It was late when I arrived home and Phillip was already in the kitchen. "Where've you been? I've been so worried about you. I thought you'd be back by six o'clock and now it's nine." I remember vividly that his face was etched with anxiety.

The gentle concern in his green eyes pushed me to tears. Tears which just would not stop. He looked so terrified that something awful had happened. When my crying eventually subsided I told him what Elle had said. He became even more concerned about me. He was so selfless.

I looked at this wonderful, kind, chubby, balding man and loved him even more than I ever thought possible. He said if we were to have a family, and this were to be the only way it could happen then we must face it together. I cried again.

Elle recommended that we use an obstetrician in London. She said that Phillip's friend Sie Patel would know someone, but I wasn't sure that I wanted Sie to know our private difficulties. Phillip reassured me. He said that Sie could be trusted and I took that as an excellent endorsement.

Not long after our discussion, we arranged to start the treatment. I'm sure that Phillip must have regretted that decision more than once. Oh my goodness, I became like a chimera and blamed the hormone treatment. One minute I was fine and my usual self, the next I was moaning or grumpy about something. The two of us seemed to spend ages waiting. Waiting for news. Waiting for treatment. Waiting to see if something had happened. Waiting to see if nothing had happened. It drove me insane.

Through it all, Phillip was amazingly calm and kind. Every negative result sent me into a spiral of disappointment. Every new treatment offered fresh hope that this time would be the successful one. After five attempts I was beginning to lose faith but Phillip never did.

He reassured me. Said that this time it wasn't meant to be, but that at some point, things would happen. I was desolate. Despondent. Unhappy.

"We knew you were going through a grim time Caroline. We were afraid to ask how things were going but knew that you needed support" said Vivie. "We never knew if you wanted to speak about the treatment or if you wanted us to ignore what was happening. There was a point when you did shut us out of your life wasn't there?" asked Bea gently.

"Yes" replied Caroline honestly. "I felt like such a flop. I couldn't bear to talk about it. Things were easier when I wasn't reminded that every day I had failed. Then one day Elle telephoned and asked if she could come and stay with me just before my sixth treatment. It was so unusual for her to ask anything of me that I couldn't refuse. She said that she would move in with us for a short while, as she needed to do research in London and she could also do with the company."

"Well, I knew what it was like to lose a baby didn't I?" asked Elle. "My work was focused on helping people to come to terms with loss and I thought if I couldn't help you, my life-long friend, then I should give up my job." "I know Elle, but you must have taken at least eight weeks off work."

"No, I didn't actually" claimed Elle. "I negotiated the time off to actually do research. Which is what I did when I stayed with you even though you didn't believe me. When you didn't need me to take your mind off things, I used the local libraries to do my research. So the situation suited both of us. It was a great opportunity to spend time with you and Phillip. Precious time, which I enjoyed."

Outside thunder rumbled overhead and the Hub was lit by the viciousness of lightning. Caroline jumped and shook her head.

"That morning when I took the pregnancy test following the sixth treatment, you can imagine how full of anxiety I was. When I looked and saw that it was positive I couldn't believe my eyes. I told you Elle didn't I that I took five more pregnancy tests that day just to be sure that my mind wasn't playing tricks on me before I told Phillip the news?" "Yes" replied Elle "but I think as soon as he arrived home he knew that there was something different about you. I went upstairs out of the way as soon as he entered the kitchen but I heard him tell you that you looked radiant. It was as if he had a sixth sense on your sixth try" joked Elle.

"I so clearly remember that evening as if it were yesterday" exclaimed Caroline in delight. "I tried to appear busy in the kitchen and seem to be nonchalant. I told him that there was a present for him on the kitchen table. When he spied the present, which was a children's book I watched his puzzled face as he opened it. Inside I had written *please read this to our baby when it joins us in July.*

I watched his reaction very closely. I saw his face light up as a smile broke across it. He jumped up from the table and hugged me so tightly I couldn't breathe. We were both overcome with relief and joy.

Phillip asked me to put on my coat and we walked the streets of London. We just walked and hardly spoke at all. We walked and walked until we ended up at Green Park. We sat on a bench and decided not to tell anyone until after the twelve week scan.

Except, when we arrived home Phillip and I talked with you didn't we Elle, long into that night about the best place to go to have the baby. Phillip was very keen for his friend Sie, your new beau, to deliver our cherished baby. They had been friends since school. It made sense as he had played such a huge part in this.

At the time he worked at the Portland Hospital. Hard to believe that after all these years he is still as dedicated to his work. He is such a great person Elle" said Caroline. "I know" replied Elle. "Hard to believe where that time has gone isn't it?" said Caroline wistfully. Elle looked at Caroline, and she felt overwhelmed with sadness for her friend.

Caroline was in her stride and continued to relay what happened after she found out about the baby. "The party we had at home to celebrate the news when we eventually decided to tell our friends was great fun wasn't it?" she beamed. "It was brilliant to gather you all in our home.

Do you remember that I asked you to stand together for a group photograph and just before Phillip took it I shouted I'm pregnant? Phillip managed to capture your reactions so we could always remember how you looked. Happy days."

"Of course we remember that moment. When the congratulations were over I organised you all back into a group for a photograph" said Vivie "but this time with you and Phillip at the front" she recollected. "As Tom took the picture I shouted, *I'm pregnant too*. Then the four of us burst into tears and the men didn't know what to do.

Yes. Great days full of hope and anticipation" exclaimed Vivie.

"It was an amazing time. I distinctly remember saying at the time that things come in threes and wondered aloud who the third pregnancy would be.

Do you recall that we all turned to Bea who looked horrified? Then a few weeks later Tom and I found out we were having twins!"

Bea laughed. "Do you remember that I gave you each a tiny box when we were celebrating at our local café soon after?" asked Bea. "Yes that was typically creative of you Bea" said Elle. '"You told us to open each box which, when we did had a single egg in each one. When we cracked open the eggs inside were little notes telling us you were expecting a baby too. Very ingenious."

"I often wondered Elle", said Vivie "how you felt to be surrounded by your closest friends who were expecting babies." "On one level I was delighted for the three of you" she replied, "but on another level I was sad for myself. Unhappy that I didn't have a partner to plan a life together. Whilst I did get a great deal of enjoyment out of my job, it was just that, a job. It didn't offer solace when I was miserable or excited anticipation about planning for the future. I knew that when I went home, there would be no-one waiting for me. No-one whose focus was to share triumphs or support through disasters. I imagined that having a partner, was very different to having friends."

"It's not all sunshine and roses y'know Elle this being in a relationship like you seem to imagine it to be. It's very hard work and sometimes you may not even like the person you're with" explained Bea.

Frank gave Bea a hard stare, which Bea sensed. "I don't mean you Frank. Although sometimes you drive me to distraction.

I'm sure that you enjoy being alone Frank. You hate it when people make any kind of noise and will sit with those custom fit Snug ear-phones to drown out superfluous noise, which I might say includes me talking to you. I mean there are people who don't bring out the best in each other aren't there?

It's possible to make a mistake in your choice of partner. To live with that disappointment day after day must be very difficult. If there are children too, that makes things much more challenging, especially if you don't have the same values. I think what I'm trying to say is sometimes it may be better to be alone, than with someone who irritates the hell out of you."

Frank laughed. "Are you trying to tell me something Bea?" he queried. "No Frank, I'm not. I'm just saying that for some people, being together may not be as wonderful as Elle imagines."

Elle recognised tension in the air and said "I think that we need to have some more coffee. The air has gone quite chilly and a hot drink would do us all some good. I'll make it" she said. "It's ok" replied Bella "Ben and I will make the coffee" and with that, they both moved away from the table and walked deftly into the kitchen.

Caroline and Bea passed a look of intrigue which Frank noticed. He sighed. Women. They notice everything, he thought, when they want to. From the kitchen he could hear the sound of Bella singing *From Time* by Drake. *'What are you so afraid of? You give, but you cannot take love.'* Frank wondered if that was him. Why did he find it so difficult to accept when those close to him showed that they loved him? He could not remember a time when he hadn't loved Bea and wondered if she knew that.

Frank looked across the table at her. He loved everything about Bea. Their eyes met briefly, he grinned at her. Bea's eyes sparkled as she stared back at her annoying husband. She thought that she could never say being with him was boring and wondered if he was enjoying entertaining their friends as much as she was.

Suddenly the tranquil atmosphere was broken by a loud crash towards the back of the café. Instinctively Frank jumped up and was in the kitchen within a moment. They thought that an angry flurry of wild punches from the wind had pummelled the kitchen window like beating an under-dog in wrestling. In this head-to-head fight, pieces of glass lay battered and bruised on the kitchen floor and jagged pieces of glass hung solemnly from the window frame.

Ben and Bella looked shocked as large shards of glass had been thrown around them onto the kitchen floor. As Ben looked down he saw blood gushing from his left leg. Frank didn't hesitate and quickly made a tourniquet out of a clean tea towel ably assisted by Bella.

Realising that it would be impossible to take Ben to the hospital as the weather was too fierce, Frank and Bella helped Ben into the café as the wind howled like an angry dog which had been left outside the Hub when it wished to shelter from the rain.

Robert dragged a cushioned chair from the far side of the café and placed it opposite to Ben who sat trembling on a little wooden chair. Lifting up Ben's leg, Robert placed it gently onto the cushion as Matilde poured tap water into a bowl, fumbled around to feel for a clean tea towel in a cupboard, walked tentatively into the café and placed the bowl at the foot of Ben's chair. At this point

Elle sprang into action, followed closely by Bella. Even in the dim light she could see that blood had gushed into the bandage on Ben's leg. Elle took charge and told Frank to undo the tourniquet.

Ben's pale face flopped onto his chest as he passed out. Within a short space of time, he had lost a lot of blood. Gently, Bella lifted Ben's chin and she looked into his handsome face. Fear snaked around her brain.

In a crisis, Bea thought that it was always useful to busy oneself as she made her way past the injured young man and into the kitchen. Caroline followed her, leaving Vivie and Tom to watch in horrified silence as others worked hard to help their immobile son who moments earlier had been laughing and full of life.

Bella could see that Ben's face was pale. She told Elle that his hand was clammy to her touch and he moved his fingers feebly. Quickly Elle bent down to feel for a pulse in Ben's wrist. She struggled to feel it. Elle's voice was urgent as she commanded Frank to lie Ben on the floor and place his feet on a chair. She asked Bella to gather blankets and cover Ben so that his body could retain heat.

Deftly she looked at the gash on Ben's leg. It was deep. She washed the surrounding area to remove small pieces of glass which were within the deep wound. A clean tea towel was tied around his leg to minimise the blood loss. She asked Frank to apply pressure to the area which gave her time to consider how to tackle the injury. Elle felt Ben's heartbeat. It was rapid.

She directed Bella to boil water which meant using one of the battery powered plug sockets. Bella thought that the saying of a *watched pot never boils* turned out to be true in this case.

She willed the kettle to boil but the seconds ticked by slowly. Elle had asked Bea to get a cutting needle and synthetic thread as the wound would need to be sutured.

In the minimal candlelight Bea ran to a cupboard where she kept a range of sewing implements. Within moments she had returned, placed the items into a bowl of boiling water, put on a pair of plastic gloves as she passed a second pair of Marigolds to Elle.

All eyes were on Elle as she skilfully began to suture Ben's wound. He opened his eyes and winced in pain. As Elle sewed, adroitly Frank washed the blood away from Ben's leg to keep the wound clean. Bea passed a cup of tea to Bella who lifted the cup to Ben's lips just as Elle completed the final stitch.

Ben shuddered awake and sipped whilst Bella gently stroked his hair. Bea gave Bella a blood pressure machine to check Ben's blood pressure. Not too bad, 110/70 will do thought Bella, after what he's been through..

The white rage of lightning momentarily lit up the Hub followed almost immediately by another torrential downpour of rain which hammered on every window and poured through the broken one in the kitchen. Thunder crashed overhead as if daring anyone to leave the safety of the café.

Frank and Tom busied themselves by covering the hollow window frame with tarpaulin, using a hammer and nails taken from what Bea called *the useful cupboard* in the kitchen.

Ben looked vulnerable under the blankets. His head turned slowly and his green eyes stared at Bella as he asked "Did I miss what happened to Phillip and Jasper?" Bella laughed, turned to her mother and said "come on, out with it." Caroline and Bea sighed resignedly, each preparing to recreate past events.

# Chapter 14 - Alfie and Minnie

Bea's blonde head tilted upwards as if seeking inspiration, then she surveyed the group calmly. "I moved into Jasper's apartment immediately after the wedding. Tom and Vivie lived with us too until they moved to New York. My new job had begun at Verbier's and I became busier than I had ever been. The hours of work were long and proved to be gruelling. I was on my feet all day, listening to the chitter chatter of my clients and making conversation with people I barely knew.

Being creative and innovative was stimulating; making small talk was onerous. One day I was listening to a lady tell me that her husband had left her for another woman. She was distraught as she told her tale of woe. Little did she know that the person in the chair next to her in the salon was the very woman who was the cause of all her problems. At times, it was difficult to keep my mouth shut. Mostly my mind was taken up with making a success of my career in London and enjoying married life.

Every day I walked through Bloomsbury, into Piccadilly and up to Bond Street. I recognised the workers who made the same journey to their own workplace, the scents associated with different buildings, and the changing styles in the shop windows. My journey was never boring.

I loved the sight of red buses making their way through the London streets, the sound of Big Ben chiming every quarter hour and the bustle of people on the pavements always pleased me, whatever the weather. Sometimes after work I would meet Jasper and we would go to the most amazing bars and clubs. Life in London was never dull.

Jasper and Phillip spent a lot of time at work, building up their business, so occasionally Caroline and I would meet and spend time exploring the different areas of London. We really liked each other's company and often enjoyed walking towards the Houses of Parliament, then looking at the great Westminster Cathedral and on towards Buckingham Palace.

In the evening, when the skies were inky blue and the stars shone, it felt as though London belonged just to us; two northern girls. The four of us made time to have breakfast together before going to work. It became difficult to imagine what life had been like in Manchester, before I married Jasper. Every so often though I couldn't help myself from wondering what part of the world Frank was exploring, then I would give my head a shake and stop daydreaming.

After a few years I was beginning to feel restless in my role at the salon. Jasper noticed and advised me to set up my own hairdressing salon. I had been saving up money, as I knew that one day I wanted to become my own boss but knowing that Jasper was behind the decision, made it easier to leave my role at Verbier's.

Having my own salon became an exciting project. I asked Caroline for her advice and the two of us began to trawl through the list of shops for sale. We visited shop after shop but found something wrong with all of them. Eventually we found a small place on Brompton Road. It was expensive, particularly as it had a two bedroomed apartment above it, but Jasper said that it would turn out to be a great investment in the long term.

I went ahead and bought the premises outright. I felt incredibly grown up when I signed the contract to start my own business.

I must've driven Jasper mad by asking him the colour of paint, type of flooring, particular lighting, different kinds of furniture and various window dressings but he never said if he was bored. I was determined that my little salon would become a success.

Caroline recommended a builder to me, Mr. Doyle, who had completed a lot of the work on her house. Together, Caroline, Mr. Doyle and I agreed how the salon would look but before I made the final decision, I asked Jasper for his opinion. He was a shrewd businessman. Jasper taught me how to negotiate order lead times, ways of obtaining the best deal from suppliers and how to detail everything in writing.

During the process of converting the little shop into a fine salon I had to make decisions which I had never before thought about. Even before a drop of paint had hit the walls, I had to tell Mr. Doyle where the plug sockets would be, how many I needed, where I wanted each wash basin to be and where the long mirrors and leather chairs would be sited.

At times when my mind was in a frazzle I would either ring Jasper or Caroline and one or the other of them would meet me for lunch, a walk and some fresh air. Through their experiences, I discovered a lot about being a manager.

Two weeks before the salon was due to open Jasper came home one evening and placed a red envelope on the dining table. I looked at it without opening it and Jasper's bright green eyes gazed into my own but I could not read his mood.

My heart pounded and I asked involuntarily if something was wrong. He remained silent. I considered the envelope, anxious about what might be in it. I stared at his face but his look was indecipherable. Softly I picked up the envelope and opened it with trepidation. Inside were two tickets to travel on the Orient Express train from Venice to Paris along with a letter of confirmation from the Bauer Hotel in Venice for a stay of three nights for the two of us.

"I thought that you needed a break" Jasper said "and a treat before your salon opens." I remember that I sobbed, tears of exhaustion and gratitude. "Caroline said that she'll look after things whilst you're away" said Jasper and I wept all the more as he hugged me.

I barely had time to pack a small suitcase that evening as we were to fly from London early the following morning. When we arrived at Venice's Marco Polo Airport it was sun-soaked and we walked about a mile to the water taxi pick up point. For forty minutes our little boat skimmed across the blue lagoon like a flat pebble.

Our first glimpse of Venice was the flamboyant array of grand buildings, dotted around the lagoon, glowing in the hazy sunlight. We could see the Doge's Palace and glimpsed the square of San Marco where throngs of people ambled. The lagoon held a myriad of water vessels, from the superbly crafted gondolas which were rowed effortlessly by the beautiful movement of the gondoliers, to a gigantic, pristine cruise ship skilfully manoeuvred by the captain and crew through the tiny lagoon of Venice.

Our small boat had to navigate its way through the myriad of boats.  As we whipped along the water the breeze provided welcome respite from the boiling sun.  My mind wandered to the time I had back-packed to Venice with Vivie, Elle and Caroline.

As we approached the Bauer Hotel, I felt disappointed because of its facade.    Its flat, modern appearance, particularly set against mostly exquisite Baroque architecture, was unremarkable.    Our boat glided alongside the hotel and docked at steps which led to the rose-coloured marble reception area.    Amazing, hand-blown Murano glass chandeliers lit up the area and in the middle of the floor was a stunning, lustrous fuchsia glass flower arrangement.  I stopped to take a closer look and was overwhelmed by the craftsmanship.

We were taken to our room which, by Venetian standards, was spacious and had a view over the tiny San Moise canal.  I peeped into the bathroom, created entirely of white marble making the room appear spacious and bright.

We were only a few minutes' walk away from St. Mark's Square but we intended to explore the whole island, not just the main tourist areas.  We unpacked quickly, ran downstairs out into Campo San Moise and peeped into the windows of some of the most exclusive shops in Venice.

We had bought a three day pass for the vaporetti when we landed at the airport and validated it straightaway so that we could catch one and have lunch on the island of Guidecca.  The short journey ended at the youth hostel where I had stayed years ago.

Jasper and I made our way to a little ostaria which had been recommended to us by Caroline. We sat at the waterfront and looked across at the beautiful church of Santa Maria della Salute. Jasper told me that the building, made of white Istrian stone, was built in 1630 by the Venetians to pay thanks to God that when they asked for the plague to stop, it did. As we ate a delicious lunch, I thought this view across the wide Guidecca Canal was tranquil, away from the chaos of hundreds of gondolas and thousands of tourists.

After lunch we ran to board a water taxi and jumped off at the Dorsoduro quarter. Above one of the entrances to the Salute church was a notice which said that no-one was allowed to ask for money inside the church. As we walked around the huge basilica an elderly woman approached me, and held out her hand to beg. The woman yelled at me in Italian because I obeyed the sign and didn't give her any money. I was frightened by this and Jasper, who had been some distance away, came to my side as the woman disappeared from the church.

I was unnerved and placed some money into a collection box to stop feeling so guilty at not helping her. When we left the church, the beggar woman was out of sight but I was sure she had put a curse on me.

Jasper was keen to visit the Peggy Guggenheim collection located in Peggy's former home in Venice. He told me about Peggy's colourful and sad history; how her father had died on the Titanic and that as an adult she socialised with many of the avant-garde artists of her time.

Jasper thought that Peggy Guggenheim had an eye for art which others, at the time, did not see. Jasper told me that Peggy had lived in London and opened an art gallery there to showcase work of the Surrealist movement.

We spent ages wandering the rooms of her old Venice home as Jasper talked through some of the works of Cubism and Surrealism. I left him to wander around the gallery as there was only so much that I could pretend that this art interested me.

I sat outside in the peaceful garden and wondered about the colourful life led by some people. The stillness of the unconventional sculpture garden must have played tricks on my mind because I was sure that I saw Frank on a little boat as it passed by along the Grand Canal. Silly to think of him at that time. Two unnerving incidents in one day. I ran out of the garden and into the museum to find Jasper.

The next day we visited the Islands of Murano and Burano. As we left the vaporetta at Murano we were almost man-handled to visit a glass blowing factory to watch craftsmen make individual glass pieces. Jasper was keen to tell me that the glassmakers had to move to Murano from the Venetian mainland because of the danger of causing a fire in the wooden city from their workshops.

These talented artisans were not allowed to leave the island of Murano to set up business elsewhere; trapped by their craftsmanship. The techniques they used were so unique that their expertise could not be equalled.

As we wandered around Murano Jasper spoke to a local man, who encouraged him to visit one of the oldest churches on the island, the Basilica dei Santi Marie e Donato. Outwardly its appearance was plain, but when we stepped inside the marble carving and mosaics were breath-taking.

Afterwards we wandered alongside the canals on our way to the main vaporetta stop, had a cold drink and waited in the searing heat. The boat was crammed with people when it arrived so we had to jam ourselves at the boat's entrance where there seemed to be fewer people. The vaporetta chugged along slowly and we both enjoyed the cooling breeze from the water.

As the boat approached the tiny island of Burano we could see a beautiful, colourful houses. Legend has it that the houses were painted in different colours so that the fishermen could see them when they were out fishing in the lagoon. We stopped outside a cerise painted house to watch a woman producing an intricate lace garment. A dying art. We both agreed that it was such an enchanting place that we vowed to visit it each year.

On our last day we decided to explore the main island of Venice. We strolled to Saint Mark's Square early in the morning before the hordes of travellers arrived by vaporetti. The shop keepers were preparing the food for the day's trade and some were swilling the path outside their shop. Saint Mark's Square was flanked by symmetrical arcades, but our main view was of the Basilica and the impressive vertical Campanile. We sat on the steps of one of the arcades and watched as life unfolded on the piazza.

We didn't visit the Basilica of Saint Mark's as we would've had to spend ages queuing when we wanted to explore the main island of Venice. We stayed on the steps of the arcade until the Torre dell'Orologio, with its mosaic of gold stars set against a shimmering blue background, chimed ten o'clock.

From there we walked along the wide promenade, at the side of the lagoon towards Arsenale where the private yachts of multi-millionaires were moored. As we headed towards the naval museum, Jasper decided to pop into one of the shops just off the promenade to get us both some bottled water and fresh fruit; I sat and waited at the waterside.

Just in front of me was moored an enormous blue and white yacht which blocked my view of the Venice Basin. I wondered why I had chosen to sit there but felt too warm to move. Lazily I watched the crew as they prepared to leave the shores of Venice.

There, right before my eyes, working on the yacht, was Frank. I hadn't imagined it the other day. It must've been Frank that I saw. He was wearing a white t-shirt with navy shorts and appeared to be enjoying life; he was joking with other crew members. I heard his distinctive laugh. I wanted to shout out to him, to catch up after all these years, he looked just the same except sun-kissed, but my mouth was dry. No sound came out when I tried to speak.

I watched him for about ten minutes, but he appeared oblivious to my presence. I wondered if I should say something as our paths may never cross again. Just then Jasper turned up at the side of me. He put his arm around my shoulder and noticed that I was shaking. I told him that the yacht had created a shadow which made me feel chilly. We walked away from the yacht, into the Biennale gardens and left Frank behind."

"I saw you that day" stated Frank baldly from across the table.

Bea looked at him with astonishment. "You did? Why didn't you speak to me then?" she questioned. "I noticed you sat on your own at the waterside" he answered flatly.

"I panicked when I saw you. I knew that the yacht was preparing to leave Venice and that I would've had very little time to find out how you were. I also realised that it was unlikely you'd be in Venice alone. It's a place of romance isn't it? No-one goes alone. I made a good job of pretending not to see you though, didn't I?" he smiled as he spoke to her.

"Yes" said Bea "but you could at least have waved to acknowledge me, ignorant git." She was a little hurt by his glib reply. "I did want to but, just as I was about to wave to you, a curly haired guy turned up, and put his arm around you. I wasn't prepared to embarrass myself in front of him" stated Frank. "You looked comfortable with him Bea as you walked away."

Frank appeared to be resentful which appeared odd to Bea as, in their younger days, it was he who had chosen to forge a life without her.

Bea was a little annoyed with Frank, and protective of Jasper so continued to talk. "I think that Jasper found me a little distracted that day. My stomach had a huge knot in it; I found it difficult to breathe.

We walked the narrow streets of Venice, browsing the shop windows, dodging tourists as they headed for the main sights of Venice, the Rialto Bridge and Saint Mark's Square. We found narrow, secret passageways as we weaved our way on foot through a maze of Venetian architecture in the backstreets of Venice.

It took some time for me to find peace again in Venice. but it came. As we sipped cold drinks and ate small snacks at an osteria which overlooked the mayhem of the Grand Canal, I looked at Jasper and felt calmer. We laughed as we watched gondolas dodge each other, tourists vie for the best observation post and Venetians who seemed resigned, but reluctant to share their beautiful island with strangers.

We were up bright and early the next morning. As we entered the reception area of the Bauer Hotel an immaculately dressed, beautiful Italian lady greeted us. "Ah, Mr. and Mrs. Butler I am Ada, your guide. I will escort you to the Orient Express."

A private water taxi was berthed at the side of the hotel, waiting to take us to the train station accompanied by Ada. She shouted instructions to the hotel's porters and the boat's captain. A real bossy boots! Like Ada, the boat didn't take prisoners as it shoved its way up the Grand Canal, past larger boats, and headed for Venezia Santa Lucia train station.

As we travelled along the Grand Canal, we could see the stark white train station as it shimmered in the morning sunshine. The building looked cool and offered the promise of adventure. As we stepped off the boat, our bags were unloaded by porters and Ada escorted us to a private check-in desk on a dedicated platform leading to the exotic Orient Express.

We were both very excited to look at this world-renowned train as it sat majestically, resplendent in its shiny blue coat of paint with gold trimmings.

We were greeted by our steward, Ralf, who promised to take care of us on the journey to Paris. We boarded the train and were led to our suite, which was formed by two interconnecting double cabins. The walnut marquetry was exquisite, our long seats were comfortable, and our crystal glasses holding the finest champagne were gulped greedily. This began the next leg of our exciting adventure.

The public carriages were vintage, and the food served on the train was cooked by skilled French chefs. We spent the afternoon in our private carriage, chatting and gazing at the stunning scenery as the train wended its way through Italy and touched the edge of Austria in the early evening. As we ate a magnificent four course dinner, the train raced along the top of Switzerland and we chatted to other guests on the train in the exhilarating atmosphere of unimaginable opulence.

We had eaten so much that when we returned to our cabin we were lulled to sleep by the hum of the rails on the track as the train wended its way through France. We awoke early the next morning to have breakfast served in our cabin by Ralf before we left the Orient Express and spent the morning sight-seeing in Paris. There was no murder on that Orient Express journey.

The break was just what I needed, and Jasper had known this. When we arrived home, I rang Caroline immediately. In her usual calm manner, she had managed to deal with the mishaps caused by the builders such as painting the main room in the salon melancholic brown instead of cream and placing the washing basins on the wrong side of the room, despite being given exact instructions. How on earth, I wondered, could such mistakes happen even under Caroline's eagle gaze?

There was a small article about the salon in the London Evening Standard which Caroline had organised. These days it would probably be more appropriate to use the Internet and appear inexorably on Facebook, Instagram, Twitter and Pinterest to generate interest which may lead to custom.

Upon our return I noticed that Caroline seemed to be radiant. I looked at her more than once to gauge her mood but never asked the reason for her happiness. I knew she would tell me in good time.

A few weeks after the opening of the salon, Jasper and I were invited to dinner by Caroline and Phillip. It wasn't an unusual gesture, there was always something happening at their exuberant home. As soon as we entered the convivial kitchen, I thought that Phillip and Caroline were bursting with news. It was delightful when they told us they were expecting a much longed-for baby.

To hear that Vivie too was having a baby was stunning. We had an evening together that was one of the happiest I have ever spent with you all. It was heart-warming to see Caroline and Phillip's joy about the baby. I would say that Phillip, who was going to be an older father, was more delighted than most. As Jasper and I left that evening, I remember feeling exhausted. I crawled into bed and had a fitful night's sleep.

For the next few days I was terribly weary. It was strange as I always had loads of energy. Matilde and Robert would often tell me off for never staying still, but right at that moment, all I wanted to do was sleep forever.

I put it down to working very hard to make a success of the salon. Jasper was worried about me and insisted I see the doctor. When eventually I gave in, I was stunned to hear from the doctor that I too was pregnant. Fancy that. Three friends expecting babies at the same time.

Seven months later I gave birth to a boy whom we named Alfie after Jasper's father. I had to leave the running of the salon to a determined and ambitious young woman named Emily but she proved to be very important. When Jasper and I welcomed our second baby Minnie into our family, Emily took over running the salon indefinitely.

I am still convinced that being a mother is the most difficult job in the world. No-one tells you how to do the correct thing so I was thankful that Caroline was around so that we could chat about things. I missed my parents so much when the children were little. They often travelled from Manchester to London, but it never felt that there was enough time to spend with them.

There were so many important decisions to make for the children such as where they would go to school, what hobbies they might like and how to guide them to become good citizens of the world. Sometimes I felt overwhelmed by that, particularly as Jasper worked long hours and most of the child-minding fell to me.

Caroline and I made sure that we made time for each other and maintained contact with Vivie by writing letters to her. We were very conscious that she was on her own in New York with the twins, Ben and Jo.

I know that you were very grateful Vivie when Elle went to spend some time with you to help when the twins were babies.  Elle, you've been the perfect God Parent to all the children.   Thank you."   Elle received this compliment with her usual gentle grace.  "It's been great fun to be part of their lives, so thank you" said Elle and raised her coffee cup in salute.

"Elle was an amazing help, particularly in New York where I knew very few people" replied Vivie.  "When I managed to stop one baby from crying the other would start.   It seemed like a permanent cycle of changing nappies, soothing babies and feeding them.

I was an exhausted wreck and Tom worked particularly long days.  You can't believe how difficult it is to get into and out of an apartment and navigate the streets of New York with a double buggy.  The local park became my haven and being outside in the fresh air was a welcome change.  Just to put on some mascara became a major accomplishment.   Oh, happy days" she said ironically.

"I have to admit, from a selfish viewpoint, I was really pleased when Tom agreed to work with Phillip and Jasper by heading up the Manchester office.  At least I was able to see you all from time to time when I could escape from being a mother for a short while.  We certainly helped each other a great deal, didn't we?

Do you remember Bea when I rang you in the middle of the night because Ben was covered in chicken pox and his eyes were bulging?

Tom had told me not to worry, especially as I had taken Ben to see the doctor earlier in the day. I was so anxious because Ben was drowsy, had a high temperature and his eyes were swollen. I felt that I just had to take him to the hospital if only for reassurance that it was just chicken pox.

Thank goodness you told me to go as soon as possible. You said that I wasn't being an unreasonable mother of a four-year old child. As soon as we arrived in the hospital, I knew something was seriously wrong with Ben. The doctor took blood tests and within an hour told me that Ben had encephalitis.

I had absolutely no idea what that meant so a nurse explained it to me in a side room whilst Ben was taken into intensive care. At that time, I didn't have a mobile telephone, so I had to rummage around for change to ring Tom from a pay 'phone. Ben stayed in the hospital for five days on intravenous antibiotics. He and Jo had just started school.

Tom altered his hours of work so that he could look after Jo. He said that she cried a lot that week as she missed Ben and me so much. I never realised that chicken pox could be so deadly as all the other mothers had said that it was a mild illness. The knots in my stomach were huge for ages. I couldn't eat properly as I was worried about Ben and anxious about how Jo would cope without him.

I lost a lot of weight. The doctors told me that Ben may have brain damage. That never happened, but he did end up with dyslexia and that we could cope with. I don't even know if that is related to his illness.

I don't suppose you remember any of that Ben, do you?" asked his mother. "No mum. I don't remember, I'm glad to say because that sounds horrific" said Ben "but I will remember today's events for a long time." He looked at Bella who whispered "so will I."

The four older women instinctively looked at each other and a subdued Frank offered to make a pot of coffee for everyone. He had found it difficult to listen to Bea's account of her past life.

Frank also had a nagging doubt about whether it was the wind that broke his kitchen window. It could easily have been the two feral lads from earlier in the day. One of them could have been the person he thought he'd seen hanging around in the alleyway earlier.

# Chapter 15 - Don't look back, that's not the way you're going

Caroline wanted to carry on talking about Phillip and began "Vivie would say that Phillip and Jasper were competitive and divergent thinkers. They had the ability to create lots of possible solutions to a problem, and not just focus on one. It was always stimulating, if not a little challenging to get into debate with them.

When we each began married life, Bea and I were very excited to be living and working in London. It was an incredibly diverse and stimulating environment, particularly for Bea who found that she was at liberty to use her creativity.

For fifteen years Phillip, Jasper and then Tom when he joined them after his stint in New York, worked hard, made sound judgements and created a successful company. The offices in Edinburgh, Manchester and London had delivered financial security, so we decided to celebrate this success by having a holiday in Italy. Obviously, we invited Elle.

We arranged for our parents to look after the children and as a treat we booked them all into the Lowry Hotel in Manchester. The children were excited as it meant that they would be able to be with their grandparents and each other for a whole week. They planned to go swimming, golfing and travel to different places in the north west of England every day and have great fun without their parents.

When we talked about our trip Tom, whose mother was Italian so had more knowledge of Italy than we did, advised that it would be better to visit Rome for the first part of our holiday and then travel to Florence by train.

With Tom's help, Vivie planned the itinerary; four days in Rome and three days in Florence. Elle arranged to join us in Rome, but she couldn't match all of her holiday dates with ours so wasn't going to Florence" explained Caroline.

Bea replied "I remember distinctly our families travelling to Manchester airport together in an entourage. Three cars full of excited people. The children were asking all kinds of questions about whether we would see the Pope, and if we would have dinner at the Vatican. At the airport we took the time to have breakfast together before we left Caroline's parents and mine with the children.

She pointed at Bella and Ben and said you two, plus Alfie, Minnie and Jo." Caroline interjected, "do you remember Bea how skittish the children were about being left in the care of two sets of grandparents? The five of them sensed that they would have a fabulous time with the doting oldies."

"You mean that they knew they would be spoilt" replied Bea. "I remember Bella sitting close by her father's side all the way through breakfast and she wouldn't let go of Phillip's hand when we reached the departure area. Phillip led Bella to a huge window to watch the 'planes land on the runway. I saw him bend down and have what appeared to be a serious talk with her which ended when she threw her arms around his neck and hugged him as if she would never see him again.

Alfie and Minnie sat either side of Jasper chattering away to him and me about all the things they were planning to do with Robert and Matilde while we were away. They took it in turns to sit on their father's knee and twirl his unkempt, curly hair. One of his idiosyncrasies was the pride that he took in his shoes. I remember the children teasing him that day about his highly polished brown shoes with tartan laces.

As we left them to go through to the departure gates, Jasper tickled the five children who giggled delightedly. If I close my eyes, I can still remember that picture so vividly" reminisced Bea. Tom smiled and Vivie said "the twins couldn't wait for us to go. They were hopping around in excitement which was a bit disappointing as I thought they'd be sad about us leaving them!" "You raised us to be independent mum and remember that Jo and I had each other so we were never ever really alone" replied Ben.

Caroline reminisced. "The six of us watched as my parents, along with Robert and Matilde, led the five children across the concourse and back to the cars. They stopped briefly, turned and waved us goodbye; all of us full of smiles and eager anticipation. Phillip shouted to them 'don't look back, that's not the way you're going' so they all strode onwards" said Caroline. "Yes, oh my goodness" cried Bella, "I remember that and how I blew six kisses to you and my father, Uncle Jasper and Aunty Bea, Tom and Vivie. To say goodbye."

Ben placed his arm gently around Bella's shoulder as he sensed her feeling of foreboding. As he touched her, she was already shaking, and he placed his lips softly on her forehead. Bella thought that the painkilling drugs which Elle had given to Ben must've weakened his usual emotional reserve.

At that moment, the café rumbled with the force of an overhead explosion, signalling a powerful thunderclap. Everybody shuddered.

Mustering her usual verve, Bea decided to continue the story of the holiday to Italy. "We arrived at Rome and decided to tackle the train service to Rome Termini, the central train station and from there, try to find our way to the hotel. I don't know why we did that" she said forcefully "except that Tom was able to guide us and follow the directions as he spoke Italian.

It was incredibly hot on the underground train, even for September. We had a suitcase each which wasn't easy to lug around on public transport especially as everywhere was awash with tourists.

With Tom's guidance, we navigated the train system and finished by taking a shuttle bus to the Cavalieri Hotel. We were definitely hot and bothered by the time we checked in. We chose that hotel as it was on a hill overlooking Rome and we thought that we'd be able to travel quickly to the whole list of places we wanted to visit."

Caroline took her cue "we didn't even unpack when we arrived, we just left our luggage in the room, had a speedy wash and met about ten minutes later in the huge marble foyer. We were so eager to start our holiday.

We met Elle in the lush gardens of the hotel and had a picnic before venturing into the city. The concierge had presented us with a guide-book so we sat down for a while and planned which sights to see first.

We agreed that we were all keen to see the Vatican and St. Peter's Basilica first so decided that we would head there. The hotel had a shuttle bus service into the city so we just jumped on the first bus we could muscle our way on to."

"I remember being dropped off near to the Basilica and, as we walked along wide strada we were unprepared for the sight as we walked through the entrance into the Vatican City" recounted Elle.

"It was steaming hot and there were thousands of tourists within the city walls. We were overwhelmed at the size of St. Peter's Square and the imposing Basilica. There were swirling queues of people from all over the world waiting reverently and patiently to view inside the church of St. Peter's.

We agreed that buying tickets to get straight into the Basilica and the Vatican had been superb foresight from Phillip. As we made our way to the front of the line, I felt so sorry for people who were queuing in searing heat without drink or toilet facilities. Not very thoughtful of the organisers.

We spent hours exploring the church and the Vatican. In medieval times, many people couldn't read, so the stone sculptures, ceiling frescos and wall paintings were used to help people imply a message. When we had finished inside the church, we wandered around the Vatican gardens which were breath-taking. I remember seeing an enormous fountain, and we stood close enough so that the water spray cooled us a little.

We were surprised to see two oak trees perfectly clipped into dome shapes, which represented the Basilica.

Slowly we struggled up Vatican Hill and climbed a cobbled stairway to see the Papal coat of arms designed out of perennial flowers coloured yellow, magenta and red. The floral displays were incredibly impressive. At the highest point of the garden was a replica of the Lourdes Grotto. We sat beside it for ages just watching the world go by" reminisced Caroline.

"It was such a peaceful place to spend the afternoon. An old lady passed-by, her rickety legs could barely hold her slight frame. She looked at me gently and whispered in Italian *'carry your cross with fortitude'* which Tom kindly translated for me. Before I had time to ask her what she meant, she had disappeared, but I found out soon enough didn't I?" stated Caroline sadly.

"It's a pity that we had such a short time in Rome" sighed Bea. "I found it too austere" revealed Vivie. "Had we been there longer, you may have found something to enjoy about it" said Caroline quietly. "I appreciated our holiday, I just thought that the architecture in Rome appeared too brutal and unwavering" said Vivie "probably reminiscent of its violent past. I was pleased to leave but definitely very excited to see Florence.

Do you remember Bea that we arrived in Florence in the early morning and the little city was bustling with people? We checked in to our hotel and couldn't wait to explore the narrow streets."

The small group of friends heard the wind whipping around the Hub, rushing up the wide street, smashing tree branches like a violent, rampaging, irate mob. Bea and Caroline shuddered in unison and stared into nothingness. Unconsciously Bea pushed away her drink and smiled sadly.

Elle leant across the table and rubbed Bea's thin arm, which jolted her out of her pensiveness. Bea turned her watery eyes towards Elle and spoke quietly "I think this awful weather is making me feel very uneasy". Robert looked at his daughter and understood her melancholy mood.

"Bea, your mum and I'll make a drink. Let's have some hot chocolate with a touch of brandy to warm our insides. We'll have some toast too with butter and that honey you like love. Is it called monkey honey?"

"No dad", laughed Bea, "it's called Manuka. It's meant to be good for your health." "Well then, it'll be just what the doctor ordered" said Matilde briskly as she bustled into the kitchen. Bella jumped up and offered to help. "Thanks Bella love" whispered Matilde, "you're a treasure. Let's get busy setting up this tray with cups and spoons. Good thing Frank had that back-up system installed for the kitchen stuff isn't it otherwise we'd be making nowt" stated Robert.

As the toast and hot chocolate, laced with brandy were passed around the table, Caroline spoke happily about their visit to Florence. "When we first saw the magnificent city of Florence, draped in bright sunshine, and set in a basin of mountains we were astounded by the historical relics and artistic masterpieces displayed on practically every street. We admired the sumptuous architecture, such beauty, particularly the Duomo built as it was out of mottled marble.

At first it was a breath-taking and calming city, which was a relief after the hectic pace of life in Rome.

Each day we strolled to the Arno River, which neatly divides the city. We went to admire the creative genius of the medieval bridges which linked the city's culture with nature and sat to admire the impressive views of the surrounding mountains.

Most of all we liked standing on the Ponte Vecchio, the oldest bridge in Florence and walking slowly from shop to shop. The shops had originally been built as houses and above them was a private corridor. It was used to connect the Uffizi art gallery with the Pitti Palace across the Arno River but we didn't have the opportunity to explore it.

When we arrived at the stiflingly hot Uffizi courtyard it was teeming with tourists and street performers. The entertainers made me feel very nervous as I thought they were a distractor for thieves, which was probable with so many tourists crammed into one place.

We all found the little city to be really charming, and as we sat in the shade agreed that when we next returned to Florence we would visit the surrounding areas too, but we've never returned have we?" asked Caroline of no-one in particular.

"It was fabulous to relax and just enjoy being in that marvellous city. We went for a meal one evening and I vividly remember Phillip's laugh echoed around the high vaulted ceiling of the restaurant and even in Italy, where they are used to noisy families like ours, he drew attention from other customers. We stayed out unusually late and, before we returned to the hotel, walked around the perimeter of the marble clad Duomo just so that we could see it in the moonlight.

We'd arranged to visit the Cathedral the following afternoon. We decided to have a moonlit stroll to the Arno River. A decision we'll always regret" she said as her countenance turned to abject misery.

"It was a very hot evening and we all sat by the side of the river and decided to paddle. We'd all had a bit too much to drink that evening; we were in high spirits. We took off our shoes and didn't stray far from the bank, but Phillip and Jasper decided they would be adventurous and swim from one side of the river to the other.

In the moonlight they stripped to their underpants and, competitive as ever with each other, started to swim. We cheered as we saw Phillip reach the other side, but we lost sight of Jasper in the darkness.

I heard Phillip shout Jasper's name repeatedly. Then Tom got into the river as he realised Jasper must have been having difficulties. Initially we thought they were messing around. We watched as Tom swam closer and closer to the other shore and Phillip jumped back into the black, icy water to seek out his brother.

We waited and waited for Phillip's head to reappear above the water, but it didn't. Tom swam and dived as we screamed at him to find Jasper and Phillip. As the sky grew blacker, and our shouts became louder, other tourists leapt into the river to help look for Jasper and Phillip in the cold, sinister water.

The Carabinieri arrived with powerful torch lights skimming the river-banks and the water for signs of Phillip and Jasper. Poor Tom had to be dragged out of the water by a diver from the Florentine police force.

Exhausted and cold he was whisked away to hospital suffering from hypothermia. The divers took over from the people who had tried to help and continued to search the deep, cheerless waters. We were frantic and shocked. I was aware that tourists stood in stupefied silence on the Ponte Vecchio as they too watched and waited with us.

Eventually we were led away by the Carbinieri from the banks of the murderous Alno River. An air of eerie calm descended on the tiny city of Florence. We joined other tourists on the Ponte Veccio and stood in mortified silence beside strangers, as we continued to watch a horror unfold in front of us. My whole body shook with fear and I vomited until there was nothing left inside me.

I was dimly aware that a helicopter hovered over the Ponte Veccio shining its beam upon the black Alno River.

The shriek of police sirens and ambulances rushed past us and screamed in unison. Everything around us seemed to stop, apart from the emergency services. There was no sign of Phillip or Jasper.

Vivie and I stood in horrified, agonising tearless dismay. We dared not move. The tension was palpable. Bea was in a shocking state. Her eyes were wild with fear and her face waxen. I hoped that possibly, by some miracle, our husband's lives hadn't disintegrated before our eyes.

I told Bea to be positive. We told each other that our arrangement to go to the Duomo with Phillip and Jasper at noon the following day would go ahead as planned and that we would laugh together about all the fuss that they caused. Somehow, we persuaded ourselves that all would be well.

But then, on the Ponti Vecchio as I looked around, an old lady stood next to me, her rickety legs could barely hold her slight frame. She looked at me gently and whispered in Italian the same words I had heard before *'carry your cross with fortitude'*.

With ominiscity growing larger inside me I knew then that Phillip and Jasper were never coming back. I turned and hugged Bea. When I looked for the old woman, she had disappeared, but I understood also that we would never ever be truly be alone."

Caroline's face was colourless, and Bea was shivering. Frank put his arm around his feisty wife and kissed her.

"Phillip and Jasper never returned. The Hotel Manager asked if we wanted help to pack our suitcases, but we declined. We drew out of the wardrobe and drawers, clothes that we knew our husbands would never wear again.

Tom and Vivie helped us with that terrible task. We told each other about the places where articles had been bought and what we had been doing at the time. We recalled laughing at Jasper's penchant for tartan laces which he always wore in honour of the first time he had met Bea in Edinburgh despite the ribbing he received from almost everyone he met.

We packed carefully the cufflinks bought as anniversary presents and the ties that would never again be knotted by Phillip or Jasper. It was a terribly painful experience. When our cab driver arrived to take us to the airport, he must have been told about our sorrow as he never asked us about our holiday or tried to make small talk with us.

In fact, we made the journey in silence. When we checked in with British Airways, the staff already knew that the return tickets for Phillip and Jasper Butler would not be needed. We were treated very delicately by everyone we met.

During the journey I held onto a jumper which belonged to Phillip and tried desperately to remember his smell. As the 'plane thundered away from Italy I remember clinging on to the jumper and wishing Phillip was by my side wearing it. We left Florence, the city which our husbands would never leave. We returned home to our anxious families, but we didn't return home with Phillip and Jasper.

I remember that my life became chaotic" said Caroline. "Tom and I had to keep the business going as there were a lot of staff relying on us for work. Also, I needed something to focus upon apart from Bella. Something which I could do in Phillip's name.

We were tireless weren't we Tom? We never allowed ourselves a minute to think. I had a seven-year old daughter to look after and an organisation to keep afloat. Tom agreed to lead the business in London and Edinburgh. I led it in Manchester. Each of us having to manage work time around the needs of the children. It was simply heart-breaking.

It took a long time for Bella, Alfie and Minnie to settle. They missed Phillip and Jasper terribly. To try to help us come to terms with our grief both families bought two large plastic bottles and cut a post hole in the middle of each. Whenever we had a happy thought about Phillip or Jasper, we wrote it and posted it.

From time to time we would open the bottles and read our notes. Each night, long after Bella had gone to bed, I would be awake trying to come to terms with the awful grief I felt and the anger that I couldn't shake off. I was so angry at the waste of life. I couldn't allow myself to have time to think. If I did, I would be lost in despair and that wouldn't do anybody any good."

"I left London and returned home to Manchester with Caroline" declared Bea. "I couldn't bear to be there without Jasper. Alfie and Minnie wanted to be closer to their grandparents. I couldn't have cared where we lived but I knew that I needed help with the children and support emotionally whilst I grieved.

Robert and Matilde were amazing. There were days when I couldn't get out of bed, and they looked after the children. There were times when I didn't even wash myself and Matilde would sit on the end of my bed and listen to me wailing about how hard and lonely life was without Jasper.

I cried so much that I thought I would never, ever be happy again. My parents were inordinately patient with me. They cooked meals, washed clothes, dealt with school issues for the children, coaxed me to go on walks with them.

Elle spent a lot of her spare time with me. She encouraged me to go swimming, and we met up for lunch at least once a week. Elle, Caroline and my parents dragged me out of my silent despair."

The wind whipped up a frenzy outside the Hub, which did not disturb the stupefied hush within the building. Frank stood up and walked to the kitchen.

Elle joined him. "You've been a terrific husband to Bea and a brilliant dad to Minnie and Alfie. Bea's very happy with you Frank."

He scrutinised Elle's eyes, turned away but said nothing. Together, in a comfortable silence, the two of them made another pot of coffee and sliced home-made lemon drizzle cake left over from earlier in the day.

Bella arrived in the kitchen in time to carry out the cake and side plates which she distributed among the friends. She heard her mother sniff but dared not look at her. She knew that Caroline's eyes would be red from crying. Bella had never heard her mother or Bea speak about that holiday. Intuitively she was aware that it was not necessary to ask any questions of either of them. That would be too painful. Today her mother had explained the passing of her father and her uncle. She did not need to know any more information. Instead, the last words she heard her father shout to her would be etched in her mind 'don't look back, that's not the way you're going'.

Bella thought that it wouldn't do to dwell on the past. She looked at Bea and Caroline. They were brave women who had forged a life after suffering much sadness.

Today's events, when she had called off her wedding to Charlie had been the correct decision. She needed to accept that she wanted a different life to the one she was likely to have shared with Charlie. She didn't want to be shackled, which, truthfully, is what she felt when she was with him. Bella and the people she loved had faced much worse than this.

She sat closer to Ben and rubbed his arm. His head turned. His face was pallid. His gorgeous green eyes stared at her, but he said nothing. Ben was thinking about the possibility of facing the loss of his beloved twin sister Jo and how he and his parents would cope. He looked across at his father. Their eyes met but neither of them spoke.

# Chapter 16 - The Manchester Hub

Vivie was obviously suffering from fatigue. Even in the dim light it was clear that the colour of her face had drawn to an ashen hue. She slumped in her chair. Tom held on to Vivie, Bea jumped up to get a glass of cold water from the kitchen, returned and placed it gently at Vivie's lips. The fresh, cold water trickled down her throat. She found it soothing but her head thumped with pain and she felt inordinately tired. Tom pressed two tablets into Vivie's hand. She shook as she raised her hand towards her face, placed the grey, oval tablets into her mouth and swallowed them with water. "I'll be fine in a moment" she whispered.

Although he did not acknowledge it to Vivie, there was a deep, hollow feeling for Tom that in the near future he might lose his wife and daughter. Tom was desperate for them both to be well again. The fear of bereavement pursued him wherever he went. Each night, before he slept, he implored God to be taken in place of his beloved Vivie and Jo.

Occasionally, his dynamic spirit felt that it could take no more. Sometimes, on his dark days, he visited the Hub to speak about his concerns with Frank. The only person who knew of his anguish. They pretended they were talking about sport.

Frank looked at Bea's face illuminated by the gentle flicker of candlelight as she attended to Vivie. He allowed his mind to wander to the evening he had sat by the fireside in Robert and Matilde's house when he was 23 years old.

Frank remembered asking about Bea and where she was working. Robert and Matilde had been incredibly kind. Frank recalled hearing from Robert that Bea was living in London and getting married, but the rest of Robert's sentence had been drowned out by the sound of Frank's heartbeat thumping in his chest, making his head ache, and his ears throb.

This wasn't part of Frank's plan. He wanted to visit Manchester, tell Bea that he had made enough money for them to set up their own business and ask her to marry him. Now he'd discovered that she was marrying someone else. His Bea. The girl who had said she would always love him. Obviously, that couldn't be true. She mustn't have loved him at all. She was going to marry a bloke called Jasper. "What kind of name was that?" he had muttered to himself as he walked home.

Frank recalled that Matilde had been so generous with her time. She knew that Frank needed to absorb the news he'd heard. She made him coffee and poured a large portion of whisky into it. Frank recollected sipping the sweet drink but had no idea how to cope with this news.

He was embarrassed to remember that he had cried. He had cried in front of Robert and Matilde. A grown man. The couple had been gentle with him, as they always had been. They listened as he explained what his plan had been.

He had wanted to whisk Bea away and live with her forever. He had never loved anyone else. In all of his journeys around the world, visiting different countries, he had never met anyone who matched up to Bea. He begged Robert and Matilde never to tell Bea about his visit or the way he felt. They reassured him that they wouldn't.

He had every confidence that they would be true to their word. They were good people. As Frank left, Robert looked into his tortured eyes and told him he would always be welcome in their home. Matilde promised to write to Frank so that he would always have some link with them and Bea.

Frank never knew that, like Bea, Robert and Matilde had loved Frank from the moment they met him. This quiet, reserved, impetuous man who felt things very deeply but rarely shared his emotions loved Bea as much as they did. Fervently they hoped that Bea was making the right decision to marry Jasper as they knew Frank would have been a wonderful husband to their daughter.

Extreme sadness befell them both as they watched Frank walk away from their home and leave behind hopes of sharing Bea's life. On her wedding day Robert had tried to make sure that Bea loved Jasper. Bea had said she did. Even on Bea's wedding day, when Robert thought that Jasper had jilted Bea, there was no way he could have told her that Frank had come back for her and left broken-hearted.

Now, as Frank sat opposite to Robert and Matilde, they couple tried to make eye contact with him. They wanted to reassure him that he was loved and cared about, that he wasn't second best in anyone's eyes. They knew that the narrative about the events in Italy would have affected him deeply.

They grasped that he always felt he didn't quite match up to the rich, confident, highly educated husband with whom Bea had once shared her life.

As if he could read their thoughts, suddenly Frank felt embarrassed and uncomfortable in his own café. He wanted to rush upstairs to the safety of the apartment but, as he rose to leave, he felt a hand on his arm. "Let me pour you a café latte Frank, and I'll put some whisky in that my beloved husband" smiled Bea as she bent down and kissed the top of his head.

Frank, who rarely showed emotion, put his arms around Bea and hugged her as if he would never let her go. He felt relieved but was discomfited when everybody cheered.

Frank sat with Bea by his side. Suddenly he felt braver. "I know that you both lived together, but how did you decide to get married?" asked Ben, as he pointed at Frank and Bea. "Somehow, you seem to fit with each other." Bea answered him. "I don't stop talking, so people don't notice that he doesn't" Bea glowed. "I don't need to talk" retorted Frank, "you do enough of it and I'd never get a word in edgeways anyway."

Bea looked at him in askance. "That's an incredible statement. When we're in this café all you do is talk about football and politics with anyone who comes in here. If I stop to speak to Vivie or Caroline when they pop in, you start banging the pots and telling me to hurry up. You do plenty of talking Frank, believe me."

He laughed. "You drive me mad Bea, because you're always on the go. Another thing, why did you turn me down the first time I asked you to marry me?" he demanded. He was on a roll. He looked straight at Bea, took a deep breath and said "We lived together. We were happy together. Why didn't you want to get married?" he asked with a courage which belied his inner anxiety as he shuddered at his own boldness.

Bea turned to stare at Frank. "In your life Frank you've never told me that you love me. When we first moved in together, we had a fabulous time, but I thought that you would've been just as happy living alone. You're very independent. You asked me to marry you when you knew I was expecting our child. I thought that you were asking me because you felt that you had to. I thought it was for the wrong reasons. I wanted to know that you loved me, but you never said it" exclaimed Bea.

Robert and Matilde stared at each other but said nothing. In a resolute manner Frank replied "I shouldn't need to say it Bea. It's obvious to anyone with eyes. I asked you to marry me and you said *yes* then the following morning you said '*you didn't believe me did you when I said I'd marry you? You know I was only joking don't you?*' Can you imagine how that felt Bea? I went to speak to Robert about you. He told me that it was your hormones playing tricks. That it often happened to women when they were pregnant. I told him simply that you Bea, were driving me bonkers and quite frankly, you still do."

Bea was unabashed. "I know" she replied affably. "Dad gave me a good, old fashioned telling off. Me, the mother of two children, expecting another and I was told off by my father" she chuckled. Robert gave her a sideways glance.

"You're never too old to be chastised by your parents" he said. Ben asked again, "I'm even more curious now. How did you end up getting married then?" Bea looked at Ben, then at Frank. "I thought that everything was complicated. Too complicated. My father was right, my hormones were all over the place when I was pregnant for the third time.

I was terrified. I already had two young children to bring up when Jasper died. I hadn't been with Frank for very long when I found out that I was expecting his baby. When Frank asked me to marry him, initially I thought that was a wonderful idea but the more I considered the prospect of him taking responsibility for my two children and a baby, it just didn't seem realistic. I thought that there was no way he would want to have the burden of two children who weren't his own and change his independent ways to settle down with a baby, me and my two children.

Initially I said yes. Swept away by the romance of it all but when I considered the massive leap that Frank would be taking, I shied away from being married to him so pretended that I had joked when I accepted his proposal."

"See what I mean?" exclaimed Frank. "It's no wonder I thought she was bonkers" he said in exasperation "it's impossible to figure out what's going on in her head." He tutted, sighed then shook his head.

Bea laughed. "Sometimes coincidences occur that are just too incredible to understand. Our child, Roberto, named after three very important men: my father, the Brazilian footballer Roberto Carlos and the Manchester United legend Sir Bobby Charlton was born ten years to the day that my first son Alfie was born.

Roberto was delivered in the same hospital, in the same room by the same midwife. That day was like reliving a very special day from my past. The only thing that was different was the man by my side. Thank goodness the midwife didn't say anything to me about a change of man.

I often wonder if she knew what happened to Jasper and had decided to stay quiet about it. She had probably seen many more unconventional things on her ward and knew to be discreet. Call me silly if you like, but it felt as though on that day Jasper handed over his precious family to Frank's safekeeping.

Frank brought Alfie and Minnie to see the new baby. I watched Frank hand the baby to the two children in turn. He was so proud of Roberto but he also wanted Minnie and Alfie to be involved with the baby. As Alfie stood by Frank's side, he gently passed Roberto to Alfie. Frank put a protective arm around Alfie and Minnie whilst the two of them stared at the tiny bundle. As I looked at the four of them, right at that moment I knew Frank would be a caring father to the three children. I knew that he would always be there for all of us no matter what. It felt as though a huge burden had been lifted from me and right then and there, I asked Frank if his offer of marriage was still good.

I asked him if he wanted to marry me. The look on his face was one of enormous incredulity. He looked down, embarrassed, rummaged in his pocket and brought out a red box with gold patterned edging. Frank passed the box to me and when I opened it there was a diamond ring. It had six diamonds on a gold band. He said the diamonds represented each one of us and showed that he thought we were all a very precious unit. Frank said the extra diamond was a memento of Jasper.

I was speechless." "Yes. I enjoyed that momentary silence" interjected Frank sardonically "I should've made the most of it because it's been rare ever since." Bea ignored him. "I put on the ring and when my parents came to visit, we both announced that we were going to get married. In the end, it all became very simple."

He had never acknowledged it, but when Bea said she would marry him, Frank had become the happiest he had ever been. He knew that he had waited a long time for this moment to materialise. It was a dream he had whilst travelling the world. Of course, he had enjoyed the carefree lifestyle when he was sailing from port to port. It had been fun to do whatever he liked whenever he chose. He wasn't answerable to anyone and he had been able to come and go just as he pleased.

Frank's nomadic spirit was at ease roving from place to place and his quiet, easy, non-judgemental personality meant that he had friends in far flung places across the globe. He found though that wherever he was, from time to time his mind often wandered back to Bea. Some things he thought, are meant to be.

Although he had not revealed anything to Bea, Frank had almost married once. He had met a Catalan girl in Barcelona when his ship had docked. He had been able to take a holiday for two weeks, arranged to stay with his friend Guillem's family in Barcelona and met Nuria. She was irresistible.

Her eyes were the colour of jet, her curly brown hair cascaded beyond her shoulders and when she spoke her quick-fire Catalan, Frank was entranced. Although he conversed in fluent Spanish, Frank had to learn how to speak Catalan in order to fit in with Guillem's friends and communicate with Nuria.

At first Nuria had pretended that she couldn't understand a word of English which forced Frank to adapt very quickly to, what to him was a totally new language. Nuria was delighted with Frank.

He was the first English man she had met who had bothered to learn to speak her language. The majority of English people she knew appeared arrogant that 'foreigners' should speak their language and not vice versa.

She was intrigued by this quiet, English man who could communicate with the people she knew in their own way. He seemed not to care what other people thought about him. She admired his astute mind, his sharp-witted approach and his keen knowledge about world politics. He obviously read a lot but wasn't influenced by the popular press. He seemed to know his own mind and she liked that.

For almost two years Frank and Nuria were considered a couple by their friends, destined to marry. Whenever Frank got the opportunity to visit Barcelona he would be there escorting Nuria to different events. They enjoyed trips to Spain's largest football stadium the Camp Nou to watch FC Barcelona play football. Frank found match days added heightened anticipation in the vibrant city which was festooned in the football team's colours of red and blue.

His passion for football was encouraged when he was lucky enough to watch some of the world's most famous footballers play at the stadium. He especially enjoyed visiting the trophy room where he could easily while away hours and revel in the club's fine history. A history even more illustrious than that of his own beloved Manchester United.

One of Frank and Nuria's favourite places to visit in Barcelona was the Sagrada Familia. As Gaudi's unfinished Gothic masterpiece, Frank found it an awe-inspiring construction.

Nuria knew the best times to call when the crowds were at their smallest so that the couple could indulge their passion for looking at distinctive architectural features like the cathedral's ornately carved towers.

Frank enjoyed observing the kaleidoscope of colour as it infiltrated the building through the stained-glass windows. He found himself to be most at peace on the days when he knelt beside one of the columns which lined the main aisle of the cathedral.

When they wished to enjoy the expansive views over their beloved city of Barcelona, Frank and Nuria took a short ride on the cable car up the hill of Montjuic. They spent time exploring the collection of art-work in the grand Palau Nacional and delighting in the spectacular water displays at the magic fountain.

The couple were able to arrange to have picnics with friends in the blistering Spanish heat which, to Frank, felt like a million miles away from cold, wet, grey Manchester and Bea.

Frank recalled that some evenings he and Nuria would walk hand in hand to the upper part of Barcelona, enter Park Guell and head for Gaudi's monument to Calvary. The park was awash with Gaudi's white mosaic walls upon which hung black iron gates shaped like butterflies.

Diminutive white buildings appeared as if they were entrancing elf-lodgings. A striking white mosaic staircase led to huge white pillars and an amazing view over the city. The couple followed paths which snaked their way around the park offering images of more ornate objects, flanked by vivid green palm trees.

Frank enjoyed the rest they had on the Plaza Natura most of all because he could spray himself with icy water from the fountain, sit on a rattan chair, drink wine, chat with Nuria and watch the world go by.

Occasionally Frank and Nuria wished to retreat from the city so would travel by train from Barcelona into the Catalonian peaks of Montserrat. The mountain offered amazing views of Catalunya where Frank and Nuria would spend half a day walking rugged mountain paths through the natural park. They would stop at brooks to drink the fresh water, before heading to Oller del Mas to drink organically produced wine from the vineyard.

Frank thought that with its labyrinthine streets and hidden squares, Barcelona bore a striking resemblance to Venice. From time to time he enjoyed walking through the public square, Placa del Rei, strolling down cobbled streets, sitting at outdoor cafes chatting with friends and discussing politics. This was where Frank and Nuria lived, in a medieval building close to the sea front. Here, he felt at home. Sun shining, close to the sea and lots of raucous laughter.

Beguiling though she was, Nuria could be bossy and wilful. She enjoyed debate and lively company. She had strong opinions and wished to share them. Nuria relished life in Spain and would not contemplate living in a grey climate when, occasionally Frank spoke about returning to Manchester. A city where the rain wasn't far away, and the sun was watery failed to appeal to Nuria.

Nuria enjoyed outdoor life, she was hot blooded and would not be tempered by a cold climate. In the end, she would not compromise when Frank wanted to spend half of their time in England and the other half in Spain. No, she had said, that would not do.

The past never seemed to be far away for Frank. Matilde had been true to her word about remaining in contact with him.

She kept the promise she had made to him when he visited her home before Bea married Jasper. When his usual monthly letter arrived one October with its Manchester postmark, Frank picked it up from the mat and ambled through the Gothic Quarter towards his favourite café.

He turned the unopened envelope over and over in his hands wondering, as always, what news would be brought to him of Bea and her family. Unbeknown to Bea, he had lived her highs and lows vicariously.

Occasionally he thought that it was madness that he still thought about her, because so many years had passed since they had seen each other. For him, the letters from Matilde made everything seem tangible, as though he were still involved with Bea's life.

For some reason, this time he did not rip open the letter and gorge greedily upon each word. Today he placed the unopened letter on the table, ordered a café con leche and looked out to sea. He imagined that he saw Bea walking towards him. Madness. He shook his head as if to fling that thought from his mind, looked down at the letter and waited.

He ordered a second drink before he finally slit open the white envelope. Frank unfurled the letter scrawled in Matilde's spidery writing. It began

Dear Frank

*This letter has been very difficult for me to write.*

Frank's heart raced. Something was wrong. He could barely think. His heart pounded so loudly that his ears vibrated with its sound. He managed to stop his hands from shaking. He was terrified that something bad had happened to Bea. That he might never see her again or hear her voice. He couldn't breathe. He picked up the letter, took a deep breath and braced himself.

*You probably remember that I told you Bea was going to Italy for a week last month. It seems bizarre that I am writing these words to you Frank, but Bea's husband Jasper and his brother Phillip were swimming in the Alno River in September. I feel that you should know that Jasper, and his brother Phillip, haven't been seen since then. Bea and Caroline stayed in Italy for eight days waiting for news of them both. They visited the river every day and hospitals in the region but there has been no trace of either Jasper or Phillip. Eventually, when they realised that there was nothing else left to do, Bea and Caroline returned home without the two of them. Bea and the two children are currently living with us as she can't face going back to her house in London. I thought you should know Frank as I feel as though you've been with Bea every step of the way. I hope you are well love and that life in Barcelona is all that you had hoped it would be. Take care. Keep in touch with us Frank.*

*Lots of love Matilde and Robert xx*

Frank felt nauseated. He folded the letter, placed it into his trouser pocket and walked towards the sea. Poor Bea and the children. Like Matilde had said, he had walked every step of the way with Bea through her mother's letters.

He spent that day wandering around Barcelona. He visited the Sagrada Familia and Park Guell. He spent hours just thinking about what to do. Finally, he reached the point where he decided to leave behind his life in Barcelona and return to Manchester to see what, if anything, arose. So that he could be close to where Bea was living.

Nuria had been despairing when he told her that he wanted to move back to Manchester with no other explanation. He had been resolute. Frank recalled that when his only son Roberto's baptism had been organised, he had asked his closest friend to be the God Father.

When Frank collected Guillem and his enchanting sister from Manchester Airport, and introduced his friends to his family, Frank thought it pointless to reveal to anyone his prior relationship with Guillem's sister Nuria.

# Chapter 17 - We don't need to live a life of quiet desperation

Frank stretched out his hand, and Bea grasped it just as there was a loud rap of thunder. The Hub vibrated. As he looked around at the terrified faces of the people assembled in his café Frank said "I think we'd agree that things have got to change for us all. We don't need to lead lives of quiet desperation. We can take control and make change happen for us. I know that Tom and I laughed at the idea of an adventure when Bea and Elle first said it, but I think we need to consider carefully an adjustment that we could make to our lives. Instead of wishing to make dramatic changes, we could think of something we could modify that would be manageable for us all. Something that we could look forward to doing."

"Well it won't be going to the gym then" stated Elle. "I don't mean something like that. I mean something significant, important and memorable. We know that we can't afford to take a gap year. We don't all have enough money to give up work, much as some of us would like that" his eyes looked towards Vivie and Bea who both shifted uncomfortably. "There's no reason why we can't all do something we enjoy" Frank said.

"What about if we each write down suggestions of what we would like to do?" advocated Tom. There was a momentary pause. "Why don't we make a list of places we'd enjoy visiting for a weekend, each month during this next year" said Ben. Everyone at the table stared at him. "What a fantastic idea", acknowledged Matilde. "We could create memories that we all share. Brilliant" she said approvingly. "Before it's too late", said Robert ominously.

"Are we all agreed on that?" queried Frank. He looked around the table.

Everyone nodded. "Right, I'll get paper and pens for us to use" stated Bea "and I'll hold the candle for you" smiled Frank "as I always have" he joked. "I've decided to find his jokes charming" said Bea. "I've got a glass jar we could use to pop in our suggestions, and we can take it in turns to take out each piece of paper" said Bea.

"This is exciting", replied Bella, "we used to have a similar jar when I was little which mum and I used. The memory jar. I can't wait to do this" she said excitedly. "You're not allowed to let anyone see your suggestion, you can only make one, and no owning up to which choice is yours either" said Vivie. "So, has it got to be somewhere we can get to on a Friday night and back on a Sunday evening?" asked Robert. "Yes, that's sounds right. Except, if it's something we can do when we have a long weekend holiday break, we can include it. Get thinking" urged Frank.

When Bea and Frank returned to the table there was much giggling and excited anticipation. Bea handed out a piece of A5 sized white paper to each person. "Ok has everyone got a piece of paper and a pen?" Each member of the group nodded.

"Right. Here goes. One choice only. You've got five minutes to choose. Once you've finished writing, fold your piece of paper and put it in this" encouraged Frank as he tapped the jar that had been placed in the middle of the table. "The jar of expectation" stated Caroline mysteriously. "Shall we each have a go at pulling out one suggestion?" asked Elle. "Yes, let's do that" agreed Frank. "Pass the jar around the table" advocated Matilde.

"Frank, as each suggestion is read out, please will you make a list of them then we can decide which month we will travel to each place" said Bea. "Oh, this is really exciting" said Bella. "Ok everyone. Here goes" announced Frank. "Drumroll Robert please" Frank said melodramatically. Robert banged on the table as the jar was passed to Vivie.

Silence descended in the café. Outside the storm erupted. Temperamentally, thunder stomped around. The rain ceased momentarily. Lightning ignited the room. Ignoring the commotion outside, each member of the group was intent on writing a proposal on their piece of plain white paper. Frank's watch showed five minutes tick by.

One by one pieces of paper were folded and placed into the glass jar. When the last piece of paper fell silently onto the white mass, Vivie picked up the jar and shook it vigorously. She placed her hand into the container and plucked out the first written suggestion, unfolded the paper and theatrically read out "Granada in Spain." "Oh, my friend Angelina spent a year living in Granada when she was studying Spanish at Manchester University. She told me about the lavish Alhambra Palace enshrined in splendid medieval history. Angelina said she used to walk in the Generalife Gardens of the Palace, sit under a tree and read. She recommended a book called *Tales of the Alhambra* which I must borrow from the library sometime soon. I think she said that it's an elegant, yet edgy city. I can't wait to go. Over to you Tom, you're up next."

Tom swirled his hand around the jar and picked out a perfectly folded piece of white paper.

He unfurled each side, looked mischievously at his friends gathered around the table and read out the name of Seville. "I've always wanted to go there" cried Bea. "I'm sure it's the home of tapas. I've read about it in Porter magazine when I was at the hairdressers recently. I think that it's a city of cobbled streets and I'd be keen to visit the Alcázar Palace as I've seen an image and it looks breath-taking."

Tom passed the jar to Ben. As Ben put his hands around the glass jar, thunder exploded in the air, followed almost immediately by lightning. The Hub shook with the violence of the storm. Bella screamed. "Sorry" she said quietly "I'm a little jumpy." Ben shifted closer to her.

Rain bashed the café window and door. Rowdier and rowdier, wilder and wilder it pounded. Outside trees reeled, leaves whirled and branches crumpled under the force of the raging storm. Bea stood up, pulled open the blind and looked outside. The sky was violet, the road glittered, appearing to be embossed with crystal raindrops, the wind wailed. Despite its ferocity, she thought there was an extraordinary splendour about this tempest. If nothing else, it had given her time to be with people she cared about.

"Where's our next destination Ben?" she shouted. "Looks like we're off to Barcelona" he said jauntily. Frank's stomach lurched, he could hardly breathe. "Brilliant. We'll be able to catch up with Guillem" chirped Bea. Frank smiled weakly. He'd never been back to Barcelona since his hasty departure.

Ben slid the glass jar to Bella.

Bella paused for a moment, closed her eyes, inhaled for four seconds, held her breath for five seconds then exhaled slowly for six seconds. This was her relaxation technique. Her slender hand reached into the jar and felt around the bottom for a piece of paper. She lifted out the note, opened it and read out the word, "Madrid". Caroline gasped. Bea patted her hand. "You said you wanted to return sometime Caroline. Now you can guide us around the city if you like. Be our tour guide" she said kindly. Caroline smiled.

Bella pushed the jar towards her mother. Caroline paused before placing her elegant hand into the jar. She swished around the paper and enjoyed the crackling sound it made in the glass jar. Dramatically she withdrew a single piece of white paper, unfurled it and placed it in front of her on the table. She closed her eyes and opened them again. "Looks like we're off to your homeland Robert. Here comes Krakow" she shouted. "Wow. I've never returned since I left with my family as a baby" exclaimed Robert. "This is exciting. Oh Robert, this is going to be an adventure and a half isn't it?" asked Matilde. Robert leaned over and kissed his wife. "We'll make it an exciting escapade Matilde."

Caroline placed both hands around the jar of expectation and pushed it along to Matilde. Shakily, Matilde placed her careworn hand into the jar and swirled around the remaining pieces of paper. She lifted one piece out of the jar slowly and deliberately then passed it to Robert. "Please will you read it Robert, I've not got my glasses with me?' "Here goes" said Robert dramatically as he banged the table. We're off to Lisbon in Portugal." The group cheered.

Robert pulled the jar towards him, rummaged around and pulled out a piece of paper. He shouted "Monaco". "Could we go to the Grand Prix?" asked Tom excitedly. "Perhaps we might" agreed Frank. Gingerly, Robert passed on the jar of expectation to Elle. "Not much to choose from now Elle" he said.

"Here goes" said replied theatrically. She placed her hand into the jar. Waited for a few seconds then chose the folded piece of paper which was at the very bottom of the jar. Dramatically she opened the paper. "We're off to Porto" she shouted. Everyone cheered. "Don't know why we're cheering. Does anyone know anything about the place?" said Ben. "Only that it produces port" replied Bella.

"Is there somewhere that any of us is hoping will come out?" asked Bea. "You can't do that, cheater" said Frank. "You have to wait patiently to see the choices people have made. You're too eager Bea." "I'm just excited" she replied.

"My turn next" said Frank "but I'll keep the tension going because I'm going to make coffee for us all and have some cake before you and I pull out the last two options Bea. How about it?" "Frank. Fancy making us all wait longer to find out where we're going" said Bea indignantly. "Great isn't it?" Frank chuckled "just to keep you all in suspense."

Bella and Caroline helped to clear the tables and stacked the dishwasher as Frank and Bea prepared the coffee. Bea cut thick slices of tiffin and Eccles cake. She placed them onto a huge plate which Bella carried into the café and placed in the middle of the table.

Caroline and Bea followed and placed coffee mugs in front of each group member.

When he sat down, Frank said "here we go. The last two places. Where will we be going?" as he looked around at the expectant faces. He grabbed the glass jar, picked up a piece of paper then dropped it. He picked up the other piece of paper and dropped that back into the jar too. "Stop messing about Frank" said an impatient Bea, "I'm dying to know where we're going and I've waited ages for my turn." "Be patient Bea" he said smoothly. "There. I've chosen", he paused, looked around, stalled then said "Stockholm". "That's brilliant" said Robert. "What an unusual choice as I don't know anyone who's been there. Can we arrange to go in the summer so that the sun might be shining?" He grinned.

"You're up last Bea" said Frank as he passed her the jar of expectation. She looked excited and giggled. Gently she placed her hand into the jar. "I can hardly contain myself" she whispered. Bea picked out the remaining piece of paper, kissed it and unfolded each edge. "VENICE. "We're going to Venice' she shouted and jumped up from the table. I can't wait to see the Grand Canal." Everyone cheered and laughed at her eagerness.

"Have you made the full list Frank?" asked Elle. "Yep" he replied "here it is. There's something for everyone here isn't there?" he asked. "It's brilliant Frank" said Robert. Bella and Ben beamed. "Can't wait" said Ben. "Neither can I" retorted Bella and they squeezed each other's hand under the table.

"Right Vivie" said Bea "what we can do is write about our adventures when we visit the different places. We'll be a bit like Michael Portillo reporting from his train travels.

This could be our best-selling novel; Ten on Tour." "Ten on tour" replied Vivie "sounds too much like an Enid Blyton story.

One thing is for sure, it'll be better than a gap year because we'll still have money coming in from work" she stated. "It'll be brilliant" replied Elle "because we don't have to live like students. We can travel in style." "We might even be able to take in a football match or two in some of those cities" suggested Frank. "Great" agreed Caroline.

"I'll give you this Bea, you're one of life's optimists" proclaimed Frank. "If you write your novel we'll show our backsides on Manchester Town Hall steps" said Frank, "you'll get arrested" interrupted Bea.

"We'd use our brilliant technological prowess to film that on our mobile 'phone" said Matilde sarcastically. "Ben and I'll upload it to You Tube for the whole world to see" laughed Bella. "It's a date" said Ben as he smiled at Bella.

Caroline looked at Frank and Tom in askance. "Great" she said. "I'm sure that's just what everyone in the world would want to look at, your spotty backsides! What a brilliant advert for our city."

"You're the working women of Manchester" said Frank, pointing at the women around the table "like bees buzzing around, busy all the time. Show the world what you can do and write a novel." Bea smiled. "Symbols of our city's industrious, pioneering and entrepreneurial spirit.

Nothing wrong with that" said Bea proudly "and now in the 21st Century we can take a degree of control over what happens to us. We can communicate with the world and tell our story."

As the smell of freshly brewed coffee hung in the air, Bea looked around the Hub and laughed.

At that precise moment a loud thud on the café door pricked the happy atmosphere. Bea leapt to her feet, peeped through the window blinds and spotted a shadowy figure as it swayed in the violent storm which raged outside. All she could see were two eyes peering back at her. She jumped and noted that the head was covered by a black hat, the face was bound by a dark scarf. Must be to ward off the bitterly cold wind and icy rain, she thought.

An outstretched, gloved hand banged again on the café door. "Bea, let me in" the voice pleaded. She turned around and looked directly at Bella. "Well, Bella, what do you want me to do?" asked Bea in a whisper. There was a long, silent pause. Bella's face turned white with fear. "Let him in Bea. I'll have to face him at some point" she replied. "Are you sure you want it to be now?" Bea asked. "Yes" replied Bella quietly.

As she yanked open the door, Bea heard the wind screech and her face was slapped by the bitingly cold air. The blinds rattled wildly as the wind swished around the café chilling everyone to the bone. The smell of freshly brewed coffee flew out into the night air.

An ashen faced Charlie, whose limbs were numb with cold, whose hair and clothes were sodden, looked beyond Bea into the café, at Bella.

"Come in love" invited Bea, it's warm in here. "We'll look after you. Let's get you into some dry clothes." Frank jumped up and, with candle in hand, led Charlie through the café, up the stairs into the living quarters. Once showered and changed into clothes Frank had pulled together, without any sartorial elegance whatsoever, Charlie walked into the living room. "What am I going to do Frank?" he implored.

Frank looked at Charlie's tortured face, put his usual reserve to one side, and hugged him. "Frank, I feel like a right Charlie". They both laughed. "C'mon lad. It's time you and Bella had a talk but before that, you need a warm drink and some hot food inside you. Bea'll look after you. She's brilliant at that.

Remember this Charlie, however painful the ending, it means there's a bright new beginning of something else ahead. You never know, you might have had a lucky escape. As someone, don't know who, once said, *marriage is an institution, and who wants to be in an institution anyway?"* Charlie smiled. "Thanks dad."

This book is due for return on or before the last date shown below.